The Deodis of Hyderabad

Rani Sarma studied in the Andhra and Osmania universities. She taught history for over twenty years when she lived in Delhi. She founded the Historical Society of Hyderabad and passionately believes that heritage should be conserved in all its forms. She is a member of INTACH and is presently engaged in many heritage and environment related activities in Visakhapatnam, where she and her husband live presently.

In the nineteenth and the early twentieth centuries, the nobles of the princely state of Hyderabad lived in palatial residences known as deodis, some 1200 of which once existed in the Old City of Hyderabad. Almost all of these traditional homes have been demolished in recent years, leaving little trace of a now vanished lifestyle.

The Deodis of Hyderabad takes you on an evocative journey into the past as the author describes some of the prominent deodis and the lives of the grand nobles who lived in them. She recreates and recaptures the ambiance that once pervaded in these stately homes and then contrasts what once was, with what is left of the deodis.

Threading its way through the past and the present, the book includes rare photographs and provides fascinating glimpses into the opulence and the grandeur of the alluring city of the Hyderabad, evoking feelings of nostalgia for a bygone era. The book aims to preserve for posterity, the memories of the deodis as they once existed.

The Deodis of Hyderabad

A Lost Heritage

Rani Sarma

RUPA

Published by
Rupa Publications India Pvt. Ltd 2008
7/16, Ansari Road, Daryaganj
New Delhi 110002

Sales centres:
Allahabad Bengaluru Chennai
Hyderabad Jaipur Kathmandu
Kolkata Mumbai

First hardcover edition 2008
First paperback edition 2019

ISBN: 978-93-5333-512-0

First impression 2019

10 9 8 7 6 5 4 3 2 1

To
Tara
and her generation
who I hope will value their heritage

Contents

Special thanks to

Nawab Mir Moazam Husain
and
Smt Lakshmi Devi Raj
without whom this book would not have been possible

Acknowledgements

Many people helped me when I embarked on the writing of the book.
I thank all of them for their wholehearted support.

I thank Prince Muffakham Jah for his words of encouragement
and for readily agreeing to write the foreword.

The two people to whom I turned to, time and time again were
Begum Meherunissa and Nawab Mir Moazam Husain. They represent
all that is most wonderful in the Hyderabad nobility. Many were the
visits I paid them to savour their company and to listen to them talk
about the old times. I am deeply grateful to both of them, for opening
their hearts and their home to me, and for letting me draw on their
remarkable memories. This book wouldn't be what it is but for their
encouragement and support. My heartfelt thanks to them for their
warmth, affection, and their blessings.

Smt Lakshmi Devi Raj was my passport to the old world Hyderabad.
She transferred her passion for the city and everything Hyderabadi to
me. The result is this book, which is before you.

Dr Ratna Naidu was a constant support to me right from the
begining; I thank her for her guidance and encouragement. My sincere

thanks are due to Robert Schick and Praful Puranik who shared my excitement and trudged with me, the lanes and the bylanes of the old city. Robert also helped me with the editing, and the sorting; he lent me a hand in the shaping of the book.

I owe a wealth of gratitude to all the wonderful people who helped me in putting the book together. Smt Mangala Devi Bhale Rao of the Rai Rayan family, spent many hours discussing her family history and taking me through the family albums, apart from feeding me 'pitla and bhakri.' Nawab Farkhunda Ali Khan spent many mornings talking about his childhood; he also introduced me to Begum Najeeb Sultana and Syed Ahmad Ali Khan, whose deodi features in the book. Dr Zeenat Sazida gave me a flavour of the old Hyderabad in the very beginning. Sri Ahteram Ali Khan spared time to tell me about Diwan Deodi, Nawab Mujeeb Yar Jung who was kind enough to talk about hunting, Dr Shiela, Sri Iqbal Karan, and Sri Tej Karan, gave me insights into the Malwala Palace apart from letting me use some rare photographs. Shyam Gopal Saincher talked about his childhood spent in the Peshkar Deodi and Dr Sadiq Naqvi and Dr Dawood Ashraf helped me by providing useful background material, Mr Narendra Luther went though my manuscript and ironed out a few rough edges in the narrative and Dr Audhesh Bawa and Prof Farooqui of Andhra University helped me to grapple with the intricacies of Urdu descriptions. Dr AKVS Reddy readily granted me permission to use the fabulous Salar Jung Museum Library and the library staff supported me cheerfully during the many days of toil among the tomes. Sri Kanaka Raju assisted me at various stages throughout the writing of the book and Smt Rekha Sekri and Sri Sekhar helped me with the scanning of the photographs. Late Sri Muthu provided the logistical support.

I am very sad that Najeeb Sultana, so full of life and cheer when I met her, is no longer with us. The pleasure of bringing out the book is dimmed for me with her loss. I also regret that my friend of many years, Sri Raja Reddy who encouraged me to write about 'Old Hyderabad' is not there to give his critical comments about the book.

Finally, the last but not the least is my own family, Gitanjali and Sanjay who were by my side while writing this book and my husband, EAS Sarma, for taking on the role he enjoys most, as my constant critic.

Foreword

The city of Hyderabad has a long history of 800 years. It begins with the Kakatiya dynasty and the creation of Golconda Fort. Today, Hyderabad has evolved from an ancient city to one that is mostly modern, pulsing with commercial, industrial and information technology activity. Sadly, modernity and urbanisation have erased many traces of the city's past heritage. Old buildings are fast-disappearing and well-known landmarks are being over shadowed by high rise buildings or worse still, flattened to make way for them. Old photographs and artifacts are finding their way out of the city. The old city is rapidly changing its character. Old structures that still stand are crumbling and the rest have receded into the mists of memories. Even more sadly, memories too have to fade.

The vibrant new phase of development is commercially driven. It has swept aside most traces of the old. Today the city of Hyderabad bristles with evidence of the latest wave of wealth. But a stranger to the city would be hard put to find traces of the city's past, its former premier residences of stateliness and splendour.

There is a real need to document that period of the city's past as reflected in its special residential buildings of that period, 'The Devdis of Hyderbad', which is the title of this book. The few surviving deoris are in a state of decay (I use one of the many alternative and equally accepted spellings). In the past, those buildings were both the culmination of a social, cultural process and showpieces for the achievements of the outstanding craftsmen and artisans who created and decorated them.

The nobles of Hyderabd who lived during the Asaf Jahi rule made a major contribution to the cultural life of the city. Those nobles lived in deodis. Men like Salar Jung I and Maharaja Kishen Pershad were not only great statesmen but were also men of refinement. They patronised poetry, art and music while some nobles took pleasure in collecting rare works of art. Others took an active interest in sports while yet others were scholars.

It is in these deoris that the Hyderabadi culture evolved Hyderabadi 'tehzeeb,' its refined way of life. The qawwalis, and mushairas and even the cuisine of Hyderabad are not without their own reputation and appreciation far beyond Hyderabad. Yet, the contribution of the refined people in the era of the deoris has gone largely unrecognised.

The author is a student of ancient Indian history and archaeology. She devoted some years to being a teacher of history but she would not accede to being termed a scholar. She is an admirer of Hyderabad, its culture and its heritage. She is deeply committed to Indian heritage and its conservation in all its forms. She has, in this book, sought to document a slice of Hyderabad's history so that there will be some record for people to understand and appreciate a particular way of life that existed in Hyderabad over the period of a century or more.

'The Devdis of Hyderabad' describes the structure of the deoris. It gives the story of some of the nobles who lived in them. It brings to life the style and the social milieu of the Asaf Jahi period. 'The Devdis' fills a gap in the history of the city and affords us a glimpse of the opulence, grandeur and the cultural effervescence of Asaf Jahi Hyderabad.

10 December 2007   Prince Muffakham Jah
Hyderabad

Introduction

This delectable book of Rani Sarma brings to mind the celebrated work of John Ruskin, *The Stones of Venice*. Both glorify their chosen city and its enticing splendour in spirit and substance. The pages of deoris reveal the creative genius of the Deccan and its florescence in Hyderabad. Likewise Lord Byron's Venice in 'Childe Harold', rising out of the waves, as from the stroke of an enchanter's wand, recalls the sovereign grace of the city of Hyderabad dowered with the historic heritage of the Qutub Shahi and Asaf Jahi dynasties. No less significant has been the legacy of the ancient noblesse and the citizens. The enchanter's wand transforms to Rani Sarma's inspired pen. Her look goes everywhere à la Marco Polo, from the halls of Falaknuma to the walls of Golkonda. Nothing escapes the questing glance. The vision of the master-builders of the deoris transmuted in brick, mortar, granite and marble has been faithfully delineated. It is resonant of what Professor Agha Haider Hasan had earlier immortalised in his book '*Hyderabad Ki Sair*' reflecting the quintessential character of the deoris and their occupants in their twilight days. Though not a Hyderabadi herself, she details the architectural features of the deoris with accuracy apt to surprise their ancestral owners.

The planning of a deori as a tout-ensemble has been deftly dealt with. In the outer precincts, the naubat khana, the gillau khana and other structural dispositions are spelt out. The interior appointments for the inmates like dalans and pesh dalans, chambers for celebratory occasions, meeting with friends and business transactions in the men's quarters (the mardana) are minutely described. So are the women's apartments, (the zenana). The general impression one gathers of the architectural pattern of the larger deoris is an amalgam of the Saracen, Persian, Moghul and Deccani temple touches, particularly in the Samasthan mansions. On a wider canvas one might mention the Char Minar and the stately Char Kamans (arches) on four sides of it, and the magnificent Makkah Masjid flanked by the Panch Mahellah palace, which are great architectural monuments symbolising the grandeur that was Hyderabad. Their growing disfigurement and neglect, particularly of the four arches, does not reflect credit on the present inheritors of this history. I will go further to say that the Nizam's government missed a great opportunity in not laying out adequate open space around Char Minar, like the Etoile in Paris, instead of sitting the Unani hospital almost cheek by jowl with this masterpiece of the Qutub Shahis.

Clemenceau, the French statesman of the twentieth century has waxed as eloquent about these monuments and their oriental city of Hyderabad, as his seventeenth century predecessors Tavernier, Bernier and Thevenot. Farishta, a contemporary of Mohammed Quli Qutub Shah, considered Hyderabad unique in the whole of India. Kafi Khan, in Aurangzeb's time, was no less profuse in his praise and extols the surpassing grace, charm and wheat complexion of our women even more so. Old cities suffer if they are denuded of their old time glamour and inimitable grace.

Certain memorable aspects of Bella Vista, its origin, layout, changing interior appointments and decor by successive occupants and throbbing tenor of life are vividly penned. I recall when I used to visit Bella Vista, where the Prince and Princess of Berar were in residence, the forepart of an elephant with an enormous head, trunk and striking tusks dominated a hall which today serves as the central meeting place of the Administrative Staff College of India.

Distinguished guests are invited to come and lecture there on the burning topics of the day.

In the book, there is a colourful portrayal of the arrival in Hyderabad of the heir apparent of the Nizam, Prince Azam Jah and his younger brother Prince Moazzam Jah, after their marriage in Nice. It might be of interest to relate my own remembrance of this happy occasion. I was one of the senior students of Jagirdar College hand-picked to form a guard of honour at the Nampally station in the full dress of the boy scouts uniform. We stood to attention, staves in hand, fringing both sides of a narrow carpet of honour, which ran right up to the edge of the platform. It was here that the saloon of the special train bringing the princes and their brides was meant to halt. Members of the Executive Council, the Umra-e-Uzzam and other prominent noblemen and senior officials of the government crowded the platform. Alighting from his car, His Exalted Highness and his family passed through our ranks. Our hearts raced but we struggled not to show. I was in my sixteenth year, and now at ninety-three, the scene stays fresh. I see the Nizam taking the salaams of the assembled dignitaries. His gaze was on the rail track which hugged the curving wall of the public garden before disappearing. Finally, the train hove in sight. Excitement ensued. The door of the princes' saloon opened precisely at the edge of the carpet. Coming out, Prince Azam Jah did the 'khadam bosi' bending low over his father's feet. Behind came his younger brother Moazzam Jah who did the same. The newly-wed princesses salaamed the Hyderabad way. I believe they had been coached to do so at Nepean House, Bombay, after arrival from Nice. The protocol presentations over, the Nizam walked past us boy scouts to his car, followed by the royal party. They were so close that I could have touched them had I dared. Princess Durre Shewar looked the embodiment of dignity. Her regal mien radiated a sort of 'thus far and no further' approach. Princess Niloufer was a vision of beauty from paradise. I had never seen one so lovely even in Hyderabad, where hourris were not rare. Her eyes darted friendly curiosity, she was all smiles and everything around seemed to arouse her interest.

I found the chapter on Bella Vista thought provoking. It both gladdens and saddens, showing what time can do and undo. There are references to the growing estrangement between the Prince of Berar and his wife, their cultural clashes and marital disharmony. The point is made about their 'irreconcilable incompatibility' and the departure of the princess to take up residence in London. My own impression of this royal couple from what I saw in the 1930's was different. Husband and wife shared the *joie de vivre* with zest. They jointly participated in constructive activities as well as in the social whirl.

In 1934, I was on holiday in Kashmir with my university professor Agha Haider Hassan Mirza, later my father-in-law. One saw in Srinagar hundreds of visitors promenading along the embankments of the Jhelum. The Prince of Berar was also on holiday. Agha Saheb and I out for a walk one morning ran into the Prince and his party. He met us graciously. I noticed the familiarity with which he received my professor and invited us to have breakfast with him the next day at the guest house at his disposal by Maharajah Harish Singh of Kashmir. Our house boat was not too far from the guest house and Agha Saheb and I strolled over. As we approached the gate, we saw the Prince of Berar jogging, with Princess Durre Shewar following close behind at the wheel of a small car. She was laughingly egging him on to continue the run. Inside the gate, we were most cordially received. The weighing machine was sent for. The Princess was keen to see how much weight her husband had shed. I saw for the first time their baby son Prince Mukarram Jah. He looked red-cheeked and healthy in his cradle, watched over by a Turkish nurse in the garden. After breakfast, we were invited to come over again in the evening for tea and tennis. When we arrived, there was a doubles game on and Princess Durre Shewar, who was playing quite well, suddenly felt giddy and nearly fainted. The anxiety of her husband was indescribable. The way he fussed over her showed how much he cared. Doctor Raj, who belonged to a well-known family of Hyderabad, was in attendance and soon brought her round. The Prince kept on repeating 'I tell you again and again not to diet, but you do not listen. This dieting is harming you.' He appealed to the doctor to stop her from dieting. The Princess smiled back affectionately.

The relations between the Prince and Princess with the ruling family of Kashmir were cordially reciprocal. Prince Azam Jah called Maharajah Harish Singh 'Uncle'. Before leaving Srinagar for Hyderabad, the Prince and Princess threw a dinner party to return the hospitality of the Maharajah. The Maharajahs of Kashmir and Jaipur attended with their families. Both the Maharajahs were heard to remark they had never seen such a variety of delicacies before and were all praise for the culinary finesse of Hyderabad. One wondered how all this 'bandobast' was managed well over a thousand miles from Hyderabad. All praise goes to the 'Amira', the catering department of the Nizam's government, which was in charge of government guest houses and state banquets.

∿

After the halcyon days in Kashmir, a progressive deterioration in relations developed between the Prince and his wife. The book touches on some of the facts which led ultimately to this tragic denouement. To one like me who had seen happiness and a radiant future for them in earlier days, echoes of a Greek tragedy resurrect.

The book also speaks about Princess Durre Shewar's keenness to learn Urdu. On the insistence of Prince Azam Jah, Professor Agha Haider Hassan put her through her paces in the rudiments of the language using his tested methodology which was *sui generis*. Agha Sahab spoke and wrote the undefiled Urdu of the Red Fort of Bahadur Shah's Delhi. It was the Urdu of Ghalib, Zauk and Momin Khan. From his younger days, his writings had established him as a stylist in Urdu literature. His personality was magnetic and people hung on his words. So did his students at the Nizam College. He was highly regarded by his colleagues and the intellectual elite. As a connoisseur of art, he was much sought after by writers on the Moghul and other schools of painting and on antiques. Princess Durre Shewar made rapid progress under his guidance. From long experience he knew how to make instruction agreeable and diversion useful. Even after their break-up at Bella Vista, the Prince and Princess kept up their individual contacts with him. It was handsome recognition of his devoted services by the heir apparent of the Nizam and by the daughter of the Calipha Abdul Majid. In later years, Princess Asra, the wife of their son Prince Mukarram Jah, also greatly appreciated his learning.

The temple adjacent to Bella Vista, like the tinkle of its bells, animates nostalgic remembrance of Hyderabad that was. It also constitutes a purple passage of the book reflecting the ganga-jumni culture of Hyderabad. The bygone glory of the deoris is graphically contrasted with skeletal walls and shattered columns of palaces. The decline had set in with fanatic forces from outside state playing havoc with our historic communal concord. The Police Action of 1948 delivered the coup-de-grace. With impartial candour, Rani Sarma vindicates the achievements of the seventh Nizam, Mir Osman Ali Khan, particularly in education and culture. His generous financial support to institutes of learning and progressive initiatives, are named. The balance is set right to the calumny of his detractors. He was judiciously liberal in his support of worthy causes. He was more discerning and modern in his transactions than his father, the beloved Mir Mahboob Ali Khan, whose munificence was proverbial. He gave with both hands in spectacular traditional charity. Mir Osman Ali Khan created financial trusts for charity and other purposes he prized. Long after his death these sustained not only his family, but many in the general public.

Our Hyderabad culture has what one might call a provincial depth. It is essential to observe culture as a measurement of depth and not of surface. We pride ourselves on this distinction. This intercourse between nature, arts and customs has produced a wealth of many-sided expression characteristic of Hyderabad. We see it in this city's monuments reared by the Qutub Shahis and the Nizams, and above all by the inspired hands of the people of Hyderabad themselves. There was a union of hearts, no need to call meetings and get-togethers to achieve integration. Integration came naturally over centuries with shared conviction, a common culture and participation in each other's joys and sorrows, as members of one large family untouched by partisan, sectarian, religious and political discord. The Nizam attended midnight mass at the Hyderabad cathedral and wrote odes in Persian on the birth of Christ.

The annual parade of the state armed forces to celebrate the Nizam's birthday was a great event. I had been witnessing it at close quarters from my school days. Sir Afsur-ul-Mulk, Commander in Chief of the army, an unforgettable marshal figure, led the parade in the 1920's. I saw the Prince of Berar, who succeeded him, do the same with full panoply of state. The Nizam took the salute and at the end of the parade departed for King Kothi Palace. The Prince and Princess of Berar, with their small son Prince Mukarram Jah in his mother's lap, sat in an open car to drive back to Bella Vista. The Naubat Pahar, Acropolis of Hyderabad, was an animated mass of humanity and thousands lined the compound walls of Fateh Maidan. It is incredible what happened next. The wall under pressure of the crowd behind collapsed. The crowd delirious with joy rushed towards the Prince's car and almost lifted it with shouts of loyalty. The car had to inch its way towards the gate. No one could have doubted on that day the love of the people of Hyderabad for the Nizam and the Asaf Jahi dynasty.

I should like to relate another event during 1946 when agitation had broken out in Nalgunda district and some people had been killed in the police firing. Sir Wilfred Grigson, Revenue and Police Minister, thought it would be a good idea to take Prince Azam Jah to Nalgunda, where the presence of the Nizam's heir apparent would have a pacifying effect. The Nizam agreed. The small town of Suryapet in Nalgunda overnight became a city of tents. Everyone who mattered in Hyderabad was there on the invitation of the government. Religious as well as political leaders, prominent personalities and the press were present. I was serving as personal assistant to Sir Wilfred and on his instruction had prepared a speech in Urdu, which was to be delivered by the Prince. I carried a tray of bank notes which was to be distributed amongst the crowds after his speech. Ignoring the written speech which he had earlier approved, Prince Azam Jah delivered an extemporary oration which came flamingly from his heart. It contained a warning to the local officials as well as assurances to the people of Nalgunda that such events would not be allowed to happen again. Then totally unexpected, he walked up to the widows whose husbands had been killed. They were huddled in a corner looking the picture of misery and misfortune. In his full regalia of state, the Prince put his arms around each of them and humbly sought their forgiveness, promising every support for them to carry on with their lives and the education of their children. There wasn't an eye that was not moist in that huge gathering. Some openly wept. With prejudice and fanaticism spreading its tentacles all over the country, such examples should be brought to the fore as a counter balancing corrective.

The account of the Dewan ki Deori is soundly researched and roentgen rayed in its search for the origins and careers of its successive owners. As a member of the integrated Salar Jung, Khan Khana and Fakhr-ul-Mulk family, I have been the recipient of many favours from Mir Yousuf Ali Khan, Salar Jung III. Rani Sarma's sketch of the Dewan ki Deori and its interior and more so of the Aine Khana revived many memories of my days there. Salar Jung kept open house and at the end of a lunch would walk up to the entrance of the Aine Khana and personally thank his guests for their company. People from several walks of life attended and his humility in dispensing hospitality reflected the nobility of his character. Before getting into his car for his daily drive, he personally took up petitions from the people waiting outside. He would whisper to the major domo behind the action to be taken on each petition. No one seeking help went back unrewarded. Throughout his life Salar Jung never paraded his gifts. It was a case of the left hand not knowing what the right gave. In the evening, dinner was quieter with only close relations.

At one dinner, just before Christmas, he asked my three cousins sitting on his right and myself alone on his left what we would like to have for Christmas. My cousins mumbled something like Meccano, toy train and cricket bat. When he turned to me, I promptly hazarded: 'Chacha Bawa, I would like to have a Sixteen Bore Holland and Holland, hammerless ejector, measured out for me.' Salar Jung was a little taken aback. He could not believe that a boy of twelve could ask for a gun made by one of the most famous and expensive gun-makers in the world. He was intrigued how at my age I could know such details about guns and their makers. He quietly asked again: 'What did you say?' I was frightened and, *sotto voce*, repeated my request. With a big smile, he said: 'Very well. Come tomorrow morning and tell Hadi (his private secretary) what you have requested and that the order should be placed in London at once for the gun.' That night I did not sleep. The next morning I rushed up the stairs to Hadi Ali Saheb's office, who too seemed surprised by the vaulting ambition of a small boy. A year later the gun arrived from London. It was a beauty. Throughout my life in many parts of the world, this precious gift never failed during hunting trips. Nor did Salar Jung's love ever.

In the reference in the book about the armoury, a variety of weapons have been named including rifles and shot-guns made by famous European gun-makers. This strikes a chord in my recollection of Nawab Salar Jung's armoury in Dewan ki Deori which was one of the finest in India. During World War II when I was serving as a Hyderabad Civil Service Special Tribes Officer in the forest areas of Adilabad District, I borrowed a high velocity rifle, 365 Jeffreys from Nawab Salar Jung since the ammunition of my own rifles had run low. A favourite black Labrador which had been a wedding gift used to be chained to a teak post of my bamboo hut every night. My hut was in a small opening on a hillock with forest all round. I had just dropped off to sleep when a commotion made me jump out of bed. My Labrador was gone and I could hear it being dragged down the hill towards the rivulet which ran below. Nothing could be done in the night. Next morning I found the half-eaten remains of my dog. I sat up in a nearby tree in the evening with the Jeffery, knowing the greedy marauder would return to finish off the remains. He did come as anticipated just after dusk. I made a clean miss with my right barrel but bowled him over with the left. It was the biggest leopard I had shot. The Gonds were as delighted as I was since he had been playing havoc with their animals. The congratulations of Nawab Salar Jung followed.

The book dwells on the inner mansions of Dewan ki Deori, the zenana where the begums held sway over numerous dependents. Fascinating vignettes are presented of the environment and tenor of life within. The names of the chief begum and dependents are not given. The reader might be interested to know that the eldest daughter of Fakhr-ul-Mulk I, Azeezunissa Begum, was given in marriage to Mukhtar-ul-Mulk Salar Jung I. The second daughter, Haidri Begum, was married to Imdad Jung; the third, Hussaini Begum, to Satwat Jung, father of Nawab Bairam-ud-Dowla, the pioneer of cricket in Hyderabad. The two sons of Fakhr-ul-Mulk were Mir Asad Ali Khan, Hissam-ul-Mulk Khan Khanan, and Mir Sarfaraz Husain, Safdar Jung Mushir-ud-Dowla Fakhr-ul-Mulk II. Such marriages show how the leading families of Hyderabad were martially connected. Nawab Salar Jung used to visit Iram Manzil frequently to pay his respects to Nawab Fakhr-ul-Mulk. He would also come to fetch my father Nawab Rais Jung and uncle Nawab Shanawaz Jung for golf at Bolaram or for polo at his private polo-ground at Begampet. He liked changing cars and would drive up in his Rolls Royce or in a Daimler or Mercedes.

Zainab Begum Saheb, wife of Mir Laiq Ali Khan, Salar Jung II, was the dominant figure in the zenana of Dewan Ki Deori. Her son Mir Yousuf Ali Khan, Salar Jung III, sustained her sumptuously. The occasions on which I had the honour of paying respects to Zainab Begum Saheb and her aunts Noorunissa Begum and Sultan Bakht Begum, daughters of Mukhtar-ul-Mulk, are happily remembered. They held regal court and radiated traditional authority mellowed with kindness and open-handed generosity. During her last illness, I often accompanied Nawab Salar Jung to her apartment. She adored him. The doctors did their best but the end had come and she passed away peacefully. My mother, Sheher Banu Begum, and Zainab Begum Saheb were closely linked through the Nawabs of Banganpalli and Masulipatam.

✒

The baradaris stand out as a landmark in the chapter on deoris. The Taramati baradari crowns the hillock in the vicinity of the Golkonda ramparts. Those of Chando Lal and Mukhtar-ul-Mulk adorn the inner city of Hyderabad. Raja Chando Lal was a patron of the arts and artists flocked to his palace even beyond Hyderabad State to enjoy his largess. Mukhtar-ul-Mulk dispensed hospitality lavishly at Lakerkot, his wooden wonder-lodge ensconced in lush surroundings on the Musi. The river then was a pellucid breast of waters and not the polluted drain it is reduced to today. When I used to go to Lakerkot in the 1920's, it still charmed though on its last legs. The artistry in timber of the finest grain boggled the mind. Its intricately carved ceiling and chiseled pillars and its superbly planned layout would have been the envy of a Kublai Khan.

The baradari of Nawab Fakhr-ul-Mulk in Iram Manzil, of a later date, was not a separate structure but an integral part of the palace. The main hall was bisected by a cluster of tapering pillars and flanked on the east by a long gallery which merged with an outer hall giving on a tennis court below and a French garden. The exit of the baradari on the west went on to a terrace with a red-tiled roof. On either side was a flight of winding stairs leading to a large rectangular open space, enclosed by swept-back wings of the zenana apartments. In the middle was a fountain in which my cousins and I swam during summer holidays. What caught the eye in the baradari were three red chandeliers; it was an elegant chamber with niches and pleasantly painted light blue. The baradari had several doors, but not twelve to accord with its name because wide windows made up the difference. During Moharram, majlises were held here attended by Nawab Fakhr-ul-Mulk and the male members of his family and the retinue of musahibins and jagir functionaries. Three 'Nal Sahebs', garbed in gold-threaded dattis, were installed on a carpeted platform during the first ten days of Moharram. In the adjoining gallery, nearly a hundred silver 'alaams' with golden dattis were installed. In the evenings, after dinner, the zenana majlises took the place over which Munirunissa Begum, wife of Fakhr-ul-Mulk, with the palace ladies presided.

Each year, during the latter half of December, this same baradari presented yet another shining facet of the ganga-jumni culture of Hyderabad. A Christmas tree festooned with small electric bulbs and weighed down with gifts for the family and guests was installed in the middle. After a go at Christmas cakes and other goodies, the much-desired gifts on the tree were distributed. The youngsters of the family followed by the more sedate elderly made for the hall giving on the tennis court where a group of Christy Minstrels from the town sang carols with gusto. Iram Manzil celebrated a truly merry Christmas as jolly as the Holi and Dusserah festivals.

During Holi, the fountain in the zenana was turned into a bubbling mass of coloured water which was squirted on all around by the younger members of the family. The female staff too joined enthusiastically. It took months for the palace walls to be cleaned up. The dance of the 'gowlis' during Dusserah followed by a large herd of marigold garlanded cattle, was watched by Nawab Fakhr-ul-Mulk from the balcony of the state rooms and by the ladies from the baradari halls. The Eid-ul-Fitr and Bakri-Eid were celebrated with equal éclat. A western style band of army veterans and naubat played by old hands were a feature of the celebrations. Unlike his western style banquets, the festive lunches for the two Eids were muglai in conception and practice. Fakhr-ul-Mulk sat on a carpeted floor of a pillared gallery called the naya makan. Members of the family squatted on both sides of the dastarkahan along with the courtiers and jagir officials. The delicacies laid out would have matched Abul Fazal's in the Aine Akbari.

An outcrop of the deoris, especially the larger ones, was of course the gate which is rightly accorded some prominence. The red arched gate of Dewan ki Deori and the double-storied of Purani Haveli, and Fakhr-ul-Mulk's Garial Ki Deori I can vividly recall. Behind the gate was Salar Jung's palace complex comprising a labyrinth of mansions, garages, stables, servants quarters and the famous Nizam Bagh, which was comparable with the Jardin de Tuileries in Paris. The main fountain was large enough to row a skiff. There were tennis courts and a well in the middle of which there was a wooden platform held by four ropes attached to corners of the well. Salar Jung used to rest on it during his swims. It was in this well that I learned to swim under his encouraging eye. Alongside the fountain was Salar Jung's library of western books in thousands in the care of a librarian. The building was modelled on the Grand Trianon at Versailles but on a smaller scale. Sometimes in the garden, polo ponies would be brought out and I have seen Salar Jung enjoy a quiet ride on his favourite named Mons.

The gate of Fakhr-ul-Mulk's Garial ki Deori in Mir Alam ki Mandi, near the Purani Haveli, was mounted by a clock whose chimes were heard all over the city. The large arched door was battened down with iron knobs and large enough to let in a fully caparisoned elephant with an amari. Inside was a spacious courtyard enclosed by double-storied wings. Behind were seven mansions, each with a rectangular courtyard with a fountain in the middle. Each had a name like Neelam Mahal, Moti Mahal, Sabz Mahal, Pukraj Mahal and so on. There were fruit trees and parterres of chambeli, champa and rose. The Deori had the privilege of the Bibi ka Alam mounted on an elephant to enter the courtyard to receive the respects and nazars of the nawab's family. An exciting thing for me as a boy was to run under the belly of the elephant onto the other side. My children and grand children were wiser not to repeat the experience.

A lofty gateway to Fakhr-ul-Mulk's country palace at Erragadda, also called Fakhrabad, now turned the Tuberculosis hospital, modelled on the gate of Falaknuma, was razed to the ground to widen the national highway to Bombay. This impressive structure could have been easily saved by turning it into an island with the national highway on either side. No heed was paid by the authorities to the protests of well-wishers. Such indifference to other monuments can be multiplied. By contrast, the restoration of the ancient Buddhist and Jain frescoes of Ajanta and the celebrated Ellora caves and monuments under the able supervision of Ghulam Yazdani, Director of the Department of Archaeology, reflect laudably on the Nizam's government.

The chapter on the City of Nobles dwells amongst other things on their fondness for games, sports and shikar. Some of the nawabs and rajahs were pioneers in Hyderabad of cricket, tennis, football and other western games. The old aristocracy excelled at polo and outdoor exercises like steeple chase, tent pegging, sheep cutting at the full gallop on horseback and cavalry manoeuvres in the country-side. They certainly could not be labelled degenerate. Of course there were some black sheep as elsewhere in the world. Salar Jung's name is known beyond the borders of India because of his magnificent private collection of objet d'art, now housed in a national museum. Little is known that a part of the present Begampet airport used to be his private polo ground. I have seen him play polo here with the world's greatest polo player of his time, Shah Mirza Beg, whose handicap, I believe, was ten. He was a close friend of my father and as a boy I had a unique honour of receiving from him, in his old age, a gift of one of his Arab ponies called Silver Bit. Nawab Bairam-ud-Dowla, son in law of Nawab Mukhtar-ul-Mulk, was a pioneer of cricket in Hyderabad. Legendary cricketers like C.K. Naidoo, Constantine of West Indies, Hobbs and Suthcliffe played at the gymkhana ground at Secunderabad in the tournaments named after Nawab Bairam-ud-Dowla and Nawab Moin-ud-Dowla. Lord Tennyson, the grandson of the Victorian poet laureate, also brought out a team from England to play in these matches.

Nawab Mehdi Jung, another sprig of the Hyderabad nobility, turned from his first love horse racing to tennis, which received a tremendous boost thanks to his all-out support. Below his palace at Mowla Ali, he had a tennis court carved out in the hill-side, where one could play under electric lights till late in the evening. He also built a spectacular tennis stadium at Musheerabad, an industrial suburb where tennis stars like Tildon, Cochet, Ghaus Mohammad, and our own Indian starter S.M. Hadi displayed their skills. Nawab Mehdi Jung's brother-in-law Nawab Sultan Ali Khan was a big game hunter who had shot elephants in the western ghats.

Nawab Fakhr-ul-Mulk in the 1870's had his own polo team and went out regularly tiger shooting in the jungles of Khartal. He kept up his horse riding in old age till the end of his life. Nawab Rais Jung, his fourth son, was a marksman and won several rifle shooting championships. Maharaj Kishen Parshad has written a most interesting account of a tiger shoot in his jagir with the sixth Nizam. Some of the

Samasthan Rajas were keen big game hunters. I have seen a photo of the young Rani of Jatphol seated with the first tiger she had shot. When serving as the second Talukdar or Deputy Collector in Gumlbarga District, I took part in a thrilling panther hunt on the ground with the Bedar Raja of Shorapur. Panthers were driven out of caves in high boulders by experienced trackers supported by a fierce pack of dogs of local breed. There are photos of the sixth Nizam out in camp for tiger hunts. The seventh Nizam showed little interest in big or small game hunting. His heir apparent, the Prince of Berar, took after his grand father. In a hall of the public gardens in Hyderabad, an exhibition was held of his trophies of the hunt which included elephants, tigers, leopards, and numerous horned game. The Prince was also keen on polo and horse racing. His horse Wavel won championship cups all over India.

The reigns of the fifth, sixth and seventh Nizams interfuse with the eminence of Maharaja Kishen Parshad, who strode Hyderabad society like a benevolent colossus. He was a scion of the house of Raja Chando Lal. Maharaja Kishen Parshad and Fakhr-ul-Mulk were intimate friends from their school days and attended the private class set up in Dewan Ki Deori by Mukhtar-ul-Mulk for his two sons, Mir Laiq Ali Khan and Mir Sadat Ali Khan. Agha Mirza Beg, Sarwar-ul-Mulk, notes in his autobiography about this private school and the relative merits of his pupils. The Maharaja twice in his life held the high office of Prime Minister as well as the unique title of Yameen-Us-Sultanat, (the right hand of the realm). Mukhtar-ul-Mulk's son, Nawab Laiq Ali Khan, was the only other recipient I know of this high honour, with the title Imad-us-Sultanat, (pillar of the realm). Further, the Maharaja was favoured with the hereditary position of Peshkar. He was the epitome of the old world courtesy, a sufi by conviction, a poet by classical genre in Urdu and Persian, a patron of the arts. He used to attend Fakhr-ul-Mulk's banquets at Iram Manzil, where to see these two leading noblemen together was an object lesson in manners at their best. Once I called on the Maharaja at his palace wearing a dastar and bugloos according to our family tradition. The room was full of people. He made me sit by his side and picking up a writing pad and pencil wrote in Urdu (translation), 'I am unhappy to see you wearing dastar and bugloos. Please take them off.' I wrote back, 'Our tradition does not permit me to do so. I beg you to let me keep them on.' He asked a second time. When I stuck to my resolve, I could see from his look that he appreciated it. Maharaja Kishen Parshad, when driving through town, had the habit of throwing coins to mendicants and others lining the streets.

So did Fakhr-ul-Mulk. I used to sit by his side in the open car holding a tray with compartments for coins of various denominations. He preferred to drive through the country side and tossed coins to people who called out to him in the villages and hamlets dotting rice fields. When Nawab Kamal Yar Jung donated a reading room to the Nizam College, I invited him as College Captain to inaugurate it. He refused and insisted that none other than the Maharajah Kishen Parshad should do it. The Maharajah was unwell when I called to deliver the message, but he came and cut the ribbon to the delight of Nawab Kamal Yar Jung and was cheered to the echo by the students and staff. Yet again in 1929, when Begum Fakhr-ul-Mulk passed away, Maharajah Kishen Parshad though advanced in years walked in the funeral cortege well after the mid-night hour. Another unforgettable moment was in 1934, when I saw the Maharajah weeping his heart out at the burial of his old friend Fakhr-ul-Mulk. Amongst the thousands present were the representatives of the British Residency and senior British officials serving with the Nizam's government. The Maharajah was then in his second term of office as Prime Minister but did not bother to conceal his grief. He too is now one with yesterday's seven thousand years of Omar Khayam. Kishan Parshad lives on, a legend of love, in the hearts of Hyderabadis.

The Paigahs of Vikar-ul-Umarah, Asman Jah and Khureseed Jah occupied a pre-eminent position in Hyderabad state. Their status was enhanced by their marriages to the daughters of the fifth Nizam Afzal-ud-Dowla. During the reign of Mir Mahboob Ali Khan, their brother-in-law, Vikar-ul-Umarah and Asman Jah held the office of Prime Minister in the post Mukhtar-ul-Mulk period. Vikar-ul-Umarah, like his friend Fakhr-ul-Mulk, was bitten by the mansion making mania. They called each other 'bhai' and recklessly indulged in their passion to build, whatever it cost. The result was perennial debts, but nothing deterred them. Vikar-ul-Umarah's legacy is Falaknuma and the palace complex at Begumpet as well as the ancestral Deori in the old city. Fakhr-ul-Mulk made structural improvement in his ancestral Gharial Ki Deori before taking up residence in Asad Bagh, now Nizam College, which he enlarged handsomely. After gifting Asad Bagh to Mir Mehboob Ali Khan, he went on to build Iram Manzil on a hill in friendly rivalry with Vikar-ul-Umarah. His next venture was the building of an impressive granite mausoleum besides on what today is the Hyderabad-Bombay national highway passing through Erragadda. Nearby was his hunting lodge, which like Louis XIV at Versailles, he transformed into a palace with a banqueting hall, reception rooms, a ball room, a private cinema hall, a vestibule and a grand staircase. Like Vikar-ul-Umarah, he feasted his eyes on the phased development of the structure, its inner decorative touches and furnishing. Deep down inside them was a thirst which permanently demanded quenching.

Vikar-ul-Umarah sent his second son for schooling at Eton. Fakhr-ul-Mulk at the same time sent four of his sons to England and the first three were admitted to Eton. On return to Hyderabad, Wali-ud-Dowla, after serving in some senior positions in government, climaxed his career by becoming Prime Minister of Hyderabad, the second recipient of this honour in his family. His two sons Moinudin Khan and Rashidudin Khan were with me at school in Madrassah Alia.

Nawab Moin-ud-Dowla, son of Sir Asman Jah, a former Prime Minister, was a sportsman and a keen hunter. On his estate at Shamsabad, he hunted with a pack of fox hounds brought out from England. He was also fond of tiger shooting and his palace at Saroor Nagar had suites of rooms displaying big game shikar trophies. Nawab Moin-ud-Dowla, when serving with the Nizam's government held several senior portfolios but never attained the position of Prime Minister which his father held. His elder son, Nawab Zaheer Yar Jung, was a class senior to me at Madrassah Alia. Moin-ud-Dowla and Salar Jung were good friends with shared interests. Moin-ud-Dowla's rolling gold cup for cricket, like Bairam-ud-Dowla's cup earlier, attracted famous players. His Paigah traditionally kept a cavalry regiment which turned out smartly on ceremonial occasions. He had charm of manner and a robust sense of humour. I witnessed both when I took out Nawab Salar Jung's cricket team which I captained, to Saroor Nagar to play against his team captained by his second son Nawab Mazar-ud-Din Khan. The match was in the cricket field of the palace. Nawab Salar Jung joined his host at lunch, which was a sumptuous affair. As team captain I had pride of place near both at the table. Their conversation in low tones was revealing. No love seemed lost between them and the Nizam. To have been with men like Maharaj Kishen Parshad, Nawab Wali-ud-Dowla, Nawab Moin-ud-Dowla, Nawab Salar Jung, Nawab Khan-e-Khanan and Nawab Fakhr-ul-Mulk warms the cockles of the heart and the lines come to mind: 'Have we not men with us royal/men the masters of things.'

To lovers of libraries in Hyderabad, this tag might recur: 'there is no past as long as books shall live.' Much has changed since the Police Action of 1948 and some of the great private libraries of Hyderabad are only a nostalgic memory. Such a one is Rajah Shamraj's. Rajah Shamraj, worthy sprig and successor of the Rai Rayan family, much looked up to in Hyderabad, was a lover of books. His other abilities, administrative and public service, and social life were outstanding. But books took precedence and he zealously promoted learning through the propagation and promotion of books. He and my uncle Shahnawaz Jung, the youngest son of Nawab Fakhr-ul-Mulk, were classmates at school and retained a lifelong friendship. I was privileged to spend hours with the Rajah in his library. He would take me from section to section impeccably arranged subject-wise and the books carefully card-indexed. He would pick out a favourite volume from the shelf and speak about it with the fervour of a lover. In the realm of books, Rajah Shamraj, Nawab Salar Jung, Sir Nizamat Jung and Nawab Ameen Jung were of the same ilk.

During the reigns of the Nizams, the Rajah Dharam Karan family inhabiting the Malwala Palace used the suffix Asaf Jahi with their names. Two sons of Raja Dharam Karan, Ram Karan and Sham Karan, my juniors at Jagirdar College were popular at games and studies. The

Rajah held the prestigious portfolio of public works during the latter years of Mir Osman Ali Khan's reign. His younger brother, Rajah Mahboob Karan was an affable figure in Hyderabad society and acted as A.D.C. to the Prince of Berar at Bella Vista. A good tennis player and social mixer, he had all the suave and finesse of an educated Hyderabadi at home with the social mores of the East and the West. A school friend of Nawab Shanawaz Jung, he was a frequent visitor to Iram Manzil and Iram Numah. An elaborate duck shoot which he arranged outside Hyderabad city in which the Prince and Princess of Berar were guests of honour was comparable with the fabled grouse and duck-shoots of the Maharajahs of Bikaner and Kashmir. I was personal assistant to Sir Wilfred Grigson at the time and was invited. While all the senior guns were comfortably seated on the bund, the younger guests were sent out to fend for themselves, waste deep in water on the other side of the lake. With all the din and bustle on the bund, the birds were not likely to wing in their direction. They flew towards our quieter concealed positions and when the bag was counted at the end of the shoot, ours was the larger contribution. The Holland and Holland gun gifted to me long back by Nawab Salar Jung had served me well on this day. Rajah Mahboob Karan's hospitality matched the very best of Hyderabad in cuisine and traditional cordiality.

Iqbal Chand, a younger member of the Dharam Karan family, was also my school fellow at Jagirdar College. We were again together at Nizam College, affiliated to Madras University. We both sat for the Hyderabad Civil Service competitive public exam, in which he stood first and I second among the first six selected. Iqbal was a first rate bowler and we both played for Madras University in the Inter-University Cricket championships. His younger brother, Doctor Harish Chander, emulated his uncle Doctor Bankat Chander, an eminent heart specialist of Hyderabad.

In the penultimate chapter, the incident at the party given in honour of Sir Richard Crofton, the abrupt quitting of the table by Nawab Kamal Yar Jung and the retrieval of his faux pas by examining a picture and returning, does not seem on all fours with his character and meticulous manners. The sons of the Khan-e-Khanan and Fakhr-ul-Mulk did not behave this way. I knew Sir Richard Crofton and his predecessors Sir Theodore Tasker and Sir Chenevix Trench in Hyderabad, and was their house guest in England in 1953. Hyderabad used to be discussed there thread-bare. No mention of such incidents ever cropped up. The reference to Nawab Wali-ud-Dowla addressing his father as 'Hello Dad', on return from England sounds somewhat in the modern idiom unrelated to those times. Fakhr-ul-Mulk's four sons, similarly returning from school in England, were kept in Bombay long enough for them to be coached by specially sent out tutors on how to behave with parents and elders. The protocol in the highest nobility of Hyderabad was not likely to be flouted with impunity.

My niece Begum Najeeb scintillates the last chapter of the book. Rani Sarma's discerning account lights up not only the gems, the jewels and sartorial splendor but the essence and spirit of the deoris' zenana. Najeeb Sultana was the daughter of my youngest sister Begum Raisunissa and Nawab Arshad Ali Khan. Her husband Ahmad, is the second son of Nawab Zaiunlabdin Khan and my eldest sister Sikandar Jehan Begum. Najeeb revealed quite early, varied talents and was the life and soul of family parties. She was witty, loved leg-pulling and was affectionate in relationships. She was a national champion in rifle shooting. She gave of her best though often assailed by adverse circumstances. Being so close to us, it embarrasses me to prolong adjectives. Her untimely death has left us shattered.

Rani Sarma before long will cast her book like the biblical bread on the waters of the world to voyage into havens of hope and merited response. I am confident it will come. Her commitment to research has illuminated the historical horizons, the genius and glory of Hyderabad. At the same time she has candidly contrasted the present status of the deoris, warts and all, with their alluring past. These endeavours deserve our accolade. The book should be a *vade mecum* for all visitors to Hyderabad and not for Hyderabadis only.

8 January 2008   **Mir Moazam Husain**
Hyderabad

Bella Vista

𝕴t was the year 2001, the month of March. I had just left Delhi, my home for well over two decades. My husband and I had learnt to love it, in spite of its harsh summers and equally punishing winters. We had learned to handle both. I loved the feel of the city; the morning walks in the sprawling India Gate grounds, routinely driving past majestic monuments like the Purana Qila and Humayun's Tomb, the pavement shopping in Janpath and Sarojini markets, and the never-ending routine of music, dance and drama at the Kamani Auditorium. 'Nothing will be the same again,' I muttered to myself as our luggage was being loaded on its way to Hyderabad. Nothing, in fact was. At that point, little did I realise that I was going to embark on a personal journey of discovery, a discovery of a whole new world suffused with glitter and grandeur. It was a world that had almost vanished and I was to get just a whiff of it.

Disheartened as I was, once I reached Hyderabad, I looked around with sudden interest as we drove through the impressive gates of what was to be our new residence. We were to live on the premises of Bella Vista, currently the Administrative Staff College of India, the former residence of Prince Azam Jah, the Prince of Berar and heir to the Nizam of Hyderabad.

It was late at night by the time we entered the grounds of the palace, but in spite of the darkness, I could make out the outlines of the ancient trees that lined the driveways. The hedges were trimmed and kept low and the grounds appeared to be extensive. My eyes opened wide as we climbed the gracious wooden staircase leading to our so-called 'flat' where we were to live. I walked through the spacious landing into the large halls and the humongous bedrooms. The graceful furniture, the deep and voluminous teak wood cupboards and the century-old bathroom fittings so charmed me, I was impatient to explore more. I stepped out onto the terrace and looked around. It was a clear night and the moon was high. I could see the silhouette of trees in the distance and the shimmering waters of a swimming pool. A spacious and well-laid-out garden stretched out below me. The breeze coming from the Hussain Sagar Lake was cool and fresh, bearing with it the fragrance of frangipani. I was enchanted by it all.

The next morning, I drew back the curtains and stepped out of the French windows, eager to discover more. I looked out into a charming courtyard, with its flowering trees and royal palms that stood tall with age. The overgrown bougainvilleas cascaded in a riot of colours from the tall trees. The palace itself stretched out gracefully in all its elegance, bathed in the early morning sun.

A young bride had come here seventy years ago, in 1931. Tall and statuesque, she was European by upbringing and was an outdoor person. She rode, swam and played tennis in a Hyderabad where women seldom stepped out of their homes. She broke the prevailing purdah system and took part in public events. She was Durru Shehvar, the daughter of the deposed Ottoman Caliph of Turkey, daughter-in-law of the last Nizam, Mir Osman Ali Khan, and the bride of Prince Azam Jah, the Prince of Berar and the heir apparent of the Nizam.

The seventh Nizam, Osman Ali Khan, had two sons, Prince Azam Jah and Moazzam Jah both of marriageable ages by Indian standards at that time. The fact that the princes had gone on a tour of Europe was known in the city, for the movements of the Nizam's family were of much interest to the subjects of the Nizam. What was not known and not expected were the marriages of the two princes to the illustrious Turkish princesses of the Ottoman family.

The Caliph, successor to the Prophet Muhammad and the commander of the faithful, at least in theory, was the spiritual and temporal leader of the Sunni Muslims the world over. By the end of the World War I, the Ottoman Empire had lost its former glory, was defeated and dismembered. Revolutionary forces led by Mustafa Kamal took over the reins of the government, and the Sultanate as well as the Caliphate was abolished. In the aftermath of these events, Abdul Majid Han, the aging Caliph was exiled to Nice with his family, where he lived in reduced circumstances. At such a time, it was the Nizam of Hyderabad who came to the rescue of the exiled royal family. A generous pension was granted to the ex-Caliph to tide over difficult times. Almost a decade later, through the intermediation of Shaukat Ali, a leader of the Khilafat movement in India, the marriage alliances were arranged for Durru Shehvar, the only daughter of Abdul Majid Han, to the elder prince and Niloufer, his niece to the junior prince, Moazzam Jah. The marriages attracted much world attention and speculation. The weddings led to the belief, in some quarters, that the Nizam had political ambitions for his sons. The weddings were celebrated on 12 November 1931 at Nice, France. It was a simple ceremony and was attended only by the immediate family of the bride. The Indian contingent consisted of the delegates from Hyderabad who had gone to Europe to attend the Round Table Conference at London.

The arrival of Princess Durru Shehvar and her younger cousin Princess Niloufer was an occasion of great joy and celebration in Hyderabad. The people of Hyderabad looked up to the foreign born princesses with awe. The daughter and niece of the Ottoman Caliph in their midst! If Durru Shehvar was striking for her statuesque figure and regal bearing, Niloufer was marked for her bubbly nature and ravishing good looks. She was barely out of school when she came to Hyderabad. A series of banquets and parties were thrown in honour of the newly married couples. The couples settled down in two richly appointed palaces in the city. What followed was the stuff fairy tales are made of, at least in the first few years after the marriages. Their arrival in the medieval city of Hyderabad brought a touch of modernity and a tumult of social activity. The princely couples spent their summers in Kashmir as the guests of the ruler of Kashmir, and special trains carrying their entire entourage left the city in great ceremony.

The British Resident looked upon the marriages of the two princes to the deposed Ottoman royal house with approval. It helped the two princesses to have the blessing of the British, particularly in matters of breaking out of uncomfortable customs like purdah, in which women had to confine themselves to their quarters and never come out in the presence of men. In an extraordinary break from convention, the Nizam took his daughters-in-law with him to important public functions, which led an English onlooker to comment that the 'Nizam was bubbling over with pride in his daughters-in-law.' The appearance of the two princesses at social functions was marked by elegance and glamour.

The Bella Vista Palace, newly renovated and decorated to receive the royal couple, came to life. The prince and the princess occupied separate apartments, as was the custom; the prince was on the ground floor and the princess in the first floor apartments, for reasons of privacy. At present, the princess' private apartment has been converted into the living quarters of the principal of the Administrative Staff College of India. For me, it was a rare experience to occupy the very rooms where the princess had once lived.

Princess Durru Shehvar worked hard to adjust to the culture of Hyderabad. Fluent in Turkish, French and English, she took pains over and acquired the local language, Urdu. She attended functions at the college for women and the primary schools for girls. She spoke passionately about primary education. A few aristocratic ladies, like Begum Wali-ud-Daula, Rani Kumudini Devi and Leela Mani, the daughter of Sarojini Naidu, gathered around her and joined her in outdoor activities like riding and tennis as well.

But hers was not a happy life. Fate played a cruel trick on her. Heir to great heritage and wealth, she thrice witnessed the loss of inheritance in her lifetime. As a child, she saw her father, Abdul Majid Han, the Ottoman Caliph, exiled to Nice. The family took little with them, except for a few faithful retainers. The second time was when her husband, the Crown Prince and Prince of Berar, was overlooked as heir to the gaddi by his own father, the seventh Nizam. The last time was when her son, Prince Mukarram Jah, was divested of his right to rule Hyderabad, when the Nizam's rule was set aside by the Indian Republic following the Police Action of 1948.

Then there was the clash of cultures between her husband and herself; she was westernised and was modern in her outlook and he was steeped in the most dissolute of court traditions. Matters came to a head over the question of the education of her two sons. Princess Durru Shehvar was keen that they should be educated, away from the court and its sycophants, a point on which there was resistance from the Nizam. In 1947, Durru Shehvar left for England with her two young sons, ostensibly to educate them in England. But in reality she carried the deeper wound of irreconcilable incompatibility with her husband. With her departure came to an end the most colourful period in the history of Bella Vista. The palace lost its sheen, never to recover it again.

In its heyday, a few hundred retainers manned the palace grounds. A swimming pool and tennis courts accommodated the princess' love of sports. Prince Azam Jah was a connoisseur of horses and had his stud farm close by. Many distinguished men of the day called on the prince, the heir apparent and also the commander in chief of the Hyderabadi armed forces. Among such distinguished visitors was Mohammad Ali Jinnah who visited Hyderabad in 1946, a year before independence. The palace was the scene of much festivity. There were banquets and dance parties for the visiting dignitaries, mostly English, and birthday parties for the children. Ceremonial military uniforms mingled with the brocade sherwanis of the nobles; western gowns contrasted with the graceful chiffon saris, however few. In all such get-togethers, Princess Durru Shehvar was always the centre of attraction and the toast of the town.

All that was seventy years ago and much water has flowed under the bridge since. The prince and princess vacated the palace long time ago and the trappings of royalty have since vanished. But memories and romance hang about the palace like the morning mist, both alluring and elusive. It takes but little imagination to conjure images of past glory. Pictures of the family adorn the walls of the palace. Durru Shehvar sits there, tinted in sepia, elegant and regal, flanked by her husband and her two young sons. Together, they make a pretty picture.

I walk around the flat, my new home, and the palace, exploring and discovering. I walk carefully in the mysterious underground tunnel built as an air raid shelter during World War II. I admire the stucco work in the prince's apartment and the view from the drawing room. I take a walk through the well-lit footpath in the garden, under the ancient gulmohar and jacaranda trees.

It is easy to transport myself to another age. If the din of the traffic and the garish billboards do not intrude upon my consciousness, I can convince myself that I am living in a bygone era. I look down at the sprawling lawns and wonder how many receptions and parties were thrown there. I imagine wrought iron lampposts throwing myriad lights, strains of music and laughter floating in the air, busy palace retainers rushing back and forth laden with heavy trays and the array of shiny motorcars driving up the motorway.

Hyderabad today is like any other city in India, growing fast and bursting at the seams. Congested roads, maddening traffic, screaming billboards and a confusion of high-rise buildings mark the city. The culture of the city too has changed beyond recognition. Anything old-fashioned is passé. Modernity of dress, speech, architecture and lifestyle is favoured. One seldom comes across the famous Hyderabadi tahzeeb today. No more does the citizenry speak the old Deccani, a charming mix of Urdu, Marathi and Telugu. Largely extinct are the grace and old-world courtesy of the past and so are the gentle speech and courteous manners. The modern Hyderabadi is a man in a hurry and the city's understated elegance has been replaced by a certain brashness.

The once celebrated weather of the city is no more. Old timers complain that the city is increasingly turning hot and humid. Ancient trees that lined the wide roads in the olden days have fallen victim to road widening and the chrome and glass of the ultra modern buildings reflect the glare on to the streets. Large tanks and lakes that existed in living memory, like the Enugula Kunta where elephants were said to have been washed in Banjara Hills, have made way for housing colonies and atrophied into pretty ponds amidst manicured gardens, where the citizenry is encouraged to go for their morning constitutionals. A regular housing colony has been built in the bed of Ma Saheba's Tank, built four centuries ago during the Qutub Shahi dynasty and the colony goes by the name 'Masab Tank.'

Bella Vista today remains an island in a fast-changing city, where a small part of the old Hyderabad lingers on. Enter its charming portals, and you enter a different world. The palace itself has remained relatively intact, barring changes in the interior necessitated by its new function as a college. The layout of the gardens has changed over the period, perhaps for the better. The old chandeliers and light fittings have more or less disappeared, although a few surprises remain; an occasional carved table here and an unexpected chandelier there, as reminders of what once was.

The present staff who man the college grounds carry themselves with such dignity and pride that they seem to belong to a different era; their old world grace and courtesy take you by surprise. When an attendant or a peon bends low to do a salaam or wish you an ordinary good morning, he makes you feel very special and important; when a bearer places a plate of food or a humble cup of tea in front of you, he does it with such grace and elegance that you wonder if you are at a nawab's dinner table. There is a whiff of the princely Hyderabad in their deportment and manner. I have often been surprised and touched by the concern and affection shown by the staff, when at a dinner with a few hundred people, a bowl of fruit would discreetly be brought to me as dessert, in deference to my vegetarianism. It is so typical of a Hyderabadi to be concerned about the needs and comfort of others and I was to notice it in all those whom I met, cutting across classes during my stay in the city.

The food that the kitchen at Bella Vista serves is very Hyderabadi. This does not necessarily mean that the cooks cannot turn out an authentic south Indian or a north Indian/Punjabi meal. Attending a dinner under the shadow of the palace in the sprawling lawns of the garden is so atmospheric that it can indeed be a memorable experience.

As a college, the palace buzzes with a different kind of activity today. Mid-career managers, civil servants, people's political leaders and even judges are trained here. The drawing room, with its wooden flooring and chandeliers, which have witnessed many banquets and ballroom dances, is now a conference hall where intellectual discussions, debates and lectures take place. It is a frequent venue for such activities, and invitations to Bella Vista are keenly sought after. There was a fleeting suggestion at some point that the hall be named after the erstwhile mistress of the palace, Princess Durru Shehvar, but that remained only a suggestion. The living rooms of the Prince of Berar have been converted into rooms for the faculty. The large room that housed his wardrobe, consisting of a few hundred lounge suits, a variety of hats, dastars and walking sticks, has been converted into a lecture hall. The prince was quite a dandy; whole shops were placed at his disposal when he went shopping. Entire bolts of cloth were purchased for him to ensure the garment's exclusivity, so that none of his subjects could attempt to wear clothes similar to his.

It is a rare experience to occupy the very rooms the princess had used. At times I wonder if the princess gazed on the same scene that I do. I notice that the jacaranda next to the bedroom is in bloom. Did she plant the tree? A train rumbles past at a distance, just as it did in her day. I am told that the engine driver had strict instructions not to whistle when the train passed the palace. The cool morning breeze is laden with the fragrance of frangipani flowers. I sit back and shut my eyes, soaking up the moment, reluctant to break the spell. Sitting on the terrace early in the morning before sunrise is an experience in itself. Each season brings surprises in its wake. In the months of March and early April, one can see the grand spectacle of thousands of rosy starlings, migratory birds from Eastern Europe, flying in swarms towards the Hussain Sagar Lake. The sight of these clouds of little birds swishing past Bella Vista is truly spectacular. Then there are the hornbills that appear in the rainy season and announce their arrival on the palace grounds with their raucous cries as they roost and breed on the massive peepul trees. On a good day, they will put up a show for you, swooping back and forth from tree to tree, sometimes across the length of the garden as fancy takes them. Come winter and there is a regular shower of fragrant blossoms from the aptly named 'rain trees' which scent the morning breeze.

In spite of the changes in Hyderabad, an imaginative mind can still recapture some of the romance of the old Hyderabad in Bella Vista. True, the train that passes in front of the palace tiptoes no more as it used to in the olden days. On the contrary, it screams past the college, forcing lectures to pause until the noise dies down. Similarly, the din of street traffic invades the interiors of the college. There was a time when the palace residents could gaze at the waters of Hussain Sagar unhindered and hence the name, Bella Vista. However, not so any more; a whole colony of unauthorised constructions has come up on the water's edge. In a strange case of 'lake grabbing', much land has been quietly disposed off for various constructions. The palace grounds, according to the Municipal Survey Map of 1915, were heavily wooded with tamarind trees. 'The fruit was plump and sweet,' an old retainer reminisces. There were also three stepped-wells meant for irrigating the grounds in the days when these were agricultural lands. The wells have been covered and the trees long since cut down to make way for the formal garden. Some trees, majestic with age and full of character, stood as recently as the year 2000 when they became victims to road widening. They were subjected to slow death by the repeated black topping of the road. Others were cut down in the dead of the night before anyone realised what was happening or could protest.

Abutting Bella Vista is a temple dedicated to Lord Hanuman and is more than a hundred years old. The existence of the temple right next to the residence of the heir apparent raises interesting questions. When the Administrative Staff College was being set up, using the Staff College at Henley on Thames in England as a model, there were a few irritants that needed to be sorted out. One of them was the noise made by the temple abutting the compound wall of the palace. It was noted with dismay that the temple bells started pealing very early in the morning, and continued to do so well into the day. 'How can lectures go on though all this noise?' wondered the Englishman who had come to help set up the college. It is strange how that comment contrasted with what had happened earlier, under a different dispensation.

It was the month of March and the weather was already turning warm. We sat on the terrace, with cups of coffee and the morning newspapers. There was disturbing news from Gujarat, where there was a carnage following the burning of a bogie of karsevaks at the town of Godhra. There were many disturbing imputations and suggestions in the newspapers regarding the communal conflagration that followed. The atmosphere was charged all over the country. Political parties were taking sides and party heads were making pronouncements with an eye on the forthcoming Gujarat elections. The communal divide in Gujarat in independent India immediately drew my attention to what I had read about Hyderabad.

In the old Hyderabad state, the majority of the population was Hindu and the ruler was a Muslim. I wondered about the Hanuman temple abutting the college premises. The temple was certainly there when Bella Vista was the residence of the prince. It was interesting that a Hindu temple was allowed to exist literally on the palace grounds, that too the residence of the heir apparent who is said to have been fond of partying all night and sleeping all day. If a train engine could be silenced from disturbing the quiet of the palace, the offensive temple could be removed too, with equal alacrity, if the authorities so desired. That the temple continued to exist and in fact flourish, said a lot about the tolerance of the prince and the culture of the city.

It is often said that in Hyderabad, the people enjoyed a composite culture. 'Ganga-Jamuni' is one word Hyderabadis are fond of using, indicating that Hyderabadi culture was a blend of Hindu and Muslim cultures. 'One was a Hyderabadi, and that was all that mattered, whether one was a Hindu or a Muslim did not matter.' The seventh Nizam, Osman Ali Khan, is supposed to have remarked often that the Hindus and the Muslims were like his two eyes. Hyderabadis hold up the example of Maharaja Kishen Pershad, the prime minister at the time of the sixth Nizam, Mahboob Ali Khan. The Nizam had no hesitation in making a Hindu his prime minister. On his part the maharaja was so liberal that he took both Hindu and Muslim wives. Then there is the story of Mahboob Ali Khan interviewing a Muslim scholar from northern India for the position of a tutor for his son. The scholar was found suitable and was almost given the job, but for the fact that the foolish man pointed out to the ruler that he had noticed that a Hindu was in charge of the royal kitchen, which according to him was not very wise and he thought it advisable to transfer the charge to a good Muslim, in the interest of the Nizam's security. That remark so incensed the ruler that the scholar was forthwith packed off to where he came from, with the Nizam remarking that anyone with such narrow-minded views was not fit to tutor his sons. There are many stories in Hyderabadi lore with a similar theme. The same Mahboob Ali Khan propitiated the Musi river, by performing harathi and offering prasad to the Goddess Bhavani when floods ravaged the city in 1908.

Old Hyderabadis are of the firm view that whatever ills the Nizam's rule might have suffered from, discrimination based on religion was not one of them. The administration treated both the Muslim and Hindu employees as equals. There is one interesting example to highlight this point.

There was a rule regarding the leave civil servants could avail of, the text of which read as follows:

A Government servant is entitled to special leave not exceeding six months for going on pilgrimage to the holy places, viz Mecca (Haj), Madina, Karbala, Baghdad, Najaf (Iraq), Mashad (Iran) or Bait-ul-Muqaddas (Jerusalem),...further that in such cases the normal ceiling four months' leave...be waived.

It was however noticed by the government itself that while the rule provided for the pilgrimage of Muslims, Christians and the Jews, the Hindus were excluded from the list. It was felt, perhaps, that the people of other religions had to travel far, to other countries but the Hindus did not. However, the Finance Department pointed out that the Hindus too would have to travel a great distance of eight hundred and thirty five miles both ways to cover the Char dhams. Moreover, some of the temples were in remote areas and the pilgrims had to reach them on foot. Much discussion followed and the amendment to the rule that followed read as:

A Government servant is entitled to a special leave not exceeding six months for going on pilgrimage to the holy places in Himalaya (Badrinarayan, Kedarnath, Gangotri and Yamnotri), Tirth, Prayag, Kasi and Gaya (chardams)...further that in such cases the normal ceiling of four months' leave...be waived.

The question of a Hindu temple abutting the palace continued to intrigue me. Curious to learn, first hand, the experience of the temple priest, I called on the old and ailing mahant. When I visited him, the mahant sat back, worry beads in his hand and a shawl thrown across his knees. The temple was undergoing renovation and the floor slabs were being replaced. The mahant did not officiate in the temple any more. His sons had taken over the job. He looked distinctly unwell; he wheezed and coughed, and was puzzled by my visit. The temple had lost much land to road widening just recently, and he looked at me with troubled eyes.

After the preliminaries, I came to the point. The mahant was relieved and happy to talk about the temple and the old times.

'The temple was built on a six-acre plot nearly three hundred years ago. Sri Ananda Brahmachari, a santh from northern India, found a murthi of Bhagvan Sri Hanuman and founded the math. The math became a shelter for sadhu santh mahathmas, who travelled from the north to the south. In 1910, the land in the possession of the math was wrongly declared as porambok and was given away as a patta. Later in 1920, Sir Ali Imam came to stay in the small bungalow when he was appointed to the Executive Council by the Nizam Sarkar. After five years, when he left Hyderabad, the Public Works Department acquired the property. The bungalow was expanded and turned into a palace; subsequently the prince came to live here.

'Those were good times,' the mahant said, dreamily. I had noticed the same glazed expression on whoever reminisced about the olden days. 'People were good. There was a lot of courtesy and civility among the Hyderabadis. The Muslims of those days respected us a lot. They respected the Hindu religion and also Hindu customs and traditions. We Brahmins were held in high regard. There was so much understanding between communities that sometimes the Muslims would ask us to perform pujas in their names in times of difficulties. When Sir Ali Imam was in occupation of the property, he granted extra land to the temple. Both the Hindu and the Muslim officers helped us whenever we needed help. When the prince was in occupation of the property we would be granted generous donations for festivals like Dipavali and Vijayadasami.

'Princess Durru Shehvar brought up her sons extremely well. They were regal in their bearing and very courteous. We used to see them go riding every morning. The mother had good control over her sons. The princess was good to everybody and was not partial to Muslims. She treated the people of all the religions as equals. There used to be forty five imli trees and three step-wells on the property. Those were the days of the plague. Many people used to migrate to the Punjagutta area and take shelter in the Lata Prasad Garden. Lata Prasad was a shahukar and had a large garden near the Punjagutta police station. The government made a plague shelter opposite the police station. The pujari of the Hanuman temple would return to the shelter after doing puja. The land in between was a vast jungle.'

The mahant had to pause to let a bus thunder past. 'Mahbub Karan of the Malwala family was the ADC to Prince Azam Jah at that time. We were facing financial problems those days. When Mahbub Karan came to the temple one day, we told him about our difficulties. He conveyed our message to the prince. Then onwards, we would be sent fifteen kilos of rice, flour, four litres of oil and fifteen rupees by the palace. Not only that, we had a lot of freedom in those days. We would get flowers from the palace. We would ring the temple bell early every morning but no one objected. It did not matter that we were right next to the palace of a Muslim prince. We were much respected.'

What the mahant told me was in keeping with what the documents of the government archives vouch for. A close scrutiny of the farmans of the seventh Nizam reveals that the Nizam made donations for the upkeep of many Hindu temples like Yadagirigutta, Bhadrachalam and even the Balaji Temple at Tirupati, which was outside the Nizam's territory and was, in fact, in British India. It is a less-known fact in India today that it was the princely state of Hyderabad that initiated and paid for the restoration of the frescos of Ajanta. What is also not known is the fact that the so called 'miser,' the seventh Nizam, made generous donations to Shantiniketan, (a sum of Rs 1.25 lakhs in 1926-27), the Banaras Hindu University, Andhra University, the Telugu Academy and for the Gokhale Memorial Scholarship.

The most interesting is the case of the Bhandarkar Oriental Research Institute of Pune. The Nizam granted funds for ten years for the publication of the epic *Mahabharat* and to build a guest house, against the advice of the finance minister Lt Col Trench. Trench protested vehemently since it was not he said, 'financially prudent', to make the grant when the state's finances were not too sound. The Nizam overruled him and the Bhandarkar Institute got the grant, not for ten years as originally proposed, but eleven, and extra funds for the purchase of furniture for the guest house! And who were the ministers who were involved in paving the way in making the grants? Maharaja Kishen Pershad, the prime minister, Sir Akbar Hydari, the then finance secretary who was a Bohra Muslim and Faridoon Jung, the minister of the Political Department and a Parsi, among others. That was the level of sophistication in Hyderabad at that time!

∿

Prince Muffakham Jah, the second son of Durru Shehvar, stood looking down at the cottage, which was a part of the original structure, next to the library. The library, a modern building constructed recently, was cleverly integrated with the palace. The cottage, the library and the palace sheltered a pretty little cobbled courtyard where white bauhinias blossomed and potted plants proliferated. The tall and lanky prince, shy and retiring by nature, had visited Bella Vista a couple of times earlier, I was told. This time round, I was there to receive him. What was more, I was able to get what may be termed 'an insider's view,' of the palace. He drove up in his tiny Maruti 800, an austerity reminiscent of his grandfather, the seventh Nizam. There was a hushed excitement among the staff on his arrival and they bent low in courtly adaabs. Prince Muffakham Jah looked around, slightly bewildered. I wondered how much he remembered of his stay in the palace.

'That is where my mother's Turkish ladies-in-waiting stayed along with our Scottish governesses and those rooms there were our class rooms,' he said, pointing to the rooms beyond. 'I cannot remember much of my mother's garden. It very much looks the same to me, except perhaps that those tall royal palms were not there. Our birthday parties were thrown on the lawns. We used to have fireworks at the end of the parties.'

It was a rare treat for me to be shown around the palace by the prince. He is sixty-odd years in age and stays in the nearby Banjara

Hills whenever he visits Hyderabad. I wondered what it meant to him to walk around the palace of his childhood, to look at the bare shell in its present state, stripped of the rich curtains, furniture, paintings and the other adornments. Did it bring back happy memories or were his memories too blurred?

The present dining room of the principal's flat was where the princes' toys were stored and the 'boys'' food was specially cooked in the adjacent kitchen. The senior prince stayed in the present principal's guest suite and the junior prince at the end of the corridor. The long corridor between the two, now partitioned, was an uninterrupted cricket pitch for the boys. Many matches were won and lost. The prince's eyes twinkled when he talked about his childhood friend, Shiv Lal, the dhobi's son who lived on the palace grounds. The young prince would signal to the boy from his window, they would make an assignation and the prince would dash down the rear staircase on a secret mission, hoodwinking the teachers and the ayahs. 'Shiv Lal washes our clothes now,' said the prince.

Prior to 1947, the palace belonged to the Public Works Department of the Hyderabad state and Prince Azam Jah occupied it in his official capacity as the commander-in-chief of Hyderabad's armed forces. After Independence, the palace passed on to the Government of Andhra Pradesh. After 1948, when Azam Jah had to vacate the palace, an offer was made to the Nizam to buy it if he so wished, for a sum of eighteen lakh rupees. Azam Jah was not interested in living in Bella Vista and preferred to move to a smaller property. The palace thus remained with the government. It was used as the official guest house in the following years. Later when the Administrative Staff College was being set up in 1957, Bella Vista was selected as the ideal location. Prior to it when the state of Andhra Pradesh was formed in 1956, a suggestion was made that Bella Vista would be an appropriate residence for the governor. That suggestion was turned down on security grounds and the neighbouring residence of the then Prime Minister of Hyderabad, Shah Manzil, was made the Raj Bhavan.

Today the principal's flat has very attractive Nirmal and Banganpalli furniture. Nirmal and Banganpalli are two villages in the districts of Adilabad and Kurnool of Andhra Pradesh. The local artisans of the two districts made attractive furniture, and it was once fashionable for the wealthy to use Banganpalli furniture in their homes. Screens made of wood with intricate designs in lacquer were especially popular. Like many traditional crafts in India, with a change in fashions, these traditional crafts too suffered a setback. The flat's Nirmal and Banganpalli furniture, which once belonged to Sir Akbar Hydari, the former Prime Minister of Hyderabad, was particularly attractive since the tables and chairs were made to French designs. Once the accumulated grime and grease marks were removed, the furniture gleamed. I would proudly display my 'antique furniture,' and sure enough, it invariably attracted attention.

Living in Bella Vista spurred me to explore other imposing mansions, the traditional deodis in particular, in the city. Sadly, I was destined to be sorely disappointed. The more I tried, the less I succeeded, for there are no stately mansions left to admire in the city today. They were already demolished. The Hyderabad of fairy tales, of fabulous wealth and opulence, is no more. The palaces and grand residences set in large gardens have disappeared without a trace. There is little but congestion, filth and clutter in the old city today.

My efforts to meet people who could tell me about the old city were equally disappointing. Reams have been written about Qutub Shahi Hyderabad, but little about the Asaf Jahi city. The few old people who remembered the city as it was were reluctant to talk. My enquiries were met with cynicism, derision and silence. It was as if the city suffered from mass amnesia. 'You have come upon the scene too late,' some said. 'What is the use of talking about times gone by?' said others. 'It was a feudal system and it is good that it collapsed. What is the good of those useless deodis, where profligates and wasters lived?' a friend demanded sternly, himself an old Hyderabadi. It was as if a hush had fallen on the city, as if there was some dark secret that they wanted to hide.

My journey into the remaining deodis was neither happy nor smooth. It evoked nostalgia, unhappy memories and even anger amongst those that I interviewed. Few wanted to reminisce as for most the memories brought nothing but pain. But I persisted in my quest in spite of the obstacles. My search, such as it is, started with Bella Vista. I was lucky to find Robert Schick, an archaeologist by profession, newly arrived from the USA and eager to explore the city, and Dr Puranik, a keen photographer. Dr Praful Puranik, a medical doctor, is no professional photographer. For him, photography is a passion and a welcome escape from work. The three of us trudged the old city week after week, starting early in the morning to beat the heat and the dust. Sadly there was not much to cover for there were only few deodis standing. We had to contend with decay and dilapidation wherever we went.

The Deodis

𝕍

In the Hyderabad of the eighteenth and nineteenth centuries, the nobles and the wealthy men of the city lived in traditional fortified residences called deodis (alternately spelled as devdis, deoris or deorhis). The three outstanding features of the deodis, as seen in Hyderabad, were their prominent main entrances, high enclosing walls and inner courtyards.

The basic concept of building deodis in the above-mentioned style was prevalent in Marathwada and interior Telengana for several centuries. Village chiefs and feudal lords lived in those deodis and in troubled times the deodi offered shelter not only to the feudal lord but to his people as well. These two regions were a part of the Nizam's territory till the States Reorganisation Act of 1956. A few typical deodis in their basic form exist to the present day in rural Maharashtra.

However, the word 'deodi' seems to vary in its meaning in different languages. This can best be understood by studying the definition of the word in different languages. Dictionaries of several languages give the meaning of the word 'deodi' variously as the residence of a feudal lord, or the chief of a dargah, with the outstanding feature being the main entrance. Security seems to be the central concern for the evolution of the concept of a deodi.

The Urdu dictionary, *Farhang-e-Asafia* gives the meaning of the word 'deodi' (a Hindi word) as the residence of a Nawab or a Raja; or the chief of a dargah, with a big main entrance, big halls, open spaces and separate apartments for men and women.

The standard Telugu Dictionary *Shabdaratnakaramu*, compiled by B. Seetharamayya identifies 'deodi' as a Hindi word and gives its meaning as the entrance of a fort or that of a 'rajanagaru' meaning the ruler's establishment.

The Dictionary of Hindustani and English (1905), compiled by John Shakespeare of the East India Company identifies 'deodi' as an Urdu word and gives the meaning as 'a threshold, a door, an antechamber or/and a porch; the doorkeeper (of such a structure) is called a 'deodidar.'

Lastly the *Adarsha Marathi Shabdakosha*, by Dr P.N. Joshi gives the meaning as 'a small platform or a niche near the front door of the house.'

Nizam-ul-Mulk, the founder of the Asaf Jahi dynasty which lasted for two and a quarter centuries from 1724 to 1948, ruled his territory with Aurangabad, which was located in the Marathwada region, as his capital. Because of the continuous trouble between the warring factions of the Deccan, the powerful feudal lords of the region built themselves fortified residences called deodis, into which the feudal lord as well as his people could withdraw during troubled times.

In the year 1763, Nawab Nizam Ali Khan, the second Nizam, shifted his capital from Aurangabad to Hyderabad. Thereafter, the focus of political activity of the Asaf Jahis shifted to Hyderabad. For decades subsequent to the shifting of the capital, trouble with the Marathas continued right up to 1795. Consequently, the feudal lords, jagirdars and nobles who moved to Hyderabad continued to build deodis as protected residences for themselves.

In the later years, even after the Subsidiary Alliance was signed with the British in the year 1798, and peace prevailed, deodis continued to be built in Hyderabad. Important jagirdars who were the close associates of the Nizam, enjoyed immense wealth and power. For them, building large and impressive deodis, lavishly decorated and serviced by retinues of well-trained servants, became a statement of power and authority. The basic structure of a deodi as it existed in rural Marathwada and Telengana was enlarged and made more elaborate in Hyderabad. The main entrance to the deodi was made more impressive and the number of courtyards within the enclosure was increased. Over a period of time, sundry structures like a khazana, tosha khana, mez khana, farrash khana and bawarchi khana came to be added to the core structure, necessitated by the lifestyle of the feudal lords who, as wealthy jagirdars, led a life of luxury. The deodis of Hyderabad were like self-contained townships in which the nobles lived with their extended families and large retinues of servants. The deodis were guarded by bands of armed men, equipped with an array of weapons. Most of the deodis of the nobility of Hyderabad came to be built on similar lines with minor variations.

By the later half of the nineteenth century, the walled city of Hyderabad had nearly 1200 deodis, ranging in size. The pictorial map of AD 1772 on display in the Idara-e-Adabiat-e-Urdu in Punjagutta and the Municipal Survey Map of 1915 reveal that the deodis were built along all the important streets of the old city. The premier nobles like the Paigahs, who were next only to the ruler in status and wealth, built their residences in Shah Gunj, a short distance from the palaces of the Nizam. The areas favoured for the homes of the other powerful nobles were the roads radiating from the Charminar. Raja Chandu Lal and Maharaja Kishen Pershad, the hereditary peshkars, and the Rai Rayans, the hereditary daftardars, had their sprawling deodis in Shah Ali Banda, close to the Panch Mahalla Palace. Diwan Deodi, the ancestral home of the Salar Jungs, was situated on the Charminar thoroughfare, on the south bank of the Musi river. The Malwalas lived on Maidan Road, close to Alijah Kotla.

The deodis varied in size; some like those of the Paigahs were extensive and occupied a whole block and, and at times, spilled over to the next. The deodis of the minor jagirdars were smaller and much humbler. They were built all over the walled city, cramped and built cheek by jowl. In marked contrast to the present, no particular distribution pattern of residences based on religion or status (apart from the deodis of the premier nobles already mentioned) can be noticed from the survey maps. There were no clusters or separate localities for the residences of either the Hindu or the Muslim nobles; they were built at random. However, the Muslim deodis far outnumbered those of the Hindus. There were some cases of women owning property too. Temples and mosques were built abutting the deodis.

While most of the prominent deodis were on main roads, others, both important and unimportant, were in narrow alleys. Very often land was carved out to build a residence for a married son or a daughter and consequently the approach to the main deodi had to be through an alley. In the early days, there was no concept of buying land and it was granted by the ruler so that a residence could be built. Land had no market value as such, for it could be had for the mere asking in the case of those who were influential at the court.

The deodis often looked drab from the outside. From the street front, all that could be seen of a deodi was its high wall and the imposing gate. In fact, in some cases like the Diwan Deodi, shops lined the outer walls. The streets leading to the deodi were narrow, dusty and crowded. But once one entered the courtyard, it was a different world altogether.

One important architectural feature that stood out in all the deodis was the large entrance. In Hyderabad, the size of the main entrance of the deodi became a symbol of the power and authority of its owner. The higher the perceived status of the lord who lived within, the larger and more elaborate the gate. Iron knobs and spikes embedded in the robust wooden gates announced the impregnability of the deodi and the tall enclosing walls gave total privacy to the residents. The raja or the nawab would ride an elephant, which was a mark of his eminence; hence the entrance to the residence had to be high enough to let an elephant and its ambari pass through it easily. The main entrance was used on special occasions, as when the master of the deodi travelled out in state or when he received high-ranking dignitaries. A small postern, inserted in the main gate, was used for the day-to-day movements of the inmates. Generally to the left but sometimes on both the sides, within the main structure of the gateway itself, was provided a niche to accommodate the gatekeeper. The imposing entrances to the deodis of the premier nobles had a jillu khana, where visitors alighted and were formally received before being conducted to the presence of the lord. On the upper floors of the entrance was the naubat khana, from where naubat played; close by would be the roshan khana, the lighting point from where, before the days of electricity, a hajjam would carry a torch and light all the lights inside the deodi.

Playing naubat was a privilege and an honour bestowed by the ruler on a few nobles in the city. Naubat was played thrice a day to mark the time of the day or on special occasions like the arrival of a dignitary or for an important event taking place in the deodi. In some deodis, the time of prayer was indicated. At a later point, under European influence, it became fashionable to have a clock tower placed over the main entrance. Before clock towers were introduced, cannon shots from the palace of the Nizam indicated the time.

The deodis were provided with a series of courtyards, set apart for the public and private activities of the inmates of the house. The enclosures ranged from the public enclosures of the men, to the private quarters of the family and the severely sheltered zenanas of the women. Behind the deodi, close at hand, lived the huge bands of retainers and servants.

Each deodi had its own rhythm of life and activity, its tone set by the master of the house. The forecourt of the deodi was strictly meant for performing official functions of the lord. The large jagirdars like the Paigahs and the Diwans not only maintained troops but also took care of the civil and judicial administration in their jagirs. They employed a large staff that operated from the peshi of the deodi. The peshis of the important nobles teemed with officials, followers and functionaries of all hues and stations, like the revenue officials, mansabdars, pattedars, vakils and so on. Thus, it became necessary for those nobles to maintain huge establishments for their official use. Moreover, the nobles' social standing in the city necessitated that they should hold court, entertain on a large scale, and hold both religious and social gatherings for the community for which they were the patrons. As such, the deodis were provided with large enclosures to hold big assemblies of courtiers, clansmen and subjects. Depending on the social standing of the owner, deodis were built in varying sizes and degrees of opulence, while the basic traditional features remained the same.

As one entered through the narrow and crowded alley, one could not have expected anything attractive or beautiful within, but the contrast between the exterior and the interior was striking. Once past the outer office/public space, one came upon the reception area. That courtyard was provided with either a simple dalan with a takhat or a beautifully decorated elaborate dalan with rich furnishings, depending on the stature of the feudal lord. Most dalans were the reception areas where the master received formal delegations or entertained guests. A dalan was an open, pillared hall, with decorated ceilings and graceful multi-foliated arches. The pillars of the dalans were made of either wood or of stone. In the latter case, they were plastered with lime and finished into graceful fluted shapes and polished till they shone like alabaster. In front of the dalan would be a pesh-dalan, which was built opposite the main structure. A pesh-dalan was a smaller version of the main dalan, identical in every way, in its composition as well as decoration. The courtyards themselves were further appointed variously with chabutras, chamans, hauzes and at a later point, marble statuary.

The dalans were the showpieces of the deodis and were furnished opulently. In the early years, guests were seated on the floor covered by takhats, carpets or durris. The musnads, where the master of the deodi sat and held court, were grand affairs; they were covered with green or red velvet cloth (yellow being the colour of the ruler) and embroidered with intricate gold and silver thread-work called karchob. There would be an embroidered or decorated canopy over the musnad, held up with silver posts. At a later point, with the influence of the Europeans, it became fashionable to use imported European furniture, and to decorate the deodis with European bric-a-brac. The inner courtyards of the wealthy nobles had beautiful wooden carvings, stucco work, and painted ceilings. The exquisitely carved wooden dalans, quaintly appointed courtyards, sweet-smelling flowering bushes and the cool comfort of deep interiors – these treasures were hidden behind the high walls that enclosed the inner courtyard of the deodi. Very few of those beautiful dalans survive today. Some of the interior decorations of such chambers can be seen in the miniature paintings of Tajalli Khan and Rai Venkatachellam, who were the famous painters of Hyderabad at the time of Nizam Ali Khan (1762-1803).

The beautiful inner courtyards were used as the meeting places of the men where religious gatherings, social functions and singing and dancing sessions by nautch girls were held. Women were excluded from such gatherings, but they could watch the goings-on from the specially provided balconies overlooking the dalan, hidden behind pardahs or chilmans. In most deodis, the inner dalans had balconies and jharokhas of finely carved trellis work. Hidden from public view, the women could enjoy music or a qawwali programme. Eventually, providing jharokhas in the principal halls became such a norm in the deodis of Hyderabad that even the British Residency, built by 1806, provided balconies around the central hall for the ladies. Chandeliers, both the hanging and the standing variety, became customary for the homes of the wealthy nobles. Commenting upon the fascination of the Hyderabadis for chandeliers, a European visitor to the city a hundred years ago wrote:

The Hyderabadists are, like all natives, mad on the subject of glass chandeliers. They have them even in the mosques, and when they are tied up in muslin bags they have anything but a religious look, but rather as if the family were out of town.

The chandeliers were kept covered for most of the year to protect them from dust and grime and more importantly, to keep away the birds from making nests. It was only on important occasions that they were uncovered.

An interesting addition to the deodi was the baradari, a feature unique to Hyderabad. The concept of building baradaris came down to Hyderabad from the Qutub Shahi period. The word 'baradari' literally means twelve doors. One example of a Qutub Shahi baradari is the Taramati Baradari, which still stands intact. It is built on a hillock and has a single large room, with arches on all sides to let in the breeze. It commands an impressive view of the Golconda Fort as well as the beautiful terrain all around. Baradaris were ideal resting places, best suited for use during the long summer months.

Wealthy nobles like Chandu Lal and the Salar Jungs built baradaris in open spaces, beyond the city limits, away from the congestion and the noise of the city. They were set in idyllic locations, either in a garden, or overlooking a water body. Chandu Lal's baradari was set in a garden, while the Salar Jungs' Lakkad Kot was situated on the banks of the Musi river. Unlike Taramati's baradari, which is a stolid structure built of stone, the baradaris of the Hyderabadi nobles were delicate double or triple-storied structures built in wood, provided with elegant jharokhas, finely carved wooden balconies and trellis work. They were meant to be the pleasure houses of wealthy men, who entertained guests lavishly with poetry, music and dance in the seclusion of these structures. Chandu Lal's baradari was said to have been built specially to entertain the third Nizam, Sikandar Jah. Chandu Lal did not get along well with his master and needed to propitiate him. Mahalaqa Bai Chanda, a beautiful dancer and a gifted poetess of Hyderabad is said to have danced for the powerful minister and his master in the baradari.

In the later years, some baradaris were built right next to the deodis, in the city itself. Of those extant, the baradari of Khursheed Jah Paigah, the baradari of Irram Manzil Palace built by Nawab Fakhr-ul-

Mulk II and the baradari of Hussaini Kothi are good examples. Another interesting feature of the baradaris of the later years was the blending of traditional architectural features with modern European construction. Both Irram Manzil and the Khursheed Jah Deodi were very western in style and were fashioned after the British Residency in a Palladian style. But they also had baradaris attached to them to be used for religious and other traditional get-togethers.

All the apartments described so far were a part of the mardana and strictly out of bounds for women. The only women that entered the men's domain freely were aged female servants, who by virtue of their closeness to the family could venture into the men's quarters carrying an occasional message or for an errand.

If the women were kept out of the men's apartments, so were the men from the women's. There were separate quarters for women called zenanas, where they were left free to carry on with their activities. Only very close male members of the household were permitted into the zenanas. A passage connected the mardana to the zenana, and the entrance of the zenana was shielded further by a heavy curtain. The entrance was fiercely guarded by a trusted woman servant of advanced years called a 'mama' who blocked the entry of all men into the women's domain. On the impending entry of the occasional male visitor, she would loudly announce the name of the visitor so that the women were alerted. Even men of the family could not get past her or enter the zenana unannounced. The mama was traditionally a loyal and old servant of the family and hence was held in high esteem in the deodi; she occupied a higher position in the hierarchy of servants and was free to enter both the men's and the women's quarters without raising a protest from either. Trusted eunuchs acted as guards and the go-betweens of the zenana and the mardana in some deodis. The provision of separate apartments for men and women—the zenana and mardana, was adhered to strictly in the deodis of the Muslim nobles but not so in the Hindu households. In the Raja Shamraj and Malwala households, married sons and their families lived in individual apartments or suites.

Zenanas had their own courtyards open to the sky and were equipped with fountains, flowering bushes and pretty chamans. The atmosphere in the zenanas was restful and slow-paced. Water dribbled in the fountains, flowering trees and plants like mynas, chameli and juhi lent fragrance to the air. Women kept birds like mynas and lal munias for pleasure. Cuckoos roosted in the trees and peacocks frolicked in the bushes. All around the courtyard were rooms, skirted with verandas or dalans. The central dalan was generally the largest and was equipped with a takhat and other paraphernalia like a hookah, a silver paandan, itardan, gulab-posh, ugaldan, a khasdan and a water container, and was kept locked when not in use. Surrounded by such silver articles of exquisite workmanship, seated on an expensive carpet or a low diwan and leaning on gau takias, the principal begum of the noble presided over the affairs of the zenana with the dignity and grandeur typical of the Hyderabadi nobility. It was customary for the women of the deodi to pay their respects to the senior begum when she held court. Guests were welcomed with itar and rose water which was sprinkled on them. The principal wives of the nobles were at times provided with separate quarters.

Deodis sometimes had their own shaadi khanas meant exclusively for the use of the family. Some had places of worship, like a mosque or a deval, meant for the private use of the jagirdar and the family. The men of the family used the main entrance to the deodi while the ladies used a side entrance, called the zenani darwaza.

There were no hard and fast rules about the way families lived. In some deodis, the whole family lived in the same building, with its many courtyards. The joint family concept was very much alive. Women worked and lived in their enclosures while the men did their own things. All the children were bundled together; they slept, ate, played and went to school together. Some jagirdars considered it infra dig to send their children to a school. Tutors were engaged at high cost to teach the children in the deodi itself. Since there were restrictions on the movements of the children, they were provided with all the facilities for play and entertainment within the four walls of the deodi.

In the larger deodis like the Diwan Deodi, married daughters were provided with independent quarters. In the Peshkar Deodi, the wives of the peshkar ran independent establishments. In Fakhr-ul-Mulk's Irram Manzil Palace which was built at a later period, married sons were given individual suites of rooms where they lived with their children. When the family met at one place on special occasions, they ate in the traditional way. A dastarkhan would be spread on the floor around which the family members sat and ate.

One rule all the deodis followed was that the master and mistress of the deodi separately held court every morning in their quarters, and it was customary for all the members of the family to be formally attired and to pay their respects to the head of the family. It was taboo to enter the presence of the elders if one was not appropriately dressed. In most households, the master of the deodi was addressed or referred to as 'sarkar' by the other members of the deodi, as well as the servants.

It was in the deodis that the famous Hyderabadi culture was born and nurtured. Be it the language, literature, music, dance, etiquette, courtesy, entertainment, cuisine or dress, they were all important and tradition dictated the norms. Transgressions were frowned upon and social standing and acceptability depended on the degree of refinement that the individuals acquired. Special care was taken to teach children the finer points of etiquette right from their childhood.

Behind the deodis lived the hordes of servants who worked in them. Clerks, office superintendents and the other staff lived in quarters, within easy reach of the deodi. The cooks, drivers, farrashes, ayahs, maalis, polishers, security guards and numerous other retainers lived in huge villages either close to the deodi or sometimes in the grounds of the deodi itself. In the Irram Manzil Palace, there were altogether nine hundred odd servants who lived in wadas behind the palace. There was a marked difference between the mansions they served in and their own humble dwellings.

The zenana had its own servants, who were of different categories. First, there were the palakadis who did very mundane menial work like cooking and nursing. Then there were those who were engaged for a salary and who could leave at will. There were also the family servants who were born in the deodi and never left it. They were like members of the family; they were in charge of the wardrobe and the valuables of the begums whom they served. The begums took good care of their servants and bonds of affection tied the ladies and the servants together. The palakadis were married off appropriately when they came of age and were even provided with large trousseaus.

Wet nurses, whom they called annas, were appointed to suckle new-born babies in the deodi. While feeding an infant in the deodi, if the nurse had her own child, the two children that the woman nursed grew up together and they were called doodh shareek bhai behen. Such children were looked after well and were treated as members of the family. Strong bonds developed between the nurses and those that they suckled, so much so that the old nurses were looked after with great care, years after the association between the two ceased. The servants were well-trained and well-versed in the etiquette of the deodi. Individual residents of the deodi had personal servants who served them for life.

The loyalty of the personal servants was phenomenal. Since the nobles were brought up in extreme seclusion and without the benefit of friends or playmates, they tended to be extremely close to their personal attendants.

The expenses of the servants at the time of marriages, illnesses or deaths were generally taken care of by the nobles. If a servant or a son of a servant got married, he would be brought to the noble for his blessings. The noble would tie the sehra and also make a gift of money on the occasion. For all practical purposes, all those that were employed in the deodi were considered to be the subjects of the noble and were generally taken care of by the master.

An interesting and humorous, if a little confused account of the servants of Hyderabad is recorded by Chenevix Trench, the revenue member of the Nizam's Executive Council in the year 1927:

There were hundreds, if not thousands, of domestic slaves in Hyderabad. All the nobles, including all the Hyderabadi Members of Council, owned them. But when (I) urged the Council to abolish slavery in the state, (I) was met by a firm non possumus. The difficulty, (I) was told, was that slavery had already been abolished, by a firman some years earlier. To abolish it again would serve no useful purpose; it would merely draw attention to its continuance and imply that His Exalted Highness' firman was ineffective. The only support (I) got was from the younger nobles, who complained bitterly that slaves were quite impossible to discipline or control. No matter how idle, dishonest or quarrelsome a slave, you could not sack him, because he had nowhere else to go; you could not sell him, because no one would buy; you could not fine him because he owned no property and received no wages; you could not even beat him because he would immediately lodge a complaint with the nearest magistrate and you would be charged with assault. Female slaves were even more unmanageable, and a very bad influence on the children. The whole situation was intolerable. So slavery was quietly phased out.

However, there was a darker side to the life of the women in the zenanas, which caused most of them much distress. While the principal wives of the nobles led lives of comfort and leisure, the other women, who were numerous did not enjoy much social status and suffered from neglect and indifference. They had to contend with boredom, low self-esteem and lack of purpose in life. Women in the zenanas did get education of a religious nature, but were tutored in little else. Most of their time was spent in pastimes like cooking, embroidery, crocheting, and similar activities. There were no avenues of expression or opportunities of being appreciated if they displayed any degree of talent in any field like writing poetry. Most of them were caught up in a web of intrigue and in the politics of rivalry and jealousy.

The second half of the nineteenth century was a period of change in Hyderabad. Englishness came to influence the architecture, lifestyle, education, spoken language and eating habits of the upper echelons of the society. The British Residency was built by 1806 and it became the fashion to build modern palaces modelled after it. Even the nomenclature of the buildings that they built changed from a 'deodi' to a 'palace.' We have the old-style deodi of the Malwalas being called Malwala Palace. Where new palaces could not be built, old structures were either modified, or new sections on western lines were added to the old deodis. This is evident in the Malwala Palace, the deodi of Iqbal-ud-Daula and the deodi of Asman Jah Paigah, where new office blocks and drawing rooms were added to the otherwise traditional deodis.

But no matter to what extent the nobility tried to imitate the English, the changes remained skin-deep. They could not move away from the traditional lifestyle. The result was that they built mansions that incorporated elements of contemporary European architecture, but also retained traditional features such as separate quarters for women. They could make their mardanas as European as they pleased, but they built their women's apartments in the strictest traditions possible. Even though premier nobles like Fakhr-ul-Mulk threw lavish parties for the British officers, the womenfolk of his family continued to stay in purdah. Even in the modern Bella Vista Palace, the living rooms of the princesses were kept discreetly away from the rest of the rooms, with just a connecting passage between the two.

In the deodis, much attention was lavished on the dalans and the reception rooms, but the living quarters were poorly built. Rooms were small and cramped and there was not much ventilation, and they had no modern amenities like plumbing. Moreover, the old city had grown haphazardly over the years. It became very crowded and a breeding ground for frequent pestilences like the plague. Whenever there were such outbreaks, it became a common practice for wealthy families to move out of their deodis until the disease was brought under control. Sir Visveswarayya who was specially invited to the city to suggest improvements, lamented in 1930 that, 'the city is old, irregularly built and unhealthy; it has to be opened out, cleaned and made wholesome.'

With the construction of the British Residency, ideas of modern living with facilities like plumbing, electricity and running water came to the city. The old-fashioned deodis with their high walls and cramped surroundings lost their appeal. Natural disasters like the Musi flood of 1908 and the plague of 1911 also prompted the nobility to move away from the walled city. Nawab Mahboob Ali Khan, the sixth Nizam, built a modern mansion and a race course at Malakpet and later the seventh Nizam moved to King Kothi across the river in 1914. The nobles followed suit and those who could afford to, built modern palaces set in large gardens, in areas like Himayat Nagar, Saroor Nagar and Malakpet. Over a period of time, the deodis of those who moved out of the city gradually fell into disuse. Their upkeep was neglected and they started to decay and money-strapped owners saw no reason to waste their resources on their old homes.

The Partition of India in 1947 and the Police Action of 1948 tore Hyderabad apart on communal lines; in the aftermath of the Partition some Muslim families from the old city fled to Pakistan. The integration of the State of Hyderabad in 1948 with the rest of India and the subsequent abolition of the jagirs in 1949 dismantled the feudal base of princely Hyderabad. With the traditional source of their incomes having been withdrawn, the nobles of Hyderabad had no other choice but to sell their property for, with the jagirs gone, the deodis were all that they were left with. Disputes over property arose among the heirs and the cases went to courts. Valuable art pieces of the deodis were sold as a prelude to dividing the property on which the deodis stood. It was ironic that a new breed of art dealers and auctioneers roamed the city to buy back pieces of immense value that were sold to the nobles a generation or so back at high costs. Paintings, articles of jade, chandeliers, porcelain and even valuable jewellery were secretly sold off in distress. One by one, the sprawling deodis were demolished. The few deodis that survived those years of turbulence finally fell to the Urban Ceiling Act of 1976, whereby the government put a ceiling on the extent of urban land that an individual could hold. There was a sudden rush to sell the land before the Act came into force and valuable properties were sold for pathetic valuations, thus ending the era of stately homes in Hyderabad. Ancient trees in gardens and orchards were felled and the land was divided into small plots and sold in a hurry, resulting in the congestion and the clutter one sees in the walled city today.

∿

Today the old city continues to be dotted with impressive looking gates, standing by themselves, without either the walls or the accompanying structures that ought to go with them. One often comes across tell-tale signs of the deodis of the past. A high wall, dark with age and a lonely arch torn out of context, are familiar sights scattered over the city. It is not uncommon to see the remnants of a handsome structure, either peeping forlornly though a narrow street, or from behind an ugly concrete structure, looking quite outlandish in its present surroundings. If one only pauses to take a closer look, the building has a story to tell.

The City of Nobles

🎋

In the aftermath of Emperor Aurangzeb's death in the year 1707, the Mughal empire fell into disarray. In the ensuing years, the Mughal subedar of the Deccan, Nizam-ul-Mulk Asaf Jah became independent, even though he continued to call himself the viceroy of the Mughals. In the year 1724, he founded the Asaf Jahi dynasty with Aurangabad as his capital. Subsequently seven generations of his family ruled the Deccan for the next 224 years, upto the year 1948, when the princely state of Hyderabad was integrated with the rest of India.

However, after breaking away from Delhi and establishing the Asaf Jahi rule in the Deccan, Nizam-ul-Mulk was very careful not to rouse the envy of the Mughals by showing signs of independence or holding an elaborate court. In fact, he declared himself the viceroy of the Mughals in the Deccan and had the Friday khutbah read and coins minted in the Mughal emperor's name. However, he started the nucleus of the Hyderabadi nobility by bestowing jagirs and titles upon his close associates. In the early years, when the Nizam was still establishing himself, a majority of the nobles were military lords. Their primary concern was to provide military assistance to the Nizam in times of conflict and war, and in return they received land grants. The income from the land was to be utilised for raising and maintaining troops.

Jagirs were also granted to the Nizam's close aides for meritorious services rendered in other fields like administration. When times were unsettled, there was the danger of the powerful nobles revolting against the ruler. To avoid such a danger, the land granted to the nobles for maintaining troops was never contiguous; the Nizam took the precaution of granting jagirs that were scattered over different parts of his kingdom.

Unlike the first Nizam who kept looking over his shoulder at Delhi, the second Nizam, Nawab Nizam Ali Khan, acquired greater independence. He shifted his capital from Aurangabad to Hyderabad in 1763. His was a period of internal stability and the beginning of an era of cultural effervescence. With the diminishing radiance of the Mughal court, Hyderabad emerged as the rallying point for artistes and poets, who flocked to the courts of the Nizams as well as their premier nobles. Both he and his prime minister, Arastu Jah, were great patrons of art, poetry and music.

Nawab Nizam Ali Khan increased the number of nobles and held an elaborate court. He bestowed large jagirs, honours and titles on his trusted followers. The nobles in turn administered their jagirs and maintained large establishments. They could grant administrative positions and other favours to people of their own choice depending on the size of their jagirs and resources. They very often advanced their kinsmen for high positions with the Nizam and hence slowly came to be looked upon as the leaders of their communities and clans. It was quickly realised that it was difficult to rise officially or socially without a patron and the patron-client relationship came to mark the character of the social structure in Hyderabad.

The nobility of Hyderabad at first comprised of those men who served and distinguished themselves at the Mughal court and came down to the Deccan with the first Nizam. They were the close associates and confidants of the Nizams and occupied prime positions to begin with.

There was a strict hierarchy in the order of the nobility of Hyderabad. At the top of the hierarchy was the Nizam, who himself was a jagirdar in a sense. His lands were called sarf-e-khas lands. Till 1857, the Asaf Jahi rulers were appointed as the subedars of the Deccan through explicit Mughal farmans. Announcements to that effect were made with great fanfare by the envoys from Delhi who were received at the city gates with great ceremony. A hillock on the outskirts of the city, Naubat Pahad, was the spot from where the announcement was made. As such, the Nizams of Hyderabad never called themselves kings.

Then there were the Paigah nobles, who claimed their descent from no less a personage than the second great Caliph of Islam of Arabia. The Paigahs distinguished themselves as military chiefs and won the favour of the first Nizam in his early years in the Deccan. They were given a commission to raise and maintain an army for the personal protection of the Nizam. In later years, in the days of Nawab Nizam Ali Khan, they rose in prominence. Jagirs and titles were bestowed on them and the Nizam also forged marriage alliances with them. That set a trend over the next hundred years, wherein royal women were given in marriage to the Paigah nobles and vice versa. As a result, the Paigahs shot into prominence and supplanted the others in the order of importance and influence. The Paigahs were not only exempted from paying revenue to the Nizam but were also free to look after the civil and judicial administration in their territories. They ran departments like education, health and public works in their jagirs.

Along with the Paigahs, there were five Hindu principalities called samasthans. They were exempted from paying taxes. They were Gadwal, Wanaparthi, Jatprole, Amarchinta and Palvancha. These along with nine other samasthans ante-dated the Mughal invasion of Golconda in 1687 and were permitted to remain independent by both the Mughals and the Asaf Jahis.

The other important nobles were the Umra-e-Uzzams, the premier nobles who were relegated to the second position after the emergence of the Paigahs as the kinsmen of the ruler. There were four families that were granted this status, the Salar Jungs, the Chandu Lal and Kishen Pershad family, the Khane Khanan and the Fakhr-ul-Mulk family. These families were also exempted from paying taxes to the Nizams. Then there were the Rai Rayans and the Malwalas who were the revenue officials. Below them were scores of other jagirdars who were granted jagirs of varying sizes. At the bottom of the ladder were the smaller jagirdars who enjoyed no privileges and sometimes jagirs were granted to them for performing specific functions.

The upper crust of the nobility belonged to a closely-knit exclusive circle, wherein birth determined an individual's status and position at court. Religious affiliation to either the Sunni or the Shiite sects or Hindu religion was of no concern. Bloodline and affiliation to a clan alone entitled a person to the status of nobility. A person was born a noble and no one could claim nobility. At any time, the most valued virtue in a noble of Hyderabad was his absolute loyalty to the Nizam. Awe and respect for the Nizam was bred in the nobles from their childhood.

The nobility lived, in keeping with their station at court and their incomes. They maintained palatial deodis in the old city, held their own courts, had clienteles and courtiers in the form of dependents, followers, musicians, poets and retainers. Even though in the early years the nobles in military service received larger jagirs and occupied more important positions, slowly the scales started tilting towards civilian and administrative functions in later years. Rewards in the form of rich ornaments and titles were one form of showing royal favour. Then the Nizam granted privileges and honours like a naqqar or a band escort, an aalam or a morchel and the permission to travel in ornamental palkis and carriages whenever the nobles went out of their deodis or in state. Some nobles were granted the honour of playing naubat at the entrance of their deodis. Nobles flaunted the honours bestowed on them by the rulers and in the early years, seldom went out of their deodis without the ceremonial escort of the drum, music or the special kind of transport that they were entitled to. In fact, not to do so was considered a slight to the Nizam. As a result, the movements of the important nobles in the city were followed by much fanfare and display. While their movements and the accompanying panoply added a quaint colour to the city, they also caused an uproar whenever they passed though the narrow lanes of the city. The ordinary people scurried and pressed themselves to the sidewalls to let the processions file past. An enchanted visitor to the city in the late eighteenth century records:

> The frequent occurrence in the Hyderabad streets is the peremptory cry to pedestrians to "make way," whereupon the syces, gorgeous with silver or gold trappings, dash into the crowd, pressing them to the right and left of the carriage, in which some nobleman or chief reclines at voluptuous ease, in some cases adding to his enjoyment by smoking a fragrant hookah of a costly make, his armed retainers, in fanciful uniforms, clattering after him upon Arab horses...Occasionally an enormous elephant tramps sturdily and slowly along (with a noble atop), it need hardly be said that everyone makes way for him, although the careful manner in which these ponderous animals tread their way though a crowd, even pushing people out of the way with their trunks, is an indication of their tameness and good nature.

To this could be added the 'sight and sound of the rhythmic hum of the palanquin bearers who alerted the crowds to their movements in the singsong way typical of them and the jingle jangle of the raths, the decorated carts attached to sprightly Gujerathi bullocks that the nobles kept for their womenfolk.' Motorcars came to the city a century later.

The court continued to follow the Mughal etiquette and there was much ceremony in all its proceedings. Protocol was strictly adhered to. The nobles presented themselves dressed in finery as per the status accorded to each of them by the ruler and sat in their appointed places in the durbar hall. When the ruler made gifts of ornaments, it was expected that the noble would present himself at the court dressed accordingly. The durbar was generally held in the evenings. The assembled nobles 'dressed in robes of Kashmir shawls and gold brocade and girt with rich kamarbands and belts, carrying gold-hilted swords under their arms' rose to their feet and stood in their places, eyes downcast, hands folded and barefooted. The Nizam sat on his gold embroidered musnad on a raised platform in the durbar hall which resonated with the strains of joyful music played by the court musicians who were seated at one side.

'The Nizam's retinue sat behind him in a semicircle, that is, those who were allowed the privilege of being seated in his presence, and in front of his musnad were ranged his principal nobles robed in neemajama, after the style of the old Moghal court, each in his appointed place. At a sign from the Nizam, the diwan approached him respectfully and presented his nazar, which consisted of eleven ashrafi; then followed the other nobles in their order of precedence. After them came the State Officials and the rest of those who had the honour of attending the durbar...the rush was so great...several persons attempting to approach the musnad at the same time caused, as was natural, a great confusion.'

After Nizam Ali Khan entered into the Subsidiary Alliance with the British in the year 1798, the jagirdars were more or less freed from their prime responsibility of providing troops to the ruler. The last battle fought by the Nizam and his men on their own strength was in 1795. Unlike the Mughal system of transferring jagirdars, in Hyderabad jagirs had become hereditary. In the absence of any major occupation and the expenditure of maintaining troops, wealth accumulated and time hung heavy in the hands of the nobles.

Assured income, security of life, freedom from major preoccupations and plenty of leisure left most of the nobles free to pursue occupations of their own choice. While some nobles were engaged in the affairs of the state, there were some others who became interested in literature, science and religious learning. Nobles like Mukkaram-ud-Daula, Raja Shamraj, Raghotham Rao, Maulvi Abdul Quayum and others established educational institutions in the city. Some took to collecting manuscripts and rare books and even coins; a few of the nobles had creditable libraries.

The Mughal tradition of miniature painting was continued in Hyderabad. Many noted painters like Danayya and Banayya lived near the Mussavir ka Naka, which in fact, was named after such painters. Many nobles took pride in collecting and commissioning family portraits, and some like the Malwalas were proud possessors of large collections. It was only after the arrival of photography that miniature paintings lost their appeal to the Hyderabadis. The modern European school of painting was introduced to Hyderabad by the French and the British. Those who could afford to do so had their portraits painted in the European style. However, the famous painter Raja Ravi Verma, we are told, did not find much favour in Hyderabad. He came to the city in the hope of getting a commission from the Nizam. He was received well by the nobles and stayed in the city for a while but the promised commission never came.

Apart from miniature paintings, the nobles also collected European art, jade, crystal, antique furniture, old manuscripts and other expensive bric-a-brac. The foremost among such were the Salar Jungs. Rai Rayan Raja Shamraj had a sangrahalay built in his deodi. Some nobles patronised music and qawwali was a popular form of entertainment. Qawwalis were held regularly in the deodis, and were occasions of great excitement. Women were permitted to sit behind the chilmans in the galleries meant for them and enjoy the music. Among the famous singers of later years were Pandit Motiram, the father of Pandit Jasraj and Shankari Bai, who enthralled the music lovers of the city. Begum Akhtar sang at the palace of the junior prince, Moazzam Jah. The tradition of inviting famous singers to the city continued well into the modern day. Bade Ghulam Ali Khan came to the city at the invitation of a Paigah noble who was a patron of music. When the maestro fell ill, the nawab took it upon himself to have him treated. Unfortunately the musician succumbed to his illness and died in Hyderabad. He lies buried in Daira Mir Momin in the old city.

Among other things, building magnificent palaces in the European Palladian style with rich appointments became a statement of the nobles power. Hyderabad was dotted with majestic palaces, set in sprawling grounds till a few decades ago. Some of the palaces had to be forfeited to the state during the lifetime of the builders themselves, as the nobles spent more than they could afford to on their pet schemes, and incurred enormous amounts of debt.

The Hyderabadi nobles believed in dressing in the finest of silks and jewels till the turn of the century. They favoured the use of the best quality himroo of Aurangabad and mushajjar of Benares. Himroo tapestries were much valued and mushajjar cloth was popular with men for making sherwanis and women for making ghagras. The two Turkish daughters-in-law of the seventh Nizam, Princess Durru Shehvar and Princess Niloufer, favoured paithani borders, which were woven in order to be stitched on saris. The two princesses were tall and graceful and they favoured saris with broad borders. Shops in the old city stocked all shades and designs of the textiles. The popularity of these textiles in Hyderabad has kept the unique weaving tradition alive to the present day.

If the Hyderabadi nobles patronised poetry and painting, they were not far behind in encouraging Hindu folk festivals either. They made generous donations for the celebration of the local festivals like Bonalu and Bathakamma. In some deodis, Holi and Rakhi were celebrated with as much enjoyment as Id.

Hunting was a major pastime for most of the nobles. The terrain from Malakpet to Saroor Nagar in the suburbs of Hyderabad was black buck land. It was reserved for the Nizam but there were vast virgin forests at a distance from the city where the nobles could indulge their passion for hunting. Preparing for a hunt was an expedition and involved major planning. Many of the premier nobles had whole armouries of weapons like gauntlet swords used by the cavalry, sailapas, short curved swords, abbasis, Damascus blades, maghrabs, Morocco blades, and short-edged weapons like the Arab jamias and the Irani khanjar. In the gun and rifle category, many brands like Holland and Holland, Greeners, Westley Richards and the like were favoured. Some major deodis had shikar khanas which liaised with the forest and district administrations to organise hunting expeditions for the noble and his friends. Whole townships of tents were erected; cooks, servants and other supporting staff were transported in advance to make the camp comfortable for the noble. Huge bands of beaters were pressed into action on the day of the hunt. Machans were erected and finally, when the hunt was over, photographs were taken with the prizes.

But not all the nobles were refined in their tastes. In the city gathered a large number of wealthy nobles, more or less free of occupation and with a strong appetite for pleasure. Life in the city had many attractions and Hyderabad became a haven for the idle rich. They found unique and innovative ways to spend their wealth and time. After 1800, entertaining European officers of the Company was an all-consuming passion for some and they spent large sums of money and went way beyond their means to impress their European guests. Sons of such nobles took to playing tennis, riding horses and maintaining polo teams. They were sent to England for higher studies. The smaller nawabs limited themselves to local pastimes like playing pacheesi, kabutar bazi, tukkidian ladna, patang bazi, jalsa and so on. The noble would patronise such activities and enjoy the game from a dignified distance. Painting and writing poetry were rare accomplishments and a few high ranking nobles indulged in them. Many aspired to be poets but very few succeeded in writing poetry of any merit. Very often the ustad – the teacher, who was engaged to correct the poetic compositions were in fact the real poets and pathetic efforts were made by the pupil – the noble to attract the attention of those that mattered.

Nautch was a traditional form of entertainment and there does not appear to be odium or stigma attached to it. In the highly conservative and respectable home of Raja Shamraj, a nautch was organised at the time of his wedding. In 1875, when Sir Salar Jung I, who was not given to frivolity, threw a state banquet to welcome the newly arrived Resident, Sir Richard and Lady Meade, one item of entertainment organised for the guests was nautch. The reporter of the London edition of the *Times of India* describes the dance in his dispatch in the following manner:

the dinner was not yet ready, and so the guests must be amused in the meantime. With that view, too, bands of dancing girls are brought on the scene. What a shock to the ideal of the European visitor must the first sight of an Indian nautch be! ... their movements in the great majority of instances are not by any means graceful...there is neither grace nor dignity nor skill evinced.

So goes the unflattering account of a traditional art form which did not meet with the approval of the Englishman of Victorian mindset. Notwithstanding what the Europeans thought about it, the local form of dance was preserved in the nautch of the day.

Mujra was another form of dance in which the dancer sang ghazals or the poetry composed by the notables in the audience. The celebrated courtesan of Hyderabad, Mahalaqa Bai Chanda was an accomplished dancer and a poet, and her company was sought after by men of refinement.

The first blow to the existing system came during the premiership of Salar Jung I, when he brought people from northern India and elsewhere to hold important positions in the state administration. Salar Jung's move was necessitated by his belief that the old nobility was not up to the task of carrying out the modern reforms he envisaged. The court became a haven for intrigue and internecine rivalry and the administration had deteriorated to a point where the British felt compelled to interfere in the internal matters of the state. The principles of governance inherited from the Mughals were not sufficient to meet the demands of the modern day administration. Moreover, in the name of tradition the nobles resisted change and reform. Decay and laxity had seeped into every level of governance. The feudal lords concerned themselves with little more than the collection of revenue. Even the revenue remittances to the state had become lax, as a result of which the state was deeply in debt. The government carried out its work on a day-to-day basis by borrowing heavily from local bankers.

A new element in the politics and the intrigues at the court were the British who were waiting for every opportunity to weaken the Nizam and his nobles and increase their own hold on the affairs of the state. The nobles on their part realised that real power lay with the British and not with the Nizam and wooed the British relentlessly. At any given point, it was hard to fathom, whose loyalties lay with whom.

When Salar Jung I became the prime minister in 1853, he was quick to grasp the situation. It did not take him long to detect the malaise in the administration. Impressed with the administrative practices in British India, he chose to introduce similar reforms in the state of Hyderabad as well. In overhauling the system, Salar Jung had to be careful not to antagonise the old nobility. They were jealous of their place in the court and would brook no change in their authority. Court ceremony and etiquette had to be preserved at all costs.

Salar Jung I soon realised that for his model of administration, he needed educated men of modern outlook. While the Hyderabadi nobles were capable of carrying out the traditional activities, the key positions at the top required persons trained in British India and he had to look outside Hyderabad for capable men. The Aligarh Muslim University at that time was emerging as an educational center under the stewardship of Syed Ahmad Khan. Salar Jung appealed to him to send men adept at administration and assured him that 'he was not going to enquire as to what caste or religion they belonged,' as long as they were good administrators. Some of the men who came to Hyderabad at his instance were Maulvi Sayed Hussain Bilgrami, Maulvi Chirag Ali, Rai Murlidhar and Dr Aghornath Chatterjee. Chatterjee was an educationist and the father of the poet and freedom fighter, Sarojini Naidu. Thus, a new generation of men of the status of the nobility was created in Hyderabad. These men rose to higher positions by sheer merit and hard work; over a period of time they were given titles and honours and became the new nobility.

The old nobility bristled and tried to prevent the entry of people like the Bilgramis into the administration. They intrigued against Salar

Jung and worked towards his ouster and there was also an attempt on his life. Disgusted with the constant bickering at the court, Salar Jung I thrice threatened to resign from the position of prime minister. It was the British who stood by him in his hour of ordeal. The old nobility was too spent and too weak to oust him and the latter was too powerful to yield. When they realised that their efforts had come to naught, the nobles retreated into the background.

The story repeated itself during the time of the seventh Nizam six decades later. When Mir Osman Ali Khan ascended the gaddi in 1911, he continued with his father's ministers. But he soon realised that the old ministers like Maharaja Kishen Pershad were too tradition-bound to carry out the modern administration that he meant to introduce in the state. Like Salar Jung I four decades earlier, he decided to appoint men of his own choice to positions of importance and he invited men trained in the western mode of administration from British India. Thus came the influx of the third batch of officer-nobles. These men were people like Sir Ali Imam from Patna and Sir Akbar Hydari from Bombay. Osman Ali Khan gave them important positions and accorded them a special place in society. However, in the eyes of the traditional nobility, they remained the first generation of title holders, and they were never accepted as the equals of the traditional nobles. An incident that took place at that time illustrates the resentment of the jagirdars against the newcomers. Once, Sir Akbar Hydari, a title holder who was appointed the president of the Executive Council, called a meeting of the Council of Jagirdars. The traditional jagirdars reacted sharply. Urgent telephone calls were made to all the jagirdars, feverish consultations were held and it was unanimously decided that Sir Akbar Hydari, a mere title holder, had no right to call for such a meeting of the jagirdars. It would have been different if Maharaja Kishen Pershad, Nawab Moin-ud-Daula or Salar Jung III had called such a meeting. Word spread about the resentment of the nobles. The intended meeting never took place. Later they made sure that a similar call for a meeting of the nobles by Sir Amin Jung too was squashed.

With the arrival of the newcomers on the scene, the realisation that there were advantages to modern education dawned on the traditional nobles. Some of them sent their children abroad so that they at least would be able to fit into the new ways. The newcomers brought in the modern and the western to the city. In fact, it was the influx of men of such varied origin and backgrounds that lent an air of sophistication to the culture of the city. The old Hyderabadis looked upon such changes as unwarranted, and in fact harmful to the Hyderabadi tahzeeb. They resented the importance given to the 'outsiders' and felt that their traditions and culture were diluted. They stuck to the age old traditions tenaciously in their deodis and in their personal lives if not elsewhere. It was this combination of the old and the new that gave rise to the fascinating Hyderabadi culture which acted as a bridge between the old and the new worlds on the one hand, and the southern and northern cultures on the other.

Commenting upon the nobles of Hyderabad, K.P.S. Menon, who served as the Under Secretary to the Resident, wrote in 1925:

...between the Nizam and the Resident, now siding with one and now with the other and carrying tales to both, stood the nobles of Hyderabad. They were men of enormous wealth and lived at the height of luxury. The most cultivated among them was Maharajah Sir Kishan Parshad, who was a scholar of Persian as well as Sanskrit, as proficient in the Koran as in the Gita. There were other personalities too, each notable in his own way: Sir Amin Jung, who had one of the best private libraries in India; Sir Imad ul Mulk and his son, to whom must go the credit of reverently preserving the precious sculptures and paintings in the cave-temples at Ellora and Ajanta; Sir Nizamat Jung, scholar, poet and politician, who built a house on the bank of Hussein Sagar lake on the model of his old college at Cambridge; Sir Farid-ul-Mulk, a Parsee, playing bridge all day with someone holding the cards for him because he was too frail; and Sir Salar Jung, a great collector, whose house was full of rare china, Satsuma bronzes and Sevres porcelain, old Persian carpets and pictures, marble statuettes and chandeliers from all parts of the world, and such historical relics as a Dresden dressing-table belonging to Marie Antoinette, a Sevres porcelain piece presented by Louis XVI to Tipu Sultan in 1788, a dagger, studded with emeralds and rubies, belonging to Nur Jehan and a Holy Koran autographed by the Emperors Jehangir, Shah Jahan and Aurangzeb. There was no other city in India, which could boast of such a galaxy of cultured, idle and versatile men.

To this, Chenevix Trench adds:

To these he might have added a Member of Council, Nawab Wali-ud-Dowlah, Eton, and Oxford, able, indolent and equally charming drunk or sober. When in his cups he used to sing the Eton Boating song and / or shoot a .22 rifle with unerring aim at silver rupees (or, preferably, gold mohurs) tossed into the air...Here you come across a society of Indians which you come across nowhere else; wealthy, well-bred, with vast estates, courteous manners and no sense of inferiority. The president of the (executive) Council, for instance, (Maharaja Sir Kishan Parshad), is an amateur artist, while the Political Secretary dabbles in English Verse...

The Police Action terminated the Nizam's rule in 1948 and a year later came the abolition of the jagirs. These cataclysmic changes struck at the very root of the old political and social order of Hyderabad, for which the old nobles were unprepared. Those who held public offices and had kept abreast of political developments in the country knew what was coming and were prepared for the changes that were in store for them.

Thus, came to an end a way of life in Hyderabad. The deodis have crumbled and the nobles have long since disappeared; but they have left behind a rich composite culture which is unique to Hyderabad.

The Diwan Deodi

If one was to travel south from the Musi river towards Charminar, on crossing the river, it would be hard not to notice an imposing gate painted in white to the left, across from the Medina Building. The gate, or what is left of it, used to be the main entrance to the fabled Diwan Deodi, the home for six diwans or prime ministers of the Hyderabad state. It was red and white in its original form and was double storied. When the Nizams ruled, the deodi occupied pride of place in the city, strategically located as it was on the Charminar main road, a short distance from the Nizam's palace, the Purani Haveli. For more than a century and a half, the deodi was the epicentre of power and influence, albeit in varying degrees, particularly when Salar Jung I was the de facto ruler of Hyderabad.

In a case unparalleled in history, six men from the same family rose to the position of diwan and the deodi was home to all of them. From the time it was built, in the last quarter of the eighteenth century, the historic deodi was an important landmark in the walled city. Syed Abul Kasim, popularly known as Mir Alam, started the construction of the deodi; he was the first of the family to become a diwan. Over the next two centuries, successive members of the family added buildings to the original structure and as the family grew in importance, so did the deodi in size and opulence. In its final form, the deodi occupied a whole block on the Paththargatti high road. It stretched from Chatta Bazaar to Mir Alam Mandi and from the Charminar thoroughfare to the Purani Haveli.

One hot summery morning, Praful, Robert and I stood across the gate, waiting for a lull in the traffic. Paththargatti, on to which the deodi opens, is the main artery of the old city and the traffic on the road makes the gate difficult to access. We had set out early in the morning, Praful and Robert with their cameras and I with my customary umbrella to brave the heat. We were under the mistaken notion that six in the morning would be the right time to beat the traffic, but we couldn't have been more wrong. Robert and Praful stood patiently for a break in the traffic to take good photographs of the gate while I fidgeted, impatient to explore the interior. After what seemed like an eternity, both of them joined me, covered in sweat, shaking their heads in frustration. 'It is almost impossible,' they said. Even at that hour, the road was not free of traffic even for a moment.

The gate is all that is left of the deodi today. The naubat khana of the gate, from where the naubat used to play in olden times does stand today, but just barely. The high walls abutting the gate have been heavily built over and billboards cover the rest, while a maze of telephone and electrical wires festoon the high arch. It is difficult to visualise that it was an entrance of eminence at one time.

We walked in, not sure of what we would find inside. We were not expecting to find much of the old deodi within the high walls. Even so, we were unprepared for what we saw. The palace grounds had obviously been sold to wholesale merchants and transport companies. Even at that hour, the place was a veritable mess; matchbox-like shops were shuttered by the ubiquitous rolling shutters and trucks were parked haphazardly in the yard. Dust and grime covered everything in sight and heaps of garbage littered the ground. Men, perhaps truckers and mechanics, slept in front of the shops and the lone chaiwala was getting ready for the day. Here and there, one saw chunks of masonry, a lone wall standing mournfully by itself, or the odd staircase leading up to nowhere. This was what had become of the once magnificent deodi, about which several visitors to the city left glowing accounts! I stared at the mess in front of me and tried to remember what I had read about the deodi when it was occupied.

In its heyday, the apartments of the deodi were so luxuriously furnished and so full of rare objects that visitors to the city, both European and Indian, would request permission to visit it. Around 1880, one such European visitor, A. Claude Campbell, left a detailed account of the deodi's many attractions.

The sprawling palace complex had many gates, but the entrance on the side of Paththargatti was the one that was used regularly. From the Charminar thoroughfare, one had to pass though a narrow passage, which led up to the deodi proper. As one entered, to the right were the reception rooms, screened from public view by red velvet curtains fringed in green and guarded by the borse ke jawan, dressed in their native uniforms. Beyond the curtain was a formal courtyard, which was the main reception area. A large marble fountain played in the courtyard and goldfish darted in the water cisterns. Exquisite European statuary, sculpted in marble and imported from different European countries, stood all around. On one side of the courtyard was the famous aina khana, the formal reception room of the deodi. The aina khana was entirely covered in coloured glass; on the columns and the ceilings small glass pieces were wrought into various shapes in Persian style and the walls of the hall were faced with large plate glass mirrors. The aina khana was furnished with a number of gilt state chairs, upholstered in crimson velvet, which once graced the court of George IV of England. Opposite the main aina khana was another structure, similarly built in glass, which was a smaller version of the main aina khana and the two structures were connected by a banquet hall.

To the west of the quadrangle and the aina khana was the library, which was stocked with many rare books. The library, with Shah Jahani multi-foliated arches, housed eight thousand manuscripts in

Persian, Turkish, Arabic and Urdu apart from 29,000 printed books! The range of topics covered by the collection is a measure of the minds of the Salar Jungs. There were books on history, archaeology, art, literature, travel, religion, social sciences and many other subjects. Though the major part of the collection was made by Nawab Yousuf Ali Khan Salar Jung III, there was quite a collection of manuscripts and books that he inherited from his ancestors, right from AD 1656. Some of the Arabic manuscripts were very ancient. One of them, a copy of the Quran dating back to 1283, contained the autographs of Emperors Jehangir, Shah Jahan and Aurangzeb. This fabulous collection today forms a part of the Salar Jung Museum Library and is open to scholars and researchers.

Close to the aina khana to the east was a small room called the Chini khana or China House, which was an unusual and a most interesting apartment. Its walls and columns were covered in antique china plates, saucers and cups, some of them very valuable; they were fitted into the walls and arranged in various fanciful designs. Silver plates were tastefully displayed in shelves. In this uniquely pretty room was placed Rebecca, an exceedingly artistic sculpture of white marble by the Italian sculptor Benzoni (1876), in the shape of a female figure draped from head to foot. It was purchased in Rome by Sir Salar Jung I when he was on a European visit. Beyond the Chini khana, to the east, was the treasury. Adjoining this apartment was the diwan khana or the durbar hall, arranged in the traditional style, with a gold embroidered musnad and takhats worked in gold thread and canopies on silver poles. That was where the Salar Jungs held court.

A subtle change overtook the otherwise traditional deodi in the early decades of the nineteenth century. European influence increased at court and interaction between Europeans and the Hyderabadi nobility, in particular the diwans, increased. Prominent citizens began to introduce elements of European lifestyle in their residences, as appointments were fitted to suit European taste. The traditional durbar halls as reception rooms did not suffice; reception rooms fitted with contemporary European furniture had to be added and more western elements like billiards rooms, libraries with English and French books and, guest suites with western toilets came to be introduced to the traditional deodi. So much so that a European visitor to the Diwan Deodi commented that sections of Sir Salar's deodi resembled a wealthy Englishman's residence!

Upstairs, above the Chini khana, were the bedrooms built in the days of Sir Salar Jung I. One bedroom in particular was furnished exquisitely in white and gold. It had a cut-glass hand basin and toilet fittings. This suite was prepared especially for the use of the sixth Nizam when he stayed at the deodi for three days to attend the wedding of Sir Salar Jung's daughter. A European chronicler records that by 1905, all the rooms were closed; the fountains had fallen dry and the furniture was shrouded under dust covers. There were other bedrooms, less expensively appointed. All this was the mardana, the exclusive domain of men. This sprawling deodi was demolished in the early 1970s.

To the west of the public place, set apart from the mardana, was the zenana. It was made up of a series of two-storied apartments, sometimes conjoined and sometimes apart, each with its own courtyard. The tone of these apartments was quite different from the men's quarters; the zenana was a world unto itself. There was none of the press of visitors or the bustle associated with court matters here; the scene that met the eye in the zenana was one of leisure, ease and comfort. Behind the deep dalans and aromatic khus curtains, the begums led a leisurely life. Water dribbled from marble fountains, birds bathed in water cisterns and young girls trained in music and dance entertained the begums. There were pretty gardens here, and shady trees and fragrant flowering bushes added to the enchantment. In the lady's section, tradition ruled. They had none of the modern western appointments; occupations and activities as well as manner of living were traditional. Visitors from distant areas came to spend days and not just hours. There was hectic activity throughout the day; numerous female servants bustled around carrying out orders. The senior begum held court, received visitors and set the tone of the household. The women of the Salar Jung household were known for their strength of character, worldly wisdom and dignity.

The deodi contained other customary buildings meant for special purposes, the khazana, the tosha khana, the mez khana, the farrash khana, the baggi khana, the motor khana and the like. A silent movie house, a great novelty of the time, was built by Nawab Yousuf Ali Khan Salar Jung III for the entertainment of the family.

After Salar Jung I, the deodi never regained its earlier grandeur. Laiq Ali Khan Salar Jung II did add sections to the old deodi but he did not live in the deodi for long. Though he too officiated as a diwan during the regime of the sixth Nizam, he did not get on well with his master. He was dismissed from the position of a diwan only a few years after he was appointed. After his sudden dismissal, Laiq Ali Khan Salar Jung II lived in self-imposed exile in Pune, never to return to Hyderabad again.

The deodi by all accounts was much larger than the diwans ever really needed. Lakkad Kot, the favourite haunt of Salar Jung I was already an old structure by 1905. Further, being close to the Musi river, the deodi had suffered much damage during the flood of 1908 and had to be repaired extensively. Some of the buildings were already in a state of neglect and many sections of the sprawling complex had fallen into disuse by the time of Salar Jung III, who was the last occupant of the deodi. His were the twilight years and the family had lost its preeminence at the court after Salar Jung I. The famous aina khana began to slowly lose its lustre.

Very little remains of the once sprawling deodi today. Other than the busy Mir Alam Mandi, the wholesale market next door, only the imposing gates of the old deodi remain. The baradari, better known as Lakkad Kot, lying across Chatta Bazaar, was pulled down along with the main deodi. A small section of the baradari, which served as an outhouse originally, has survived. This ramshackle structure, which is on its last legs, has Shah Jahani arches and carved woodwork affording a tantalising glimpse into the once beautiful baradari. Presently it houses a motor mechanic's shop. We wandered around the desolate yard, pock marked with structures of 'unredeemed ugliness.' Stray dogs roam where the aina khana once stood, hawkers peddle their wares in the zenana khana and motor mechanics lounge where the library had once stood.

The deodi did not prove to be a happy place for any of its masters. Except for Salar Jung I, not one of the diwans of the long line of six, enjoyed peace of mind. All of them fell to the cupidity of the rulers and jealousy of the court nobles. Mir Alam, the man who set the family on the course to power and fame, was even imprisoned for four years in the Golconda Fort.

Mir Alam, Diwan of Hyderabad from 1804-1808, a migrant from Persia, played a key role in Hyderabad's affairs in the last quarter of the eighteenth century. He was able to win British support and was appointed to represent the Nizam in the war with Tipu Sultan. When Mir Alam returned home victorious after the defeat of Tipu, he was accorded a hero's welcome. The Nizam sent his personal elephant to receive him and directed his nobles to receive Mir Alam outside the city gates. Receptions were thrown in his honour and celebrations followed, but his moment of glory was tinged with suspicion. A case was made out by his enemies that a sizeable portion of the booty that fell to Hyderabad's share, found its way into Mir Alam's private coffers. It was also whispered, rather openly, that he had appropriated Tipu's state jewels. Thereafter, Mir Alam was disgraced, stripped of all his privileges and imprisoned in the Golconda Fort. A few years before his death in 1808, he regained his former position at court and was appointed prime minister, a position he held for barely four years.

With the prize money that he had received at Srirangapatnam, Mir Alam built a tank which was named after him, and a chain of sarais on the two important trade routes, leading to Masulipatnam and Pune. The well-known Mir Alam Mandi, the wholesale market abutting the Diwan Deodi, was named after him. It was as if by his humanitarian gestures, Mir Alam was trying to exonerate himself in the eyes of the public, and perhaps those of Allah.

For Mir Alam, building the deodi on a lavish scale must have been a matter of reasserting his position in Hyderabad. Though he was not a wealthy man to begin with, he came into a lot of money during his tenure in office. When he led a delegation to Calcutta, he received a substantial amount, a sum of Rs 5,000 a month as salary, apart from being granted a generous allowance of Rs 100,000. Then there was the considerable prize money from Srirangapatnam. Moreover, the diwans of Hyderabad received huge amounts as their salary. A diwan was known to have received two annas worth of income out of every rupee that the state received, amounting to one eighth of the state's income. Perhaps Mir Alam started construction of the deodi after he became the prime minister.

The sun was high by that time we reached Mir Alam Mandi. It took me a while to readjust my eyes to the scene in front of us, for the hectic activity of the market was at variance with the ravaged condition of the deodi. Mir Alam Mandi continues to be a popular wholesale market and traders and merchants continue to throng to it as they did a couple of centuries ago. Aromatic herbs and spices, vegetables of all descriptions, fish, meat and condiments are all for sale. Lorries lined the street beyond, customers bustled around and dogs and cattle strayed unhindered. The air was thick with the stench of rotting vegetables and the aroma of spices; it was a typical Indian market scene. In the middle of all this confusion, one could hear the peal of Hindu temple bells.

If we wonder why Mir Alam took the trouble of building the noisy mandi right next to so grand a deodi, the answer was not far to find. The shops in the mandi were rented out by the family, as were those abutting the high walls of the deodi. In the days of the Salar Jungs, the deodi stood in the middle of a busy market place, the interior of the deodi contrasting sharply with the bustle and the chaos outside. The rents from the shops accounted for some part of the income of the diwans.

On the edge of the market stood the century-and-a-half-old residence of Siddi Ambar, who was the Sudanese housekeeper of Salar Jung I. The house appeared untouched. One almost expected the powerful African to look out of his bedroom window upstairs and shout orders to his soldiers. He perhaps looked out on to the same scene that we were witnessing. Nothing much had changed in the intervening time except for minor differences; the bullock carts have given way to lorries and the city folk of Hyderabad dress differently today. In the olden days, as they still do today, market places in Hyderabad looked colourful but were also at times troubled. Men of different races, regions and languages stalked the market; there were fierce looking mercenaries looking for employment, idlers looking for trouble and regular soldiers loaded with weapons hanging about the markets; Afghans, Baluchis, Pathans, Rohillas, Punjabis, Siddis, and Turks scouring the market, engaged in buying and selling and perhaps merely whiling away their time. Street brawls were frequent, as were attacks on foreign and native traders. The Nizam's security guards stood alert everywhere, for trouble was common at such places.

There is an interesting account left behind by a European observer about the men who haunted the streets of Hyderabad at that time. He writes:

There is probably no other city in India, which at the present moment contains a larger collection of fierce armed men, ready for any sort of strife and excitable and difficult to manage. One has only to visit its narrow picturesque and very dirty streets, and note the groups of wild ferocious-looking men, armed to the teeth, lounging about the palace gates of the different nobles, or strutting about on their own account...Every one above the social status of a coolly seems to think it necessary to carry about his person a perfect museum of offensive weapons. A long matchlock, in some instances an English rifle, a wicked looking curved sword, a brace of pistols, or a revolver and as many knives and daggers of sorts as he can hang about him, form the ordinary promenading paraphernalia of a denizen of

Hyderabad. Europeans often wonder what possible motive can induce men to burden themselves of cartloads of arms that these people carry as naturally and constantly as an Englishman sports a walking stick. The countenances of most of these gentry bear a savage and a reckless expression.

It must have taken all of Siddi Ambar's ingenuity to control the vagabonds, take care of the traders and run the mandi profitably for the diwans.

ᔕ

After Mir Alam, the next famous occupant of the deodi was his great grandson, Mir Turab Ali Khan Salar Jung I (1829-83), the fourth member of the family to become diwan.

Few ministers in modern times can lay claim to as much credit as Salar Jung I as a statesman, an administrator and a manager of matters. He was responsible for laying the foundation of modern Hyderabad. He inherited a state frozen in medieval times and on the verge of financial collapse. By the time he was done with it, Hyderabad was well on its way to becoming one of the front line states in the country. As the co-regent for the child Nizam, Mahboob Ali Khan, Salar Jung I was the de facto ruler of the state. In that capacity, he was instrumental in bringing about radical changes in the administration. Impressed with the methods and the efficiency of the British-administered states, Salar Jung borrowed British models but adapted them to suit local conditions. Departments like the judiciary, police, health, education, customs and a host of others were set up in Hyderabad for the first time.

Salar Jung I worked from his deodi, making it the virtual seat of power in those days. At any time of the day, elephants, horses, palanquins and every other mode of transportation crowded the entrance to the deodi, which teemed with people. Harried vakils carrying dispatches to and from the Residency, high-ranking nobles and officials engaged in serious state matters, anxious petitioners and self-appointed pairavikars all waited in different parts of the deodi depending on their status and nature of work; busy arzbegees carried petitions back and forth and chaubdars carrying long staffs announced visitors. The deodi bustled with highly charged activity. Never again was the palace to occupy a position of such eminence and never again was a diwan so totally in control of the state's affairs after Nawab Mir Turab Ali Salar Jung I.

Apart from being the diwan, Salar Jung I was also the co-regent of the child ruler, Mahboob Ali Khan. In that capacity, he had to maintain a close relationship with the representatives of the British. Moreover, he depended heavily on the Resident to support him against the local nobles who resisted his reforms. As a result, when the revolt of 1857 rocked the country, Salar Jung threw his weight behind the British and scotched even the feeble efforts made by a few 'disgruntled nobles' to join the 'mutineers.' However, he was no sycophant of the British. Paying allegiance to the British was an act of political expediency with no emotional strings attached. He was ready to go over their heads if need be, to protect the interests of Hyderabad. Towards this end in his dealings with the British he stuck a fine balance between defiance and conciliation, now giving and now hedging, depending upon the need of the hour. The ultimate good of his state and the dignity and authority of the ruler were what mattered most to him. He fought bitterly to recover Berar, unfairly retained by the British long after the dues of the Hyderabad forces were paid for. In an act of daring defiance of the Government of India, he raised loans in the London money market to finance the railways in the Hyderabad state. He went over the heads of the officials of the India office at Calcutta and used his contacts with the Prince of Wales and Queen Victoria to establish the Nizam as a sovereign ruler and an equal to the British monarch.

The British, on their part were wary of the sagacious noble. They found him to be reticent and dignified and not at all like the other ministers of princely India, who constantly tried to curry favour with them. It was obvious they were both impressed and intrigued by the minister. An English journalist who happened to attend an official reception thrown by the minister at his residence observed:

At the top of the steps, waiting to receive the guests, stands the first statesman of India, the subduer of the Calcutta Government, the outwitter of the poor Mr. Saunders, the defender of the little Nizam...here stands Sir Salar Jung, smiling that pleasant smile of his peculiar to himself among all men, and unique among the native men of India...(On receiving the guests) when His Excellency shakes hands with you, how is it that he directs his eyes clean over your head? Is it to show that the deed he is performing is an act of official courtesy and not of a private friendship? "You individually are nothing, but the uniform you wear shows you to be a servant of the Empress of India, and so you are a welcome guest of her "Faithful Ally (the Nizam)!"

The above description aptly sums up the attitude of Salar Jung towards the British.

Once the banquet is over and it is time to leave', the journalist goes on to write, 'there is a crush at the place of exit, we move forward step by step. The carriages get away...we say adieu to our illustrious...(host)...who hands me a couple of thin bottles of attar of rose,' and he writes, rather petulantly, '(he) once more examines my cranium to see whether I use hair dye or whether I show symptoms of getting bald!

It must have irked the officer that the minister should treat the British with such indifference. Incidentally the same reporter goes on to mention that Colonel Meadows Taylor, the literary celebrity, also attended the banquet. He is said to have 'attained an advanced age, and looked very feeble, requiring assistance to walk.'

There was another duty that Salar Jung I needed to perform in the capacity of co-regent to the child Nizam. On him fell the responsibility of bringing up the three-year-old future Nizam. His task was to see that neither the British nor the courtiers took advantage of the tender age of the Nizam. An incident, of a most disturbing nature had taken place recently and Salar Jung continued to smart from it:

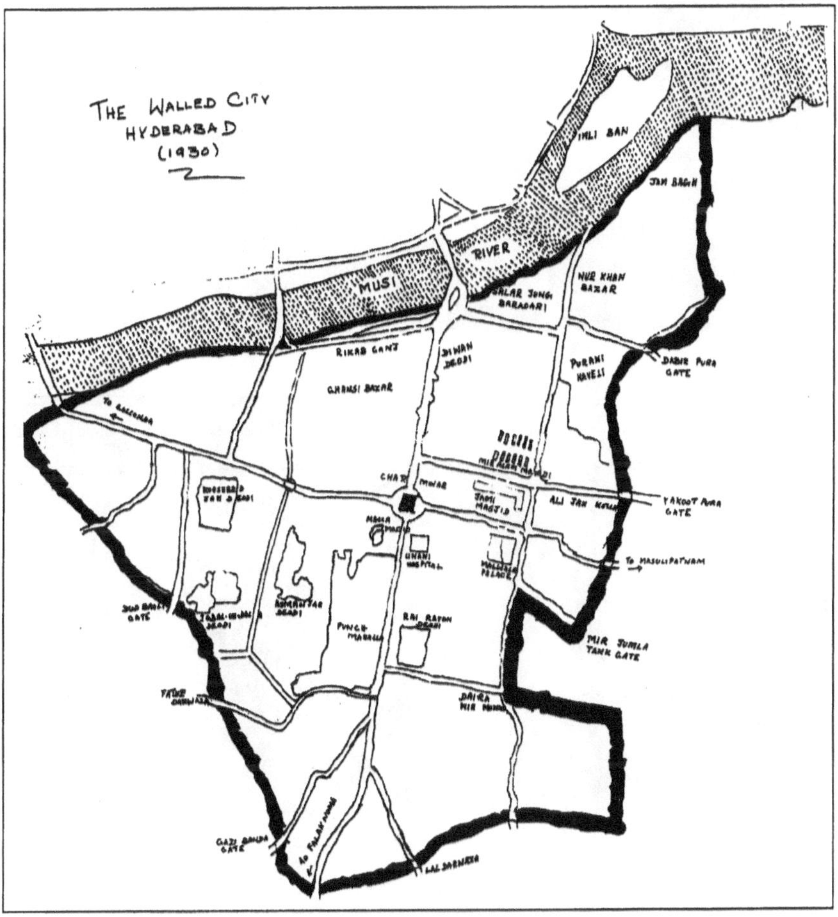

THE WALLED CITY
HYDERABAD
(1930)

IMLI BAN

JAM BAGH

MUSI RIVER

SALAR JUNG
BARADARI

NUR KHAN
BAZAR

RIKAB GANZ

DIWAN
DEODI

PURANI
HAVELI

DABIR PURA
GATE

GHANSI BAZAR

To GOLCONDA

DOGRA PARADE

CHAR MINAR

JAMI MASJID

ALI JAH KOTLA

YAKOOT PURA
GATE

MEGHA
KMANA

GHANI
HOSPITAL

MOKALLA
PALACE

To MASULIPATNAM

TABLIGH NAGAR
DEODI

AURANGZEB
DEODI

PUNGA
MAGALLA

RAI BAYAN
DEODI

MIR JUMLA
TANK GATE

SULTAN BAZLI
GATE

FATEH
DARWAZA

DAIRA
MIR MOMIN

GAZI BAGH
GATE

To FALAKNUMA

LAL DARWAZA

A map of Hyderabad, 1930.
Courtesy: Dhirajlal Dangoria

Bella Vista lit up for an occasion. Courtesy: Salar Jung Museum

The wedding of the princes, Azam Jah and Moazzam Jah with the princesses Durru Shehvar and Niloufer respectively in Nice, France. Courtesy: Mr Narendra Luther

Bella Vista today; as the Administrative Staff College of India. Courtesy: Administrative Staff College of India.

*A happy family, Prince Azam Jah, Durru Shehvar
and their first born, Prince Mukarram Jah.
Courtesy: Mr Narendra Luther*

*Durru Shehvar with Prince Mukarram Jah.
Courtesy: Kumudini Devi*

*Prince Azam Jah with his two sons.
Courtesy: Smt Lakshmi Devi Raj*

Princess Durru Shehvar on a holiday in Kashmir.
Courtesy: Kumudini Devi

The Nizam's contribrition to the Bhandarkar Oriental Research Institute.
Courtesy: Dr Dawood Ashraf

The musnad of Raja Shamraj in the diwan khana of the Rai Rayan Deodi.
Courtesy: Smt Mangala Devi Bhale Rao

A nautch in progress at a deodi. Courtesy: Smt Mangala Devi Bhale Rao

A typical street scene with a deodi in the background. Courtesy: Smt Mangala Devi Bhale Rao

A successful hunting expedition. It was considered respectable to be hunters and sportsmen. Courtesy: Begum Fazluddin Khan

A zenana. It is a part of the Purani Haveli, one of the palaces of the Nizam. Courtesy: Princess Esin Women's Educational Centre.

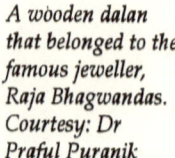

A wooden dalan that belonged to the famous jeweller, Raja Bhagwandas. Courtesy: Dr Praful Puranik

The Diwan Deodi in 1947. The Delhi Gate facing the deodi was subsequently demolished as it was felt it obstructed traffic Courtesy: Salar Jung Museum

One of the rooms of
the Diwan Deodi.
Courtesy: Salar
Jung Museum

Yousuf Ali Khan, Salar Jung III
Courtesy: Smt Soona Mirza

The famous
Lakkad Kot of
the Salar Jungs
which overlooked
the Musi river.
Courtesy: Salar
Jung Museum

The family portrait of the male members of Nawab Inayat Jung. Courtesy: Mr Asghar Ali Hussain

A Muharram procession on the banks of the Musi river. Courtesy: Salar Jung Museum

The seventh Nizam, his family and his nobles on a visit to a deodi. Courtesy: Smt Mangala Devi Bhale Rao

The Moti Bungalow of the Peshkar Deodi. Courtesy: Dr Sheila Karan

The aina khana of the Peshkar Deodi, since demolished. Courtesy: Dr Sheila Karan

The dining room at the Falaknuma Palace. The table could seat a hundred people. The acoustics of the room were such that what was said at the head of the table could clearly be heard by someone sitting at the foot of the table. Courtesy: Salar Jung Museum

The reception room at the Bashirbagh Palace, said to have been one of the most opulently furnished palaces in the city.
Courtesy: Mohammad Qutub Yar Jung

A banquet at Khas Bagh, Peshkar Deodi.
Courtesy: Salar Jung Museum

A langar procession passing infront of Deodi Asman Jah. The deodi occupied the entire street.
Courtesy: Glimpses of the Nizam's Dominions by A. Claude Campbell, Bombay and London, C.B. Burrows, 1898.

The entrance to the Rai Rayan Deodi.
Courtesy: Smt Mangala Devi Bhale Rao

An elephant with an ambari atop, passing
through the main entrance of a deodi.
Courtesy: Smt Mangala Devi Bhale Rao

Raja Shamraj II
Courtesy: Smt Mangala Devi Bhale Rao

Muharram decorations at Peshkar Deodi Courtesy: Dr Shiela Karan

A langar procession passing in front of the maharaja's deodi. Courtesy: Dr Shiela Karan

Lord Curzon flanked by the sixth and seventh Nizams at the maharaja's palace Courtesy: Salar Jung Museum

Raja Shamraj II in
his library.
Courtesy: Smt Mangala
Devi Bhale Rao

The inspection of
troops at Chandu
Lal's Baradari.
Courtesy: Dr Shiela
Karan

The collection of Raja Shamraj's miniature
paintings at the Rai Rayan Deodi.
Courtesy: Smt Mangala Devi Bhale Rao

Chandrabhuvan, the modern drawing room of the Rai Rayan Deodi. Courtesy: Smt Mangala Devi Bhale Rao

The inner courtyard of the Raj Rayan Deodi. Courtesy: Smt Mangala Devi Bhale Rao

Rani Ambika and other members of the Ladies' club with Princess Durru Shevar. Courtesy: Smt Mangala Devi Bhale Rao

The diwan khana of the Malwala Palace.
Courtesy: Mr Tej Karan

The fluted wooden pillars rose to hold the delicate Shah Jahani arches of the pavilion of the Malwala Palace.
Courtesy: Mr Tej Karan

A detail of the decorated work on the ceiling of the Malwala Palace.
Courtesy: Mr Tej Karan

Najeeb Sultana's 'flat,' the only surviving part of the once sprawling Saram Jung Deodi in Malakpet. Courtesy: Dr Praful Puranik

Syed Ahmad Ali Khan in his drawing room, surrounded by what is left of his inheritance. Courtesy: Dr Praful Puranik

Najeeb Sultana with her wedding finery. Courtesy: Dr Praful Puranik

It had been a set practice in Hyderabad that the Resident on approaching the 'presence of the Nizam,' had to take off his shoes and squat on the floor like the rest of the nobles. It had been so until the death of Afzal-ud-Daula, the fifth Nizam (1827-68). But when Mahboob Ali, a child of three years, succeeded as the Nizam, the then Resident, Mr C. B. Saunders declared that he had no intention of carrying on with the charade. He declared that he intended to go into durbar with his shoes on and sit on a chair. An agitated Salar Jung informed the Resident that he would not be able to contain the incensed nobles, the Pathans and the Rohillas of a highly volatile nature, if their lord was thus insulted. A determined Saunders informed his army to stand by and to sack Hyderabad if they should hear as much as a shot from the palace. He also ordered a telegraph wire to be fitted from the palace to his camp at Secunderabad. It had become a battle of wills; an eyeball-to-eyeball confrontation. The Resident entered the durbar with his shoes on, sat on a chair and survived the incident. However, Salar Jung was deeply wounded and vowed not to yield any more space to the British.

Salar Jung had an even more difficult task at hand, that of protecting the child from the dissolute ways of the court; he was worried that the nobles related to the royal family by marriage might take advantage of the child. He had to ward off both the dangers without appearing to do so and it took all his ingenuity to achieve his aim. He achieved this by instituting heightened levels of court etiquette and established it as a barrier between the ruler and the rest of the court. He insisted that all the nobles show utmost respect to the child, often exaggerated as to border on absurdity.

To illustrate his point, he made use of every important occasion for the ritual of paying respect to the child Nizam. Sir Nizamat Jung, who served the seventh Nizam as a minister half a century later, records, quoting the personal physician to the Nizam:

On the anniversary of the Nizam's birthday and on Idd days, traditional custom demanded that nazars should be presented by the Diwan and the chief nobles at formal durbar. But as the child Nizam could not hold durbar, the Diwan proceeded to the royal palace to pay homage. Mounted on a majestic elephant, richly adorned in silver ornaments and surrounded with armed retainers (Arab, Afghans and others) forming a long procession, he arrived at the palace in juloos. Etiquette forbade entry into the courtyard of the palace except on foot; he had to alight at the outer gate and stand respectfully with his face turned towards the mahal, where his royal master was supposed to be. There he made his salaams, his right hand touching the ground as he bent low and then touching his forehead as he rose each time. This he repeated at the entrance of the next courtyard, and so on until he arrived at the spot beyond which none was allowed to pass. No court dignitary, no chamberlain or master of ceremonies was there in attendance, but some privileged female servant had to convey his humble nazr to his august master with his adaab. The message was received not by the child Nizam but his grandmother, who acknowledged it by sending to the Diwan her blessings in return. On his departure the Diwan repeated the salaam ceremony at each of the gates exactly as before until he reached the main entrance on the road.

As a contemporary Englishman comments:

All this even though, every one is aware that he, and not the child, was the virtual ruler of the state!

Another amusing incident, recorded by yet another Englishman, throws light on the same matter. It was strictly against the etiquette of the court to present oneself to the ruler without being appropriately attired in the traditional dastar, the headgear and the bugloos, the girdle. Once, when the Nizam was paying a visit to Golconda, he (the Nizam), boy-like, ran into Sir Salar Jung's room, and found the minister taking a siesta. The minister had taken off his girdle! Now, to be in the Nizam's company without a girdle was a heinous offence. And the minister at once handed over to the little Nizam fifteen gold mohurs. The next morning he sent him 1,500 rupees to complete the fine!

♪

The Diwan Deodi was bordered on its eastern side by the Chatta Bazaar. Today, the bazaar continues to be a busy market center for paper and printing material. Over the bazaar stands an interesting looking arch, which acted as a bridge and connected the deodi to the garden beyond. It was in this garden, overlooking the Musi river that the famous Lakkad Kot of Salar Jung stood. The Lakkad Kot, also referred to as the baradari, was an integral part of the deodi at one time. It was a three-storied wooden structure, set in a charming terraced garden, equipped with fountains and a huge hauz. The baradari was the traditional mardana of the deodi. It was an enchanting mansion affording comfort and privacy; it was cool, secluded and luxuriously appointed. Its carved wooden arches, delicately patterned jharokhas, the airy rooms and the spacious halls made it an ideal place to relax and to entertain. The cool breeze that wafted in from the river through the twelve doors of the baradari kept it cool through the summer months. It was also a quick get-away for the diwans, who could slip away quietly, unnoticed, via the bridge. This is where Sir Salar Jung I and several of his ancestors repaired to when they wanted to escape the hordes of petitioners and sycophants who pursued them day and night.

From the upper floors of Lakkad Kot, one had a panoramic view of the Musi river. The Musi was not much of a river even in those days; it was only in the rainy season that it showed some spirit. It seldom went into spate, but when it did, as in 1908, it could be devastating. When the flow of the river shrank to a trickle and the riverbed went dry, it looked as if the whole city descended upon it. At such times, the view of the river as seen from the baradari was quite enchanting; it was a microcosm of life in the city. On its banks grew vines and water melons; dhobis spread their washing on the dry sand dunes in a tapestry of colour and design, and elephants and cattle wallowed in the muddy pools. Hindu women offered prayers on festival days and the diyas and the floral offerings they made floated gracefully down the stream.

Another not-so-pretty sight visible from the upper floors of the Lakkad Kot, close to the Delhi Gate along the Musi river, was the sati mound where Hindu women threw themselves into the funeral pyres of their husbands. It seems strange that the powerful minister would build his pleasure house overlooking such a disturbing site. Records show that sati continued to be observed in Hyderabad up to the days of Salar Jung I, who put an effective end to it in 1875.

Salar Jung made extensive use of the Lakkad Kot for both public and private entertaining and it was the venue for many state banquets that he threw on behalf of the Nizam. Entertaining was taken seriously and banquets were grand affairs. Hyderabad put its best foot forward, particularly when foreigners were in attendance.

On December 21 1875, the London edition of the *Times of India* published a detailed account of one such banquet. The occasion for the celebration was to welcome the new Resident, Sir Richard Meade and his wife Lady Meade. The welcome festivities commenced with a state dinner given by the government. The venue for the banquet was the baradari of Sir Salar Jung; the guests were predominantly British officers. With a large cantonment at Secunderabad close at hand, the assemblage was a very large one. A great majority of the guests were of course military officers, all dressed in military uniforms. The plain black coat of the civilians was not extensively seen.

The hour of invitation was 6:30 and shortly before that time the roadway over the great Hussain Sagar tank was active with vehicles of every description driving along, towards the (old) city; handsome carriages drawn by a pair of high-stepping grays, bullock coaches plodding their way slowly and other manners of conveyance. A noisy swaying crowd gathered along the road to view the procession of vehicles and the assembly of guests; a body of the Nizam's police maintained excellent order. Darkness had by that time closed in, and the moon had not yet shown her face over the eastern horizon. Mounted lancers were drawn up inside the city gate to welcome the guests. The guests entered the extensive domain belonging to the 'virtual ruler' of the Hyderabad state, namely, Sir Salar. They drove up through avenues of trees and alighted at the foot of the terraced garden and were received by the first statesman in India, Sir Salar Jung, 'smiling that pleasant smile of his.'

The garden and the baradari were decorated attractively with oil lamps, flower pots and festoons. The gravelled walks all over the garden were concealed by white durries. Numerous lights were planted within globes of coloured glass along the flowerbeds. Jets of water whirled and splashed with a pleasant tinkling sound. The copings of buildings, which overlook the garden on all sides, were thickly set with coloured lights. The oil lamps were so arranged as to form the legend, 'In honour of Sir Richard and Lady Meade.'

All the military officers present were in full dress, and from the variety of uniforms the spectacle offered to view was a very gay and animated one. In the crowd moved a number of 'native swells,' attired in silks and satins overlaid with gold embroidery. Nearly all the 'natives' present were resplendently dressed conspicuous by the 'barbaric sized pearls and gold.' All of them, high and low, were armed with an array of offensive weapons. 'The officers of the Paramount Power were simply nowhere by the side of these lustrous beings encased in emerald green and shining effulgent in burnished gold.'

At 7 o'clock, a flourish of trumpets and a brass band accomplished 'God save the Queen;' bands of dancing girls were brought on the scene, which was not much appreciated (by the Europeans). The tables were handsomely laid out. Dinner finished, the company retired to the upper part of the building, whence to view the exhibition of fireworks and the spectacle concluded with a grand naval engagement conducted from opposite sides of the garden reservoir.

✧

Nawab Mir Turab Ali Khan Salar Jung I stands tall among the statesmen of India. His fame and reputation as an administrator, as a collector of art and as a philanthropist had spread all over the country during his lifetime. People flocked to him with requests for jobs, for financial help and for quick and ready justice. News of his fabulous wealth and generosity had reached all over India, so much so that Ghalib, the famous poet of Delhi, once wrote to him asking for financial support. Ghalib always lived beyond his means and was deep in debt. To placate Salar Jung, he wrote a qasida in his honour hoping that Sir Salar would make a large donation of money. The qasida and the request arrived in Hyderabad when Salar Jung was in mourning for the death of his father-in-law, Nawab Fakhr-ul-Mulk I. A whole year of mourning had just been declared. A year passed. Ghalib kept pressing his student, the famous poet Zauq, into service to pursue the matter. After the mourning period, Salar Jung became preoccupied with other matters, and the money never came. That must have been one of the rare occasions when the great noble failed to answer a call of distress.

In the eastern quarter of the old city, near the Mir Jumla Tank in Daira Mir Momin, lies the family burial place of the Salar Jungs. Mir Momin was a famous Shia saint, who migrated to Hyderabad during the Qutub Shahi rule. Mir Alam and many other members of the family lie buried in the enclosure, beyond the ancient tombs. There, on a raised platform lies the grave of the greatest statesman of Hyderabad, Salar Jung I. For years after his death, mullahs used to read the Quran near his grave and pilgrims would cover his grave with jasmine flowers and pray. Those who sought his intervention on their behalf left behind bundles of petitions at his grave, hoping that, somehow, that very act would solve their problems. Such was the respect and faith Nawab Turab Ali Khan Salar Jung commanded during his lifetime.

ᔓ

Nawab Yousuf Ali Khan Salar Jung III, whose collection of artifacts is famous as the largest 'one-man' art collections in the world, was the last member of the family to live in the deodi. His name and, in fact, that of the whole family is immortalised in the Salar Jung Museum which houses the artifacts that the deodi yielded when it was demolished.

Salar Jung III died in 1949 without leaving an heir. In the absence of a direct descendent, the government appointed a committee to administer the Salar Jung estate; but in a true Hyderabadi style, wrangling began among the various claimants to the property. In 1951, to institutionalise the art collection of Salar Jung, the Government of India created the Salar Jung Museum. The bulk of the exhibits for the museum were drawn from the personal collection of Salar Jung III, and the museum initially was housed in the deodi itself. In 1968, the museum shifted to a new building specially built for that purpose. Once the litigation ended, with the descendents of Salar Jung choosing to live elsewhere, the deodi fell into disuse for a few years. Finally, it was declared unsafe for habitation and was demolished in the early 1970s. With the mindless demolition of the deodi, Hyderbad lost one of the most celebrated residences. With it went the memories of two centuries, not only of the family but also of the city itself.

Mir Yousuf Ali Khan Salar Jung III, the last in the line of the great Salar Jungs, was born in Pune, where his father, Salar Jung II, was living in self-imposed exile, having fallen out with the sixth Nizam. Yousuf Ali Khan had an unhappy childhood. His father died when he was but a child of twenty-four days, and his family lived under reduced circumstances. Fortunately royal favour was restored soon after and a young Yousuf Ali Khan returned to Hyderabad with dignity and honour. Soon the family jagirs and the title of 'Salar Jung' were restored to him.

For all the advantage that his wealth and lineage afforded him, Yousuf Ali Khan did not fare any better than his father. He too did not get along well with the seventh Nizam. He resigned as prime minister in mid-1914, barely two and half years after he was appointed. He was spurned by the ruler as quickly as he was favoured and condemned to official oblivion even before his career had time to blossom. Shocked and humiliated by that inexplicable turn of events, Yousuf Ali Khan retired from public life, never to return to it again. For the rest of his life, he remained a lonely and tragic figure, haunted by the ghosts of his illustrious ancestors. Life came to a full circle for the Salar Jungs, as

Yousuf Ali Khan's emotional exile began. His were the twilight years; the days of glory and power were over for the Salar Jungs.

However, it is a quirk of fate that Salar Jung III alone is remembered in present-day Hyderabad, while the rest of the family, including the illustrious Sir Salar Jung I, has been consigned to history books. Free of public duties, Salar Jung devoted himself to the administration of his enormous jagir at Kuppal. His family estate comprised an area of 1480 square miles and had a population of 2,000,000 (*Pictorial Hyderabad, Bk II*). The estate contained ten law courts and three jails; the revenue per year came to 15 lakh (1.5 million) rupees. The fabulous Salar Jung wealth was still intact and Mir Alam's legendary jewels were still in the family. Adding to it, Yousuf Ali Khan made some shrewd investments in a number of companies such as Nizam's State Railways, the Shahbad Cement Factory, Siganreni Collieries, the Tajmahal Hotel of Bombay, the Scindia Steam Navigation Company and many other safe and profitable concerns.

While the management of his property took up considerable time, his real interest was the collection of artifacts. He was like a man possessed and his passion for collecting art became an all-absorbing obsession. It was as if he wanted to erase the pain of rejection and failure by indulging in the more pleasant things of life. All his wealth went into the acquisition of beautiful objects. Room after room in the deodi were stocked with art objects that arrived from all over the world, some not even opened from their protective packing at the time of his death. His reputation as an art collector spread not only in India but also abroad; catalogues poured in through the mail, he was besieged by art dealers. If anybody had to offer family heirlooms for sale, Salar Jung used to be the first person to whom the objects would be shown. He had agents in all the important cities of the country, who scoured the markets for valuables. He was also known to frequently purchase from Christie's and Sotheby's. He travelled abroad frequently in pursuit of artifacts. Over the years, the sprawling deodi, with its large halls started to look like a warehouse; the art pieces were strewn everywhere, on tables, chairs and in every conceivable corner. He did not let his servants dust or rearrange his collection; partly for fear of theft and partly for fear of breakage. He had a wonderful retentive memory and at any point he could recall where a particular object was kept. A time came when the deodi could not take in any more objects and they had to be stored in his other palaces. His Saroor Nagar Palace, for example, was stocked with many beautiful objects.

The collection included all the sundry bric-a-brac that crowded the Nawab's life – from the armies of tin soldiers he played with as a child to a priceless collection of jade; antique bronzes; marble statuary; textiles, far eastern art, an eclectic assemblage of paintings, jewellery, ivory and rare illuminated manuscripts, some dating back to the Mughal period. Some of these are of great value, some ordinary and others both childish and idiosyncratic.

Those who knew Yousuf Ali Khan remember him as an affable, courteous and generous person. He must have inherited his grandfather's trait in that respect. Whenever and wherever he showed himself, he would be mobbed by hordes of petitioners; he would receive all the petitions with equal courtesy and his secretary would process them. He gave away generously even when he knew that some of the petitions were not genuine. He was a lover of music and literature and a keen sportsman; a part of the present airport in Begumpet was the private polo ground of the Salar Jungs. Yousuf Ali Khan was an ace polo player, and among those with whom he played the game were Sir Winston Churchill and the renowned player, Shah Mirza Baig, who was originally from Hyderabad. He was deeply religious but was no religious bigot. During the month of Muharram, when the Shia community of Hyderabad went into mourning to commemorate the martyrdom of Husain at Karbala, Yousuf Ali Khan would hold mushairas and have famous artists visiting the city and rendering ghazals to a private and select gathering in his deodi. Such activities, perforce, had to be kept low-key since the orthodox members of the community frowned at such frivolity during the month of mourning.

If Yousuf Ali Khan's public life remained unfulfilled, so did his private life. He could not form a meaningful relationship with any woman. He remained a lonely man and died a bachelor, in spite of the fact that he was one of the most sought-after young men in town. The nawab's name was romantically linked to those of many young ladies. One of the ladies in question was Padmaja Naidu, the daughter of the freedom fighter and poetess, Sarojini Naidu. Padmaja belonged to one of the most prominent and intellectual families in the city. Her grandfather Dr Aghornath Chatterjee and mother Sarojini Naidu were celebrated figures not only in Hyderabad, but also in the national scene. Padmaja was said to possess a vivacious and a sunny nature; what she lacked by way of good looks, it was said, she made up by her temperament. She alone, among Sarojini Naidu's children, was said to have inherited her mother's wit and sparkle. It seemed for a while as though her affections were returned. But if the city expected to hear the news that the romance was to result in matrimony, they were to be disappointed; the rumours died as suddenly as they had sprung up. Nothing came of the relationship and what went wrong is not known. Padmaja, however, was known to be heart-broken and was said to be on the verge of an emotional breakdown. There were a string of young ladies whose names figured in the gossip of the city. But nothing came of these associations either.

Leila Wellinker, a young lady of singular charm, who later married the famous filmmaker, David Lean, came closest to marrying the nawab. She was still in her teens, young and highly impressionable. Moreover, her engagement to Prince Salabat Jah, the step-brother of the ruler Osman Ali Khan, had just been broken. He caught her on the rebound, so to speak. Salar Jung was, by then, a man of the world at the age of forty-four, and was endowed with his famous charm of manner. They were both socially very active and he was captivated by Leila's vivacity. Eventually the matter reached the advanced stage of a formal engagement. Zainab Begum, Salar Jung's mother, gifted the bride-to-be with traditional jewellery in keeping with the local tradition. This time round it seemed as if the nawab was finally going to tie the knot and settle down to matrimony. Then again the inevitable happened;

a heart-breaking standoff between the lovers led to the cancellation of the engagement. Many contemporary observers felt that there was something wrong with the nawab. How else could one explain the string of broken engagements? Those who knew him personally, think otherwise. As for the nawab, both matrimony and emotional security seemed to have eluded him.

ᔑ

Rasheed is a dapper old man of seventy-odd years. He was one of the hundreds of retainers who worked in the deodi in the time of Salar Jung III. His main job was to run around the deodi carrying messages and running errands for his seniors. The older retainers liked to keep him close by since he was nimble-footed. As a result, he knew the layout of the deodi well. When the deodi was converted into a museum, some of the staff of the nawab was transferred to it. Rasheed was one such member of the museum staff. He lives in retirement now and comes to the museum to draw his pension. I came upon him after a long search. He was elusive as he was reticent.

'Why do you want to talk about the bygone times, saab?' he said when I first met him. 'Woh zamana guzar gaya hai. Those days were different and those people were different. Ab kuch bhi nahi bacha hai. Only memories.'

He was even more perplexed when I asked him to take me round the deodi.

'What deodi do you want to see? There is no deodi now, only the walls remain, nothing else.'

Not deterred by his cynicism, Praful and I had arranged to meet him one afternoon, soon after his afternoon prayers at the entrance of the dargah of Hazrat Abbas, which had been enclosed by the deodi at one time. I was confident that he would be knowledgeable, even allowing for memory lapses and exaggerations.

The Hazrat Abbas Dargah predates the deodi; it dates back to the Qutub Shahi period. The deodi of the diwans grew all around it, enclosing the dargah within its high walls. Even though the deodi has been demolished, the dargah stayed intact. It retains an air of antiquity in spite of repeated renovations; its high walls, which apparently were a part of the original construction, shield the shrine from the busy road beyond. In fact, other than the gates, the dargah is the only part of the deodi that is still intact now.

We walked into the dargah one afternoon while waiting for Rasheed. A man, frail and bent, sat in a corner of the dargah, a rosary in hand and an old woman was sweeping the floor. Inside the shrine, incense burned and garlands of jasmine and rose petals covered the aalams. The mutavalli, whose family has been taking care of the dargah for well over four centuries, lives on the premises. He showed us around and invited us into his house. Over a cup of tea, he told us, 'It was Mir Alam who started the construction of the deodi. He is said to have come loaded with money after defeating Tipu Sultan of Mysore. He brought jewellery on camels, they say. His booty consisted of fabulous jewels, pearls, rubies and emeralds. What good did all that do him?' he said, sipping his tea. 'Hyderabad has changed so much. Everything is so different! Gone are the ruler and his nobles. Their wealth is gone too and nothing is left. But the dargah continues to attract devotees. Such is the power of faith!'

For all his initial reluctance, Rasheed was a good guide. He pointed out interesting places as we walked: 'On the tenth day of Muharram, a procession of aalams used to be taken out of the dargah every year. On that day Sarkar and his zenana would pay a visit to the deodi to witness the procession. About fifty cars would arrive, carrying the royal party, many of them Rolls Royces with their windows covered with curtains...Sarkar's zenana stood there,' he told us, pointing to the shops on the first floor, which replaced the upper floors of the deodi 'and watched the procession of the aalams. For days before the visit of the royalty, the deodi would be thrown into a frenzy of activity. The rooms overlooking the dargah, which were kept shut throughout the year, would be opened for the use of the zenana. They would be aired and swept; the floors would be covered with farrashes. Sarkar sat in the aina khana, with the nobles standing behind him; the ladies were conducted to the rooms overlooking the dargah, which were specially prepared for them. They would watch the procession, make their offerings and witness the maatham. Khoob maatham hota tha, saab; der raat tak chalta tha. The courtyard of the dargah would be splattered with blood,' he reminisced. I shivered in spite of the afternoon heat.

'As long as Sarkar was in the deodi, all of us, servants and officials huddled in corners, our senses alert and hands folded. Everyone had to be appropriately dressed; our elders used to tell us what we should do and what we should not, when Sarkar visited the deodi. We had to train ourselves to stand still; you could not move a muscle in your body in the presence of the ruler and you could not even lift your eyes as long as Sarkar was present. I remember the scene as clearly as if it happened yesterday. We used to tremble with fear and even the important ministers used to stand behind Ala Hazraat (the Nizam), hands folded, their heads bent.' Suddenly a gleam came into Raheed's eyes. 'Nawab Saheb (Salar Jung) bhi darte the, Sarkar se', he chuckled, 'but he was afraid of him for a different reason. He was afraid that the ruler might take away his precious art pieces and he seldom showed him the most valuable pieces of his collection!'

We walked around the grounds of the deodi, trying to get a sense of the place; Rasheed pointed to the spot where a plaque once stood, indicating the levels to which flood waters of the Musi river had risen in 1908. We walked past the no longer existent Naya Makan, built by Nawab Laiq Ali Khan; Purana Makan, Zenana Khana, the formal courtyard and so on.

'I cannot recognise the place any more,' Rasheed complained. 'All the landmarks have disappeared. There used to be huge step-wells, lovely gardens, tennis courts and very beautiful buildings with carved woodwork; the first ones to go were the trees and the baolis are now filled up. There used to be a huge baoli there, where Nawab Saheb used to swim, sometimes his nephews used to join him. Can you see that spot in the middle of the well? That was the place where he would rest and soap himself. All that has gone now, the beautiful buildings were pulled down and their contents were auctioned. How do you expect me to show you anything now?' Rasheed grumbled.

'Narasayya, a Hindu Brahmin, took care of the khazana. Ranga Rao, also a Brahmin, was the cashier. G. Venkatachalam was the art adviser. A thousand people serviced the deodi and fifty people were constantly on attendance on Nawab Saheb. The stables had two hundred horses; clothes for Saheb came from Europe and sometimes from John Burton of Secunderabad. Food was carried from the bawarchi khana to the dining table under an armed guard.

'There used to be a beautiful garden here,' said Rasheed, with a sweep of his hand; we were standing in front of an empty space, where Nizam Bagh had once stood. 'Nizam Bagh was a beautiful palace. It was very grand. Nawab Saheb's birthdays were celebrated there. People would give him presents, read poetry, and present addresses. Nawab Saheb was not like the other nobles. He was genuinely loved by everybody.

'The deodi had a total of 200 rooms. Nawab Saheb wanted to make a museum and display the art objects that he collected; he had all the plans ready but did not live to see it made. Saheb really loved the pieces he bought and valued them. He knew what was kept where and if anything was missing, he could immediately detect its absence. The servants had to be careful; they were not permitted to dust the pieces, lest they should break them. He told them not to touch his valuables. Nobody, not even the senior servants, ever touched them unless he specifically asked for them.

'There used to be a big oval table in the aina khana; interesting articles the various merchants brought for sale would be selected carefully and they would be placed on the table along with the prices of each piece. Nawab Saheb would go through the merchandise. These were articles like swords, daggers, vases, guns, paintings, and others. R.W. Dueskar was an artist and he used to live in the deodi. Nawab Saheb would consult Dueskar and Venkatachalam before selecting art pieces to buy. Nawab Saheb had a trained eye and could easily spot a good piece when he saw one; he would select a piece or two of value, write down the offer price and initial it. The paymaster would pay for it. The art pieces were arranged in seventy-seven rooms.

'Salar Jung III was heartbroken when the jagirs were abolished. He went to meet Sardar Vallabhai Patel, the then Home Minister of India, who was in town at that time. He came home late that night. We do not know what happened. He kept to his apartments after that. Every one was worried. Two days later, he died. Heart attack, they said. He used to live in the Naya Makan, built by his father, which was more modern than the rest of the deodi. That was where he died.' Rasheed's voice went soft. 'The next day, his body, covered in a shawl, was placed in the dalan. Many people, including General Choudhury and all the other nawabs and the big people in the town came rushing. A huge crowd collected outside the deodi, people wanting to know what happened, some wanting to see the body and some idlers, out of curiosity. The deodi was at once put under protection. The body was washed at noon in the hauz, in the quadrangle where he lived. Many people, friends, relatives, servants followed the body to Daira Mir Momin; the procession was the biggest I have ever seen. Of course, the Nizam Sarkar's funeral procession was bigger than that. There was so much affection, such courtesy, insaniyat aur pyar mohabbat in those days; they were grand days; those days are gone for ever, saab,' Raheed whispered.

'After the death of Nawab Saheb sab barbad hogaya, saab', Rasheed continued after a brief silence. 'All of Nawab Saheb's valuables were photographed, documented, sealed and put in the bank vaults of the Imperial Bank at Sultan Bazaar. After the valuables were removed, for days and days, auctions of the contents of the deodi took place. We pulled out clothes, suits, shoes, scent bottles, cutlery, crockery, vases, sheets, floor spreads, lights, tents and all sorts of things from the tosha khana, the mez khana, farrash khana and so on. It was heart-rending to see the beautiful deodi stripped and pulled apart like that. There were four ivory chairs, which had been presented to Tipu Sultan by the French government, which were still in packing at the time Saheb died. They were purchased at a cost of Rs 80,000. These chairs are in the museum now. Un yadon se bahut takleef hota hai, saab.'

We had been sitting on the grimy steps of a shop facing the Chatta Bazaar. The heat of the afternoon had abated and shadows had begun to lengthen. It had been a long day for all of us. It was time for Rasheed's evening prayers, but he seemed not to notice. We stirred ourselves and prepared to leave. After bidding farewell to Rasheed, as we walked out of the gateway, I saw an old gentleman with a flowing white beard, wearing a fez cap and dressed in a faded sherwani walking towards the Dargah of Hazrat Abbas. It was almost as if nothing had changed. The old gentleman walked slowly, leaning heavily on his walking stick. That, perhaps, is the last generation which cared for the deodi. After his generation fades, very few in the modern times will remember what the Diwan Deodi was all about. Another slice of Hyderabad's memories would be lost for ever.

Peshkar Deodi

The year was 1910 and the day, the fifth day of the Islamic holy month of Muharram. The hour was 2 p.m; the place, Peshkar Deodi. The occasion was the display of the langar procession.

The balcony of the Peshkar Deodi was festooned with colourful banners and buntings. On it at a vantage point were gathered, high ranking dignitaries of Hyderabad. The most distinguished of those assembled were the Resident and his staff, civil and military officers, European visitors to the city, the Hyderabadi nobles and all those who merited an invitation from the prime minister. In a happy coincidence, the prime minister was residing in the Peshkar Deodi of Hyderabad. For Maharaja Kishen Pershad Bahadur had risen to the position of a prime minister and he combined in himself the positions of both a peshkar and a prime minister. It had been the tradition for the langar to pass in front of the diwan's residence first, and then move on to the Panch Mahalla Palace, where the royal entourage witnessed the procession before it passed on to the Peshkar Deodi.

There was an air of expectancy about the gathered guests on the balcony. Farther down along the Charminar main street, throngs of people had already taken their positions; they had journeyed from the nearby villages and towns to witness the spectacle. The motley crowd of pressing humanity was in particularly high spirits; they were lively but orderly. It was amazing that it should be so, since most of the men who gathered there carried mean-looking lethal weapons and belonged to different religions and nationalities. One could hear the hubbub of different languages and dialects spoken. They included Siddis, Rohillas, Pathans, Marathas, Turks, Sikhs, Persians, Punjabis, Parsis, Madrasis, Bengalis and Europeans of all nationalities. They made an attractive picture in their colourful clothes and a variety of headgear.

The langar procession was an event that had come down to Hyderabad from the Qutub Shahi times. The background of the event was that in the year 1594, Prince Abdulla, son of Sultan Quli Qutub Shah, left Hyderabad for Golconda mounted on an elephant, with a large body of nobles and attendants. Shortly after leaving the Purana Pul Gate, the elephant became uncontrollable and charged into the crowd and then ran off into the nearby jungle with the unfortunate prince on its back. The prince's mother, Hayat Baksh Begum, became very alarmed for her son's safety. She ordered that food be placed at various places high on trees, so that both the elephant as well as the prince, could reach it. She vowed that if the prince returned safely from the ordeal she would make a chain of gold similar in thickness and weight to that used for the fastening of elephants as an offering. After an agonising wait of six days, her son did return safely, whereupon the grateful mother proceeded to fulfil her vow. She had a massive gold chain made. The prince carried the chain in a procession of all the nobles and troops of the state and went to the shrine of a Shia saint in the city and offered thanks for his safe return. After the ceremony, the gold chain was broken up into pieces, which were distributed among fakirs and beggars of the city. From that day onwards, the procession became an honoured tradition in Hyderabad. The Nizams, although they were not Shias, followed the tradition right up to the modern day. It was the last Nizam, Osman Ali Khan, who put an end to that practice.

The procession was an annual feature in the city's calendar and was a much awaited event. It consisted of all the troops of Hyderabad, both regular and irregular; scores of elephants beautifully painted and decorated with colourful trappings, camels gaily caparisoned, horses with elaborately embroidered headgear and the troops in colourful costumes. The pageant was long and colourful, and consisted of endless irregular troops of Arabs, Pathans, Afghans and Sikhs; then there was the Myseram Regiment (Monsieur Raymond's Regiment), the Nizam's Afghans, the Peshkar's Sikhs, the Lancers, the Artillery, the Infantry regiments and the regular troops of the British. The most impressive figure in the procession was the figure of the kotwal, who paraded seated in a hauda on a stately elephant. The eye catching part of the procession was the running, hopping and whirling of the Arabs and the Siddis in a kind of a war dance. Equally attractive was the long line of royal horses clad in bright yellow livery. As the colourful procession passed by, there was muted applause from the dignitaries in the balcony and lustier cheering from the crowds below. Finally, the event came to an end and the guests of the maharaja prepared to leave. The prime minister stood at the entrance of his sprawling deodi, seeing off his numerous guests, with that grace and courtesy, which he was so famous for.

༈

The prime minister, Maharaja Kishen Pershad Bahadur, Yamin-us-Saltanat, and GCIE, (Grand Commander of the Indian Empire, a title granted by the British) traced his descent to Raja Todar Mal, the celebrated revenue minister of the Mughal emperor, Akbar. When Nizam-ul-Mulk Asaf Jah came to the Deccan, Rai Mulchand, the fifth descendent of Todar Mal, accompanied him. Since then, the family played an important role in the affairs of Hyderabad. While generations of men from that illustrious family held important positions in the Nizam's court, the two outstanding members of the family were Raja Chandu Lal and Maharaja Kishen Pershad. They both started as hereditary peshkars but rose to the position of prime ministers. Their family deodi was hence called the Peshkar Deodi.

Raja Chandu Lal was a quintessential court noble who had mastered the art of intrigue and manipulation. During his time, there were different forces at play in the court of the Nizam; the British and the old nobility. The British had already signed the Subsidiary Alliance with the Nizam and were expanding their control over the ruler, and Nizam Sikandar Jah, backed by the old nobles, was putting up a stiff resistance. Chandu Lal was a British protégé and was disliked by the Nizam. Chandu Lal played one group against the other with consummate skill; he sidelined the authority of the Nizam, kept the British in the dark, defrauded the state exchequer with the help of the private banker Palmer and Co, amassed great wealth and acted as the principal power in the state for well over thirty-five years.

Finally when he was forced to resign, the Nizam had to grant him rich jagirs, a bonus of a crore of rupees and a pension of Rs 3000 per month. Even then, Chandu Lal walked away with important official documents of the state to be in a position to control the Nizam!

Chandu Lal's deodi stood in the heart of the old city, close to Charminar. His pleasure house, the baradari, stood in the outskirts of the city. The baradari was a wooden mansion of lofty proportions and intricate wooden carvings. It was surrounded by attractive gardens and water hauzes. Chandu Lal entertained lavishly in his baradari. The famous courtesan of his time, Mahalaqa Bai Chanda, regularly entertained Chandu Lal's guests. His most important mission, of course, was to mollify the ruler, Sikandar Jah, with whom he had a strained relationship. Other guests at his receptions were the officers of the East India Company.

✵

Maharaja Kishen Pershad Bahadur, the great grandson of Chandu Lal, also controlled the affairs of the state of Hyderabad for well over thirty-five years, in two separate spells. The difference between the two men was that unlike Chandu Lal, Kishen Pershad was one of the most respected and loved prime ministers of the state, he was His Highness' childhood friend and companion. In contrast to his ancestor's strained relationship with the ruler, the maharaja's devotion and loyalty to his master bordered on worship. His love for the ruler was such that it was believed that the prime minister wept in private, long after Mahboob Ali Khan had departed from this world.

Kishen Pershad was a member of a select group of young pupils who shared space with the Nizam himself. Mahboob Ali Khan was barely three years old when he became the ruler. He was under the direct guardianship of Sir Salar Jung I, who was responsible for the education and upbringing of the child Nizam. Salar Jung selected a group of companions, appropriate in family background and nobility of birth, to be classmates and playmates for the child king. The two sons of Salar Jung, along with Kishen Pershad, Fakhr-ul-Mulk and several other scions of the nobility of the court made up the classroom. The young men were trained in western principles of administration as well as the elaborate Mughlai court etiquette, which was still in practice in Hyderbad.

In Hyderabad at that time, government posts were largely hereditary. Appointments to important positions generally went on expected lines. In spite of his closeness to the ruler, the maharaja's rise to power was not so smooth. Although he was appointed to the position of deputy peshkar, other honours were slow in coming. When his maternal grandfather, Narainder Pershad, died in 1888, the position of peshkari he held was not automatically bestowed on the heir, his grandson. This was a major setback to the young maharaja. On the other hand, his rivals succeeded in proposing that the position of peshkar should be abolished and the jagirs attached to the position should revert to the state. This was an alarming situation; without the income from the jagirs, it was very difficult for the maharaja to maintain the huge establishment of the deodi and the family. To add to his woes, the Nizam recognised him as the chief mourner after his grandfather's death and consoled him as such. That meant that he automatically became the head of the family, a position that brought with it enormous responsibility, without the family income. The maharaja bore his difficulties with dignity and carried on with the family responsibilities stoically. Being a noble of the highest order, he could not turn to anyone for help. Mahboob Ali Khan, the Nizam, who was generally apathetic to the affairs of state, was loath to assert his authority vis-a-vis the warring factions at the court and help his childhood companion. As was his wont, he took his time in resolving the matter. When he finally took the decision to invest Kishen Pershad with the position of peshkar, the good news was conveyed to the maharaja in an unusual manner. The langar procession which traditionally passed through the Peshkar Deodi, had stopped doing so since the death of Narainder Pershad, Kishen Pershad's grandfather. Now, it was directed that the procession pass through the maharaja's deodi, leaving no one in doubt as to the position that the maharaja was to occupy in the near future. It was typical of the Hyderabad of those days that the fortunes of great nobles changed in the twinkling of an eye. Thereafter, the maharaja's troubles were over and ten years later, the maharaja became the diwan, the Prime Minister of Hyderabad, a position next only to that of the ruler. The two childhood friends came together again and this augured well for the state.

The maharaja was a man of many interests. He was a member of the Freemasons Lodge and took an active part in the social life of the city. He was a scholar in Persian, Arabic, Urdu, Sanskrit and English. He was also an accomplished poet, a calligraphist, a painter, a photographer and a good cook. He was given the title of Shagird-e-Khas Asaf Jah, an honour seldom bestowed by the Nizam on anyone. The maharaja was the author of fifty-seven works in Persian and Urdu and also of a few books in Marathi. He composed poetry under the pen name 'Shad'. His ghazals, qasidas, rubaiyats and other genres of classical verse in Persian and Urdu made him well known in literary circles. The maharaja's court teemed with writers, artists and poets from different parts of India, whom he patronised with generous gifts and donations. He supported many struggling writers like Fani and was a friend of the poets Dagh, Iqbal, Sarojini Naidu, Aamir Minai and others, who were household names in the literary world. He would hold annual mushairas which were attended by poets from all over the country. Other nobles followed his example and held similar gatherings of poets and of course, the guest of honour at such gatherings was the maharaja himself. His popularity in the literary circles was such that years after he died 'Shad Memorial Mushairas' were held in Hyderabad right up to 1947, and were attended by literary luminaries of the Urdu world like Shabbir Husain Josh, Jigar Moradabadi and Raghupathi Rai Firaq Gorakpuri, among others.

The maharaja's acts of charity and generosity are legendary. He is said to have tossed fists full of coins to the poor whenever he drove out of the deodi. As a result, the legend says, after his death, when his body was cremated, his hand stood out, his palm and fingers stretched open! The maharaja's lifestyle often outran his means. But living beyond one's means was a common matter among the nobles of Hyderabad in those days. Mundane matters such as personal finances were left to the paid servants to worry about. The maharaja was no exception.

The death of the sixth Nizam in 1911 affected the maharaja very deeply and in more ways than one. With his death came to an end the years of position and power for the maharaja. Osman Ali Khan, the seventh Nizam, who succeeded Mahboob Ali Khan was a man with modern views. He has been described as the most capable administrator after the founder of the Asaf Jahi dynasty, Nizam-ul-Mulk. He was young and energetic and was impatient to introduce modern methods of administration in the state. Like Salar Jung I half a century ago, he was not sure if the old nobility of Hyderabad was up to the task of tightening the sagging administration. He is said to have remarked in private, that 'old ropes cannot hold new tents!' Moreover, the ugly monster of court intrigue reared its head again. Questions were raised about the maharaja's loyalty to the young Nizam. The old and loyal noble was accused of campaigning against Osman Ali Khan's claim to succeed his father. Consequent to the turbulence at the court the maharaja fell from the position of pre-eminence he had so far occupied. Those were days of depression and loneliness, and feelings of rejection took their toll on the otherwise sanguine personality of the maharaja. Life was never the same again for him. It was at that time that opium started taking its effect on him. His once magnificent physique lost its tone. The photographs of the maharaja taken in later years show him slouching and looking apathetic. However fortune favoured him after fourteen long years of neglect and oblivion; Osman Ali Khan apparently reconsidered his opinion of the maharaja for he appointed him the president of his Executive Council in 1925, the position the old noble held until 1936.

The maharaja was a much-married man. He had seven wives, three of them were Hindus and four were Muslims. His family lived in the large and rambling ancestral Peshkar Deodi, built over a hundred years, for each incumbent added buildings to the original deodi. Each wife had her own palace, servants, kitchen and establishment. The children of his Hindu wives had Hindu names, while those of his Muslim wives bore Muslim names.

The Peshkar Deodi was located in Shah Ali Banda; the area is at present popularly known as Bela Chandu Lal and is famous for khoya or khova. Today, the deodi has changed beyond recognition. It is difficult to imagine that it was the very place that once witnessed important events that changed the course of Hyderabad's history. The tall gates that once provided access to the deodi still stand. Of the cluster of buildings that once formed the deodi, like the aina khana, Khas Bagh, Lal Bungalow, Moti Mahal, Shad Manzil, Zenana Mahal, bawarchi khana, baggi khana and so on, just a handful of these structures still stand in different states of ruination. Fortunately, all those structures that are still habitable are being put to different uses in their altered forms. The deodi today houses a hospital, a school and a shaadi khana and provides living quarters to a dozen or more families. The large enclosure is cluttered with construction and the high walls that once enclosed the deodi, stand only in part.

The famous aina khana of the Peshkar Deodi, similar in construction to the one at Diwan Deodi, was the venue for many distinguished gatherings. A particularly attractive building in the deodi was the Khas Bagh with a high ceiling, tall wooden pillars and artistic multi-foliated Shah Jahani arches. It was a wooden structure, built in a baradari style so typical to Hyderabad. It was decorated with very rich adornments like chandeliers, full-length mirrors, carpets, paintings and expensive furniture. In its heyday, the Khas Bagh witnessed a lot of grandeur and was the scene of much action, as it was the venue for banquets, dancing, musical soirees and cocktail parties. Sometimes after cocktails, the guests would saunter through the garden to the nearby Lal Bungalow, another structure within the deodi, where they would sit down to a sumptuous meal. As the prime minister of the state, the maharaja had to entertain frequently. It was in the Khas Bagh that important people like the governors general were received and entertained. Of the many distinguished people who visited the deodi were Lord Curzon (1902) the Prince and the Princess of Wales (1905), and Lord Hardinge (1911). The deodi had a well laid-out garden complete with a pavilion, ornamental walkways, a rose garden and so on. The maharaja entertained his most important guests there. European guests, both men and women attended banquets thrown by the maharaja along with a sprinkling of local ladies but the female members of the peshkar family kept away from such gatherings. Not a trace of that magnificent garden remains today.

Generally, guests would be received in front of the Khas Bagh and escorted inside, where they would be seated formally in the order of their position at the court. Traditions that ruled such seating were strictly followed and any deviation from such arrangements could cause grievous breach of protocol. The British tried time and time again to infringe on such rules. It was a matter of great irritation to the Nizam's court and caused much friction between the two powers. The visit of Lord Curzon to the maharaja's deodi resulted in one such event.

Lord and Lady Curzon paid a ceremonial visit to Hyderabad, ostensibly to promote friendship and goodwill between the Nizam's and His Majesty's government. However, the reason behind the visit was not as innocent as it appeared to be. The real purpose behind the visit was to arm-twist the Nizam into closing the issue of ceding the cotton-rich state of Berar to the British permanently. The cession of Berar to the British had been a tricky issue and needed to be handled with care. Curzon pressed into action his skills at persuasion, pressure and guile. In so doing, Lord Curzon tried to drive a wedge between the Nizam and his nobles by favouring one against the other. One of the dignitaries he favoured with a visit was Maharaja Bahadur. There is a photograph taken in the Khas Bagh of the maharaja's deodi, which bears eloquent testimony to the incident.

Curzon was at his wily best and he was playing the age-old game of divide and rule. He selected Nawab Fakhr-ul-Mulk, a premier noble and a close friend and confidant of Mahboob Ali Khan, to be used as a pawn; Fakhr-ul-Mulk was an outgoing man, widely known to be on friendly terms with His Majesty's officers. He entertained them lavishly and what was more, his three sons were educated in England and were even received by Queen Victoria! From the time he arrived at the maharaja's deodi, Curzon made it a point to demonstrate his easy friendship with Fakhr-ul-Mulk with pointed references to his son's education and their upbringing. He also insisted that Fakhr-ul-Mulk should sit down to pose for the official photograph. An agitated and embarrassed Fakhr-ul-Mulk politely tried to decline the invitation but the governor general did not let the matter rest. To Fakhr-ul-Mulk's consternation, the surprised Nizam bade the noble to obey the honoured guest; the red-faced noble sat down for the photograph with the dignitaries but with a quaking heart. The matter was made worse for the noble because there were the other nobles like Shahab Jung, the home minister, Afsar-ul-Mulk, the commander-in-chief among others, his friends and close associates and equals in rank, standing behind the ruler, whereas he alone was singled out by the governor general and asked to sit down. He realised that he was the victim of the Englishman's plan of dividing the court and weakening the ruler but he was helpless at that moment to do anything. Later, after Berar was permanently signed off and the governor general had departed and when the nobility were closeted with the ruler, a bitter Nizam looked at Fakhr-ul-Mulk, his childhood friend of long years and said accusingly:

'Do rangi chhod ke, ek rang hoja,
pighalkar moam hoja ya sang hoja.'

Fakhr-ul-Mulk returned home that night, crushed in spirit and deeply hurt; he, a childhood associate of the Nizam was suspected of treachery and betrayal!

When the scene was enacted in the Peshkar Deodi, the maharaja, a close friend and confidant of both Mahboob Ali Khan and Fakhr-ul-Mulk watched the drama unfold helplessly, not sure how to avert the misunderstanding. It was only later, when tempers had cooled, that he was able to mediate. At Falaknuma Palace where the nobles met the ruler, he was able to help Fakhr-ul-Mulk by easing the tension. In the presence of the assembled nobles, Fakhr-ul-Mulk approached the Nizam and pointed out to him that he did not carry a single honour like a knighthood bestowed on him by the British, but that his breast was adorned by the honours handed down to him by the Asaf Jahs alone. It took Fakhr-ul-Mulk's repeated professions of loyalty and the soothing words of the maharaja before the noble could be restored to the affections of his master again.

Another distinguished personage who visited the maharaja at his deodi was Rabindranath Tagore. The last Nizam, Osman Ali Khan, had granted an amount of one lakh and a quarter to the poet, to institute a Chair for Persian studies at Shantiniketan. Rabindranath Tagore made a special trip to Hyderabad and sought the intervention of the nobles of Hyderabad, particularly the maharaja, for an increase in the grant. He was received with great courtesy and warmth by the maharaja and presented to the ruler.

∽

If dressed in a sherwani and dastar, a sarpech and his grandfather's pearl necklaces, Shyam Gopal Saincher may pass off for a younger version of Maharaja Kishen Pershad. The photographs of the maharaja taken in his early youth show him as a powerfully built, athletic and handsome man. As Kishen Pershad's grandson, through his youngest wife Rani Draupadi Bai, alias Tahniyat Mahal, Shyam inherits some of his grandfather's good looks, if not his fame and wealth.

The maharaja's family's fortunes, built over several generations, melted away in just a few decades after his death. It is true that the maharaja lived beyond his means during his lifetime; his enormous expenditure of supporting poets and artistes, handing out of substantial amounts of money to various causes and his lavish lifestyle had imposed a heavy burden on his finances. To add to this, he married seven times and had to support a large family. He was naturally heavily in debt by the time he died. The Nizam, out of respect for the late noble, paid off at least part of the maharaja's debts. The substantial property, one of the largest in the state of Hyderabad, was handed over to the heirs free of encumbrances. Yet in a matter of a few decades, the family had run through the enormous wealth of the peshkars and reduced themselves to penury.

The neglect of the deodi had started even during the maharaja's lifetime. Towards the end of his life, the maharaja had more or less retired from public life. After he ceased to be the president of the Executive Council in 1936, he did not entertain much. The death of his favourite wife, Draupadi Bai, depressed his spirits. Years of taking opium, a habit favoured by most of the nobles in the city, had taken its toll on his health. He had become reclusive and withdrawn.

During his childhood, Shyam's family lived in Khas Bagh, in the ancestral deodi in the old city. He has distinct memories of Khas Bagh, where he spent his formative years. He remembers the palace as a large but dusty structure with faded grandeur and tarnished mirrors. He remembers seeing a lot of valuables lying about Khas Bagh, gathering dust and uncared for. Furniture, paintings, pictures, guns, photographs and other valuable items were all over the place, some under lock and key and some not. The house was large and had many doors. A large number of people walked in and out of the house as they were used to in the earlier years. It was almost a case of any one being able to walk away with anything. Shyam remembers seeing enormous quantities of family jewellery, not yet divided amongst the heirs. 'Believe me, now that I run a jewellery shop, I can recognise a good jewel when I see one; what we had in our deodi was unbelievable, both in terms of quantity and quality. Pearls, emeralds and diamonds of such size and quality are rare to come by; my blood turns to water when I think of all that we lost. My brothers and father were poor managers and neglected to take care of the estate or the deodi. They lost everything due to sheer negligence and apathy. Matters were left to the managers, there was no personal supervision of the assets. Everything was lost before my time,' he says. Though all the palaces inside the deodi were shut down and bore a deserted look, there was a horde of servants in attendance. The family continued to live in the style that it was used to, even after the jagirs were abolished. The family was perpetually cash-strapped. A number of expensive cars were parked in the motor khanas, some of them not as much as started in years because there was no money to buy petrol to run them. Paying the salaries of the large number of servants was a burden. Day to day living had become a struggle.'

Expensive paintings, guns, and cars disappeared right in front of Shyam's eyes; they were sold for paltry sums. Property was mortgaged again and again to pay off creditors. Finally in the early eighties, Khas Bagh was demolished and the beautifully carved wooden pavilions were sold as scrap.

The Paigahs

The word 'Paigah,' means high rank, and was first granted as an honorific title to Abul Fateh Khan Tegh Jung by the second Nizam, Nawab Nizam Ali Khan, in recognition of the services rendered. To begin with, the Paigahs were military chiefs in the employment of the Nizams of Hyderabad and provided the household troops to guard the person of the Nizam. The second Nizam bestowed titles and generous jagirs on Tegh Jung and gave him the position of a premier noble.

The Paigahs claimed their descent from the personage of the second great Caliph of Islam, Hazrat Omar. One of the descendents of Hazrat Omar, Shaik Fareed-ud-din-Khan, migrated to India and was noted for his piety. He became a famous saint and lived in the Montgomery district of Punjab, now in Pakistan. Fateh Khan's grandfather was a governor of Shikohabad during the reign of Aurangzeb. It was his father, Khair Khan, who was at the court of the Mughal emperor Muhammad Shah of Delhi and came to the notice of the first Nizam, who invited him to join him during his campaign in the Deccan. Khair Khan attached himself to Nizam Ali Khan and proved to be a great asset to his master during the early years of his campaign. He won a decisive battle against the Marathas in the year 1745. His military prowess and fierce loyalty won him the respect and affection of the Nizam, who bestowed jagirs and titles on him. Khair Khan died in 1752, leaving behind a wealth of goodwill and reputation in the Nizam's court

Tegh Jung proved to be a worthy son of his father. He was said to be a giant of a man, who stood six and a half feet tall and rode a very big horse. Stories of the valour and courage of Fateh Khan Tegh Jung describe the fierce loyalty and devotion that he displayed for the Nizam. Impressed by his devotion to the family, the second Nizam, offered him the position of a prime minister. But in answer to such an honour, Tegh Jung is supposed to have remarked that he was a soldier and not an administrator and he declined the job. Tegh Jung was averse to the idea of self-glorification and firmly believed that he should concentrate on protecting the Nizam and not fritter away his time and resources in self-indulgence. The story goes that when Nizam Ali Khan, who was very fond of him, asked him to build himself a garden, he raised a disciplined army instead and informed his master that it was his idea of a garden. In keeping with his personality, he neither left behind a large deodi nor much money to his descendents, for he spent most of his revenue on raising troops.

It was during the time of Tegh Jung's successor that the family's wealth began to grow. When he died, his son Fakhruddin Khan was a lad of ten years. The Nizam's respect and affection for Tegh Jung was such that he took the boy under his wing, educated him, bestowed large jagirs, a mansab of 10,000 cavalry and gave him his daughter, Bashir-un-Nisa Begum in marriage. He was the first member of the Paigah family to marry a lady of the royal household. Unlike the other nobles, whose jagirs could be rescinded at any time, the Paigah jagirs were bestowed on them in perpetuity. Moreover, a sanad was issued in 1834 by the second Nizam that exempted the Paigahs from paying the customary chouth to the state. Along with the collection of revenues, the Paigahs also looked after the civil and judicial administration in their jagirs. The head of the Paigah family carried the title 'Shams-ul-Umarah' meaning 'the sun amongst nobles', a title that was to define the position the Paigah nobles held in Hyderabad for the next two centuries.

Nawab Fakhruddin Khan helped the British to defeat the 'mutineers' during the revolt of 1857. He remained a close confidant of the Nizams throughout his life. He distinguished himself as a scholar and had many books translated from English and Arabic into Urdu and Persian. He was interested in engineering, chemistry, physics, mathematics, geography and astronomy. The credit of opening the first large school in the city goes to him. He also had his own astronomical observatory, which was equipped with instruments imported from Europe. Thus, the first two men of the Paigah family were distinguished, one as a soldier and the other as a scholar.

It was during Nawab Fakhruddin's time, that the famous deodis of the Paigahs were built. The construction of Jahannuma and the other two named after their last occupants and known by those names in Hyderabad, namely the Khursheed Jah Deodi and the deodi of Iqbal-ud-Daula were started during the time of Fakhruddin. He is credited with personally designing the very attractive Palladian structure later known as the Khursheed Jah Baradari.

Over the following decades, the Paigah nobles grew in influence. Marriages between the royal household and that of the Paigahs brought them closer together. Their proximity to the ruler made them feel that they had an overriding claim to all the important positions in the state. The Paigah nobles of later generations held positions of power from time to time. Being very closely related to the royal household, they were treated with deference and tact by all the others. The other important nobles took every care not to hurt their sensitivities. On their part, the Paigahs zealously guarded their position at the court. They often crossed swords with any one who posed a threat to their importance.

That rivalry was particularly acute during the prime ministership of Sir Salar Jung I. The Paigahs resented the control Salar Jung exercised on the child Nizam Mahboob Ali Khan, and also his hold on the affairs of the state. At their insistence a Paigah noble was made a co-regent to look after the young Nizam. In spite of such an arrangement, the trouble between the Paigahs and Salar Jung I persisted. Matters came to such a pass, that the beleaguered prime minister thrice came close to resigning from his position. Decades later, when maharaja Kishen Pershad became the prime minister, he avoided confrontation with the Paigahs at all costs. He mollified their egos by showing extra respect to them. For example, when the maharaja became the prime minister of the state, some of the Paigah nobles had to salute him when they led their troops during the langar procession. The maharaja, being the diplomat that he was, tactfully withdrew from his balcony when the Paigah nobles filed past his deodi to spare them the embarrassment of saluting him. Such were the sensitivities of the nobles of the time. Members of the Paigah families like Asman Jah, Vicar-ul-Umrah and several others held important positions as prime ministers, but only for short tenures.

In addition to being related to the royal family, the Paigahs were also the richest nobles in the state. In 1784, the annual revenue of Tegh Jung amounted to thirty-six lakhs of rupees and soon rose to fifty two lakhs in the following years. Over the following century, the Paigah jagirs were divided among the heirs repeatedly, and hence individual shares of income fell sharply. In 1881, they were divided for the last time into three houses, the Asman Jahi, Khursheed Jahi and Vicar-ul-Umrahi Paigahs. Around 1918, the annual income of the Asman Jahi Paigah was seventeen lakhs, the Khursheed Jahi Paigah, fourteen lakhs and the Vicar-ul-Umrahi Paigah, twelve and three fourth lakhs.

In spite of such riches, the Paigahs were often heavily in debt due to mismanagement of their jagirs. The estates had often to be placed under the supervision of able administrators to put them back on track and straighten out their finances. The families waited anxiously while their estates were under the care of the administrators and they went into great demonstrations of joy and happiness every time the jagirs were restored to them.

The Paigahs built their deodis in close proximity to the royal palaces, their locations themselves being a mark of honour. They were built to the west of the Mahboob Chowk on the Amir-e-Kabir Road, and its neighbourhood. The deodis of these nobles were larger than any others in the old city and naturally more opulent.

The Paigahs were prolific builders. The real need to raise and maintain troops for the Nizam ceased when the ruler signed the Subsidiary Alliance with the British in 1798. With no major preoccupations to divert their attention, the members of the family seemed impelled to make statements of wealth and power by building fabulous palaces and decorating them with rich adornments. They built large deodis and lived in the old city before the urge to move out to modern palaces overtook them.

The oldest was the Jahannuma, where the head of the family entertained originally. In his monumental work, *The Glimpses of the Nizam's Dominions* written in 1898, A. Claude Campbell recognises Jahannuma which means the 'reflection of the world', as one of the oldest palaces in the city.

To the west of the Chauk, he writes, 'is the city palace of His Excellency the Nawab Sir Asman Jah…the old portion of which was built on Oriental style by His Excellency's forefathers, and which is, today, one of the oldest…To this the Khana Bagh was added, in European style by the present Nawab twenty years ago, this portion being elegantly furnished in English style. From this part of the palace, the Langar procession is witnessed by European friends of the Nawab. Until the Khana Bagh was erected, entertainments were held at Jahannuma palace, which is noted for its spacious gardens, handsome fittings, in Oriental style, and many other interesting and charming details.

Asman Jah was related to two Nizams; he was the grandson of the third Nizam and the son-in-law of the fourth Nizam. He occupied important positions during his lifetime. He was appointed as the co-regent to the child Nizam, Mahboob Ali Khan and in 1887, he represented the Nizam at the Golden Jubilee of Queen Victoria. Subsequently he was appointed as the prime minister of the state from 1887 to 1894.

The first Paigah deodis were built in the traditional style of a typical Hyderabadi deodi but on a more elaborate scale, with a series of inner courtyards and all the other features appropriate to a deodi of powerful nobles. Those were the days of immense power, authority and wealth, since the family's jagirs had not yet been divided. Their deodis were likened to 'a palace of the Arabian nights.' In the later years the Paigahs took to building 'palaces' in the European style.

Asman Jah was greatly influenced by everything English. He added a whole new section to the old deodi in the then fashionable European style. This new building incorporated Palladian and Romanesque architecture, had Corinthian pilasters, elliptical, and semi-circular arches and stucco work of lime. The outer walls as well as the main entrance to the deodi are so European in conception that the deodi is in marked contrast to the rest of the old city. It looks quite out of place in the otherwise medieval-like neighbourhood of the Mahboob Chowk and its environs. In 1869, when Asman Jah was appointed the Minister of Justice, the deodi doubled as the high court. Opposite the deodi was an abdaar khana, a water point where people could get a drink of fresh water on hot days.

If the Jahannuma was located inside the Asman Jahi Deodi, it has disappeared without a trace. All that remains of the deodi today is its outer wall and the main entrance of the deodi. The inner courts and structures have been razed to the ground and a regular colony of houses has sprung up in its place. Ragpickers rummage in the garbage piled high in front of the once grand deodi, and a cycle mechanic sets his repair shop on a makeshift platform at its entrance. There is not a trace of the earlier grandeur or eminence. The once great Amir-e-Kabir Road displays neither the grace nor dignity that it was once famous for.

At some distance from the deodi of Asman Jah, is the deodi of Iqbal-ud-Daula. Iqbal-ud-Daula was the title given to Vicar-ul-Umrah, who was the prime minister of the state from 1894-1901. The Iqbal-ud-Daula Deodi came to the Paigah nobles of the Vicar-ul-Umrahi branch. Of all the deodis in the old city, this indeed is one of the best preserved. The deodi, which covers the entire length of a street, is built in lofty proportions and is once again a blend of the European and the Oriental styles of architecture. The jillu khana, which is outside the main entrance, is damaged and heavily built over and almost covered by modern construction. The main gate and its massive wooden doors and the naubat khana above the gate are in a fairly good state of preservation though. Through the imposing gate, one enters a spacious courtyard, where the offices and European reception rooms were once located. A gallery of rooms, now ramshackle, looks out on to the road. A private mosque of dignified proportions abuts the deodi. A school, quaintly called the 'Ethics School', is located in the gallery of the rooms upstairs now. Children bound up and down the rickety stairs and spill over into the spacious courtyard when the school gets over.

The rest of the forecourt, its innumerable rooms, galleries and apartments all around the sprawling courtyard, are in a decrepit state. At least a dozen families, if not more, occupy them now. An assortment of rags and gunny bags act as curtains to screen their kitchens and living quarters. Children play gilli danda in the once busy yard, and chicken scratch the ground and scamper around as we walk. Elderly men lounge on charpais and smoke beedis while young men stare insolently while we walk past. The once grand circular drawing room, where the European guests were entertained, serves as a class room for the Ethics School, but there are large portions of the deodi that are totally abandoned as they are unfit for human habitation. We walk around gingerly, braving the sagging floors and the crumbling side-walls, to get a glimpse of what lies in those rooms. These are the extensions to the modern drawing rooms, specially built to entertain the European guests. Quaint designs and intricate stucco work peep through the peeling plaster and the exposed brick work; there are no oriental decorations here, not even in design. The ornamental patterns are mostly European in style.

Once past the European sections of the deodi, one enters a different world altogether. My eyes take a minute or two to adjust to the shaded apartment in front of me. What meets my eye is very different from what we left behind in the forecourt. We walk past the connecting vestibule and step right into another world.

It is the Rangeeli Haveli, we are told, and the dalan was a part of the old deodi. It was used for social gatherings and special occasions. One is taken by the harmony and the compactness of this gem of a dalan with its delicate pillars that rise to hold the roof and the graceful arches that screen the glare. A narrow staircase leads to the gallery in the upper floor overlooking the dalan; elegant windows provided with wooden shutters afford an excellent view of the goings on down below. Women of the deodi, when permitted, would have sat behind those shutters and watched the goings on in the dalan. Fortunately, this part of the deodi along with the pesh-dalan is intact, and what is more, it is in use. A karate class is in progress and a wedding reception is scheduled for the night, we are informed. Preparations are on for the reception; the once elegant pillars are painted in florid colours and decorated with childish floral designs. They are, no doubt, meant to look colourful and attractive in the artificial neon lighting by night. The courtyard is hemmed in by high walls, but it was not so at one time, the courtyard had opened on to yet another enclosure, or so the tell-tale signs of brick work indicate. The place is abuzz with activity; students clad in white karate clothes are practicing karate kicks. We come away feeling relieved that as long as this quaint part of the deodi is put to such commercial use, it will receive a modicum of maintenance. The colour of the paint applied recently may look garish and the designs painted on the pillars might look immature, but the structure itself is taken care of.

Other parts of the deodi are not so visible to begin with. They are blocked from view, and the residents bar entry to strangers and trespassers. We qualify on both accounts. There has to be more to the deodi than just the Rangeeli Haveli, we feel. We pick up courage and start searching around, trying to find the rest of the deodi. We begin to feel like snoopers, for that is what we are doing. People glare at us forbiddingly. There is an old style wooden door in one corner. It is firmly closed. Beyond that door could be the zenani section of the deodi. The grounds are extensive and the treetops soar above the buildings. We rattle the knocker to attract attention, and are greeted with an angry 'andar ana mana hai!' So we move on to another part of the deodi. We look around bewildered, not knowing where to begin. It is tantalising. We know that the rest of the deodi is right there, if only we knew how to get there! At the risk of incurring the wrath of the inmates, we duck low and walk past some more living quarters, past a kitchen and startled looks, lifting a grimy screen here and muttering an apology there, guilt written all over us. They have been living there for decades and we have no business invading their privacy. We step out of the warren of tenements and out of the gloom. Suddenly, we feel as if we stepped back a hundred years. We stand back to take it all in.

It is a large rectangular courtyard enclosed on three sides by attractive shallow dalans. There are galleries of rooms over looking the courtyard on the first floor. They are abandoned, shut and empty. The windows stare down at us with vacant eyes, their wooden shutters hanging loose and glass window-panes cracked. The ditch in the middle of the courtyard is what is left of a water cistern. It is brimming with rubble and discarded plastic bottles. A fountain must have played here at one time, but there is not a trace of it today. However, the ornamental lamp posts that illuminated the courtyard at one time still stand. There are enough indications to suggest that this courtyard leads to yet another courtyard, or perhaps another haveli. We cannot tell, as the entrance is barred. A hastily built brick wall blocks further view. On the fourth side of the courtyard is the deodi's large ornamental diwan khana. It looks large and promising from where we stand. Explore the courtyard further we must, provided we make our way through garbage. The structure is pretty ramshackle and signs of neglect and decay are all too obvious; the lime plaster barely covers the brick and the stone core of the structure and the shell-like gloss of the walls is pitted and scribbled over.

As far as the diwan khanas of Hyderabad go, this is the biggest that we have seen so far. It comes as a surprise after the squalor and the clutter that we had seen all around. It has a harmonious composition of long graceful arches and delicate ornamental pillars that taper delicately. The lime-plastered pillars have lost their shine, but the basic structure is still intact. Centuries of dust and grime cover the decorative designs on the ceiling. There are viewing galleries with delicate shutters on three sides of the large hall; the jaalis of the upper floors meant to provide privacy to the ladies are thick with dust and cobwebs. The once delicate wooden shutters are mouldy and frayed. The grand hall has not had a lick of paint in perhaps a century or more and giant cobwebs hang from the ceiling instead of brocade and silk. The empty shell of the diwan khana resounds with hollowness. The intricate designs on the ceiling are still intact and so are the hooks from which the chandeliers once hung. At one time, women must have sat in the upper galleries, hushed by the presence of the men below but expectant and excited nevertheless; a musical soiree, perhaps, was to take place soon, or maybe a poetry session? The murmur of voices and the rustle of silk from below must have found its echo in the smothered smiles and the tinkling of bangles in the galleries above. A blend of itars, henna and musk, khus and rose, depending on the season, must have blended with the floral fragrances of mulcheri and jasmines. The diwan khana and its polished walls must have glowed in the light of the chandeliers, as did the jewels worn by the guests. A pigeon rises suddenly, startling us and breaking the spell. The pretty images have vanished and all we see is peeling paint and chipped plaster.

We had entered the diwan khana from the wrong end of the building since its entrance is blocked too. The elegant structure is put to a different use today; it is used as a chicken coop. There is loose dust under one's feet instead of Kashmiri carpets and a foul smell assails our nostrils instead of the fragrance of itar. It is dark and damp inside. Fine feathers rise like a cloud with every step we take. Urchins who gathered to gawk at us tell us that a film shooting had taken place there once and it was for a fighting scene. The local hero, they tell us, starry-eyed, beat up the villain. We come away perplexed, trying to imagine the hero fighting a villain under the Shah Jahani arches!

The owners of this charming structure moved out of the old city more than a century ago. Its owner, Nawab Vicar-ul-Umrah had built a fabulous palace called the Falaknuma, credited to be one of the most outstanding palaces in India at that time. Italian architects designed it and workmen from Florence executed it and most of the furnishings were imported from Europe. It was so beautiful and built at such cost that the nawab ran into enormous debt. Later, he had to gift his palace to the sixth Nizam, who was in fact, his brother-in-law, who paid off the nawab's creditors. Once Falaknuma was given away, the nawab built himself another palace in Begumpet. No wonder he did not pay attention to the old deodi. The old home, left to the vagaries of nature, was shut down and abandoned.

We have to retrace our steps now. We know that there is a lot more that we should see. But it is not to be.

∿

At a distance of a quarter of a mile from the Iqbal-ud-Daula Deodi, is the palatial baradari that belongs to Nawab Khursheed Jah, popularly known as the Khursheed Jah Baradari. Calling this handsome Palladian structure with high Corinthian pillars a baradari is a misnomer; the only reason the Hyderabadis would have done so is that it has twelve doors and windows. That is where the similarity with a baradari ends, for the rest of the building is very European in design and execution.

Predictably, the baradari was where the master of the deodi entertained. The living quarters were located at a discreet distance from the baradari, no doubt hidden behind high walls. The baradari was a showpiece, decorated with very rich and expensive furniture, chandeliers, glassware, paintings and other ornamental items, to be used only when there were important guests to entertain and kept under wraps the rest of the time. Banquets and formal receptions were held there. The Survey Map of 1915 shows that the baradari stood in the middle of large and open grounds; attractive gateways gave access to the grounds and a high wall enclosed the yard. When the Paigah nobles lived there, the grounds had chabutras, fountains and hauzes; there were formal gardens and also a vinery.

Historical accounts show that the grandfather of Sir Khursheed Jah personally designed the building and laid the foundation stone around 1860, well after the British Residency had been built and when it had become the rage in Hyderabad to build palaces in its imitation. The superstructure was hardly raised nine feet high when that nobleman died; it was left to his son, the father of Sir Khursheed Jah, to complete the construction, who made improvements to the original design. From an architectural point of view, it is said to rank high among the palaces of Hyderabad. Prior to 1948, it was very richly furnished and was famous for its many attractions. There was a fine collection of armaments, including the armour of the family's illustrious ancestor, Abdul Fateh Khan Tegh Jung. On display were his steel chain mail and cap which were peculiar in shape and weighed twenty pounds. His picture occupied the pride of place in the baradari.

While the rest of the nobles of Hyderabad were content with maintaining well-stocked stables, Nawab Khursheed Jah Paigah maintained ostriches along with horses. Those birds were trained to be ridden. They ran very fast, we are informed, although they were difficult to manage and 'caused great merriment to the onlookers.' The deodi occupied the entire block, and its sundry buildings, like the baggi khana and the daftar khana, were located in the next block.

Another peculiarity of the Khursheed Jah Deodi was that it was protected by a platoon of female soldiers, called Zafar Pultan which meant the victorious platoon! The platoon derived its name from the successful expeditions that it had carried out against the Marathas in the previous century, in the days of the founders of the family. The soldiers of the platoon were not mere ornaments, they were 'proper' soldiers. It was just that like everything else in Hyderabad at that time, their roles lost their original significance; they were reduced to guarding the female quarters of the Paigah nobles. The soldiers of the platoon dressed in uniforms, played a 'band' of their own and carried out exercises under the guidance of their 'officers.'

In a refreshing change from the other deodis of Hyderabad, the grounds adjoining the baradari are still attached to it. They are open, vacant and barren. At present a college is located in the baradari and the grounds are utilised as a playground by the students. Every now and then one hears a rumour that the government is planning to set up a heritage museum in the deodi. It would be an excellent idea if the authorities decide to do so, since the structure is in a good condition and the extensive grounds are intact. The location is perfect too, lying as it does close to the Chow Mahalla Palace of the Nizam and the Charminar. Rumours, however, have remained but rumours. Meanwhile the building itself is deteriorating. Hundreds of students bounding up and down the delicate structure does not augur well for the aging structure.

Hyderabad was strewn with the palaces of the Paigah nobles at one time, each vying with the other in terms of grandeur and opulence. The grandest of the palaces are the Falaknuma and the Bashir Bagh palaces, both of which were built at a great cost and furnished at an even greater expense. Falaknuma survives today with diminished grandeur while the Bashir Bagh Palace was demolished in 1960 and has made way for a shopping centre. Other palaces have survived too and are now being used as office buildings, shaadi khanas, clubs and private residences.

The Rai Rayan Deodi

To the north of Charminar, when the blaring of horns and the tinny film music that emanates from the roadside eateries do not drown it out, there is an interesting sound that one can hear; a sound that is as old as the city itself. It is the rhythmic tapping sound made by the traditional silver smiths, beating silver into thin foils called waraq. Artisans have been working at the same spot for centuries, from the Qutub Shahi times. The thin silver foil that they make is used to lace the celebrated Hyderabadi paan and sweetmeats; it is also used as an essential ingredient in the Unani medicine. Once you hear that insistent tap tap, you know that the Raja Shamraj Deodi is close by. Walking past the Mecca Masjid and the Unani Hospital, which face each other, amidst the noise and confusion of little shops selling fruits and other eatables, one comes upon an interesting looking gateway. The gateway is interesting since it harmonises three different styles of architecture dating back to three different periods. The arch, which is tall enough to let an elephant pass, is Qutub Shahi in style. The clock, which was added later, is decidedly English, and the topmost chattri is very Hindu in ornamentation and style. While a gateway of such elegance looks incongruous and out of place in the present surroundings, some fifty years ago, it was an integral part of the streetscape of the city, and one of the many such ornate and imposing gateways that dot the city even today. If one walks a little further, one sees a row of shabby shops, whose owners were engaged in traditional occupations at one time and provided services to the deodi. The shehnaiwala, for example, will tell you that his ancestors used to play shehnai on all the festivals and important occasions in the deodi at one time. His people were artistes then, there was dignity and pride in working at the deodi. Now that the deodi no longer needs his services, he has to eke out a living by playing humdrum film music at sundry weddings, where 'people cannot tell the difference from one raga to the other'. Gone are his pretensions to dignity or talent.

The spiked wooden doors of the gate are still in place, though they have not been used for decades. The gate itself is whitewashed and the clock still ticks. One is told that it has just been put right by the Municipal Corporation in an attempt at renovating old structures! The upper floors of the gateway overlook the busy street outside. Before the clock was installed in 1904, naubat played three times a day from that floor to indicate the time of the day. Guarding the gate stood a ferocious looking Arab. In the days when the ancestors of Raja Rai Rayan Dayanatwant Shamraj (II) Bahadur lived in the deodi, the Arab must have carried a curved knife or in the later years, a long matchlock gun. Ordinary people must have thought twice before approaching him for permission to enter the deodi.

Beyond the gateway, nothing else appears to be the way it once was. A broken jalli protrudes out of the rubble; it must have formed a part of the jharokha at one time. One sees an interesting looking ornamentation here, and a piece of stucco there. There are crudely built half-finished houses, built without a care for either the layout or order. Iron rods jut out indicating that further construction is on and a confusion of electrical wires rises in the sky. This, at one time, was the famous deodi of Raja Shamraj.

Raja Shamraj (II) Rajawant Bahadur, and his ancestors arrived in Hyderabad at the express request and invitation of the first Nizam, Nizam-ul-Mulk Asaf Jah. The founder of the family, Krishnaji Pant was a watandar of Deogarh, which lies in the present day Dualatabad district of Maharashtra. Krishnaji Pant's administrative skills came to the notice of the Mughal emperor, Shah Jahan, who appointed him as a munsabdar at his court. Krishnaji Pant served the emperor in that capacity for thirty-five years. On his death in AD 1688, his two sons, Moro Pant and Naro Pant, were appointed in his place and they continued to enjoy the favour of the Mughal emperor. It was in the Mughal court that the two brothers came into contact with Nizam-ul-Mulk, the future founder of the Asaf Jahi dynasty, who was then the subedar of the Deccan. During the years of turbulence, between 1720 and 1724, the two brothers stood loyally by the side of the Nizam. Subsequently the family settled down in the Deccan in the employment of the Nizam from 1740 onwards. Moro Pant was appointed as the peshkar in the year 1748. After his death, his brother, Naro Pant succeeded him to that position. Thus began the long association of Raja Shamraj's family with that of the Nizam of Hyderabad. Descendents of Krishnaji Pant continued to play an important role in the affairs of Hyderabad and successive generations were granted munsabdaris and jagirs. They came to be granted with many royal privileges like the use of a palki, the display of an aalam, morchel, chattri and chamar, the beating of a naqqar during public appearances and the honour of wearing court jewels on ceremonial occasions. Many titles like Rai Rayan, Dayanatwant, Dharmwant and Raja were bestowed on them. The family played an important role during the Nizam's wars with the Peshwas, and, at a later point, with Tipu Sultan of Mysore. The Pants were said to be skillful diplomats and were employed in the delicate negotiations Hyderabad had with the Peshwas. They were so artful in resolving tricky matters to the satisfaction of both parties that the Nizam and the Marathas appreciated them and rewarded them.

During the eighteenth and the nineteenth centuries, the Rai Rayan family held munsabs of 5,000 to 7,000 zat, and jagirs worth Rs 48,000 per year. Over the years the family had accumulated considerable wealth and, by the time of Raja Shamraj II, who was the last of the line, the family held 120 villages in its control, in Telengana, Marathwada and Karnataka. Prudent by nature and meticulous in account keeping, the Rai Rayans took good care of their jagirs and were considered to be one of the richest families in the princely state of Hyderabad.

The Rai Rayans were much respected and held in great affection by the Nizams. There were several instances of the royal family displaying great concern and tenderness towards the Rai Rayans through out the two and a quarter centuries of their association. The family records show that when the young wife of Raja Shamraj I (1765-1822) died and left behind two sons, the Nizam and his begum were greatly concerned. The boy's father, who was quite young himself, had remarried. Fearing that the step mother would not be able to take care of the children adequately, the second Nizam, Nawab Nizam Ali Khan, and his wife, Bakshi Begum Saheba, took the two children under their care. They built a kothi right next to their own palace and took care of the children's education and upbringing. When the boys came of age, the Nizam and his begum had their thread ceremonies performed as per the Hindu tradition and appointed them to important positions in the Nizam's peshi. Another eighty years down the line, the story repeated itself again. When Raja Lakshmanraj, another minor, lost his father, the then Nizam took him under his protection. He was brought up with great care and given the benefit of excellent education. When he was married in 1892, the invitations were issued over the signature of Nawab Vicar-ul-Umrah, the prime minister, on behalf of the Government.

∿

What is left of the deodi of the Rai Rayans, lies at a short distance from the Panch Mahalla Palace of the Nizam, which, incidentally, has also been demolished. The Rai Rayan Deodi started as a small house, built on traditional Maharashtrian lines. It was a humble dwelling, built with the courtyard and the deogarh as its focus. The original house had an internal well that supplied water to the kitchen over the centuries. Over the next two centuries, the later generations added rooms and whole sections to the deodi. Despite the ravages of time, the original section of the house with its exquisitely carved woodwork has survived, and so has the deogarh, where the family's kuladevta, Renuka Mata is enshrined. Renuka Mata was so sacred to the family that generations of Rai Rayan men bore the name 'Renuka Das' along with their other given names. Below the deogarh were built a few underground rooms, where the family could take shelter in troubled times.

The Rai Rayan's concerns for security when they first settled in the city were quite understandable. Theirs was a prominent Hindu family, living in what was predominantly a Muslim city. They had just arrived in the new city; the memories of the fierce battles between the Marathas, who were staunch Hindus and the Mughals, who were Muslims, were fresh in their minds. Moreover, in the city roamed fierce looking men with volatile tempers, carrying dangerous weapons. The streets were not safe for any one to walk in, it was believed. The underground rooms, hidden discreetly below the family shrine, gave them a sense of security, however fragile. The fact that the deodi was located so close to the Nizam's palace must have been a matter of some solace. Many Maharashtrian Brahmin families, which migrated to Hyderabad more or less at the same time, also settled down around the deodi; they looked to the deodi, which was heavily guarded, for protection.

However, there are no records to show if the rooms built underground were ever used. On the contrary, there is every indication to show that the goddess Renuka Mata, and her devotees, survived safely over the centuries among men of intemperate dispositions. When the city was torn by communal riots during the Razakar movement in 1947-48, and even as many Hindus fled the city, loyal Arab guards continued to guard the deodi and both Raja Shamraj and Rani Ambika remained in the deodi, unharmed. Since Independence, the old city has been subjected to some of the worst communal riots that the country has witnessed. Right through that period, long after the Arab guards were withdrawn, Renuka Mata continued to receive regular worship. At present, members of the family and their old associates gather in full strength to celebrate Dussera, as per the family tradition.

In that sense, a part of old Hyderabad has survived, in more ways than one.

∿

About half a century ago, the first thing that a visitor to the deodi would have noticed on entering its premises, was how different it looked from all the other deodis in the city. The Rai Rayan residence incorporated many Hindu architectural features while retaining the basic forms of a typical Hyderabadi deodi. In the later years too, at a time when the rest of Hyderabad was going to great lengths to adopt European features in their residences, the Rai Rayan Deodi continued to stay traditional.

Perhaps the only concession made to the new trend of westernisation was the addition of a clock to the gateway and the provision of a formal drawing room with European furniture. Even then, the European drawing room bore the Sanskrit name, 'Chandrabhuvan' meaning 'the mansion of the moon.'

In its final form, the deodi incorporated all the features customary to a deodi of a nobleman. It had a series of courtyards, allocated to public and private uses, well laid out formal gardens, ornamental dalans, a diwan khana, an elaborately furnished drawing room, a well-stocked library, a museum, and other sundry buildings like a farrash khana, baggi khana, motor khana and so on. There was no separate bawarchi khana since the food was cooked by Brahmins inside the traditional kitchen, which was a part of the original structure.

The frontage of the deodi was adorned with statues of elephants with ambaris, serving as a support for the jharokhas. The pillars supporting the portico and the decorative arches were of a style known in Hyderabad as the 'regional Mughal variation.' Figurines of 'Deepa Lakshmis' welcomed the visitors through the main portico and a flight of steps led to the first of many courtyards.

As in the case of all the other deodis of Hyderabad, the main courtyard was the focus of the house. The musnad where the head of the family received visitors on ceremonial occasions was located in the main dalan. A pavilion in a typical Rajasthani style, polished to look like marble, was provided with the usual paraphernalia like a takhat and gau takias made of red velvet and embroidered in gold karchob work. Honoured guests like the Nizam and other distinguished visitors to the deodi were entertained there. Social and religious gatherings were held in the courtyard. The dalans were deep and provided with the typical multi-foliated arches; an ornamental hauz stood in the middle of the attractive courtyard. Chandeliers hung from the ceiling and family portraits adorned the walls. In later years European furniture was placed in its recesses.

There were a series of courtyards, earmarked for different uses. The internal courtyards were reserved for private use. One such courtyard was meant for large gatherings such as marriages. Weddings were lavish affairs and both men and women took part in the ceremony. Hindu Vedic rituals were strictly followed. Pandals were erected and decorated with torans of mango leaves and other traditional designs. Marriage feasts were held in a different enclosure, the ground for which was specially prepared, for the guests were to be seated on rows of wooden peedhas decorated with silver motifs. After the grounds were watered and swept, women laboured for hours over the intricate rangoli designs to decorate the area where the peedhas were to be placed. The family's ensemble of gold and silver plates was taken out of the vaults for the occasion. Seated on the row upon row of peedhas, the guests were served the specially prepared wedding feast by Brahmin cooks. This feast was naturally confined to the community of Maharashtrian Brahmins. The others were entertained to regular receptions in the formal garden on the following day.

One major difference between the deodi of the Rai Rayans and those of the others in the city was that the women of the Rai Rayan family did not observe purdah. Though the Rani had her own private drawing room, the Zenani Diwan Khana where she received visitors, it was maintained to make her Muslim guests feel comfortable rather than to provide privacy to the women of her own household. The deodi did not provide for independent quarters for women. It is interesting to note that the family albums of the Rai Rayans carry photographs of generations of Rai Rayan women whereas it is hard to find photos of women in the albums of the other deodis. Even if the women were photographed, the pictures were kept strictly private.

At the back of the house were the kitchen and the dining section. The family dining place was simple and there were no lavish dining tables or tableware here. The family members ate sitting on the floor, on wooden peedhas decorated with the customary silver motifs. The family ate out of silver plates. The Rai Rayans' wealth was such that the family was supposed to have possessed five hundred silver plates, complete with katoris and all, which were taken out of the khazana and used on important occasions and a few gold sets of a similar nature.

The Rai Rayan men were deeply religious; they were brought up in a strict Vedic tradition. Protracted Hindu rituals and the chanting of the holy scriptures dominated their lives. There were separate enclosures for conducting religious ceremonies, for drying clothes, for pujas, for feeding the Brahmins and for making chandan paste. The elaborately designed kitchen was equipped with numerous rooms for storing pickles, grinding masala, cutting vegetables, storing condiments and so on. True to the Hindu tradition there was a separate maternity room, set slightly apart, where women were confined during the long hours of labour and childbirth. The deodi was also provided with underground rooms, meant, perhaps, as thekhanas, to be used in the hot summer months. It is also possible that the rooms were meant for another use too, that of providing shelter to the family in troubled times. A flight of wooden steps led to these rooms and they were kept closed for most of the year.

The last member of the line, Raja Shamraj II, added a museum, which was famous for its marble statuary, ivory carvings, ornamental clocks, Chinese artifacts and other interesting objects. He also built a vast library which had 44,000 books and the people who visited the library vouch for the fact that it had books on a variety of subjects and topics. What is more, the books were no mere ornaments; the owner of the library had read them all; most books had his pencilled notations in the margins.

The strong room of the house was located in the basement. As revenue collectors of the state, the Rai Rayans were the custodians of many revenue records. It was in these vaults that the family's valuables, like gold and silver, were kept. Traditionally, a Brahmin clerk was in charge of the vault. During the time of Shamraj II, a Telugu clerk called Gaurayya, a Brahmin by birth, was in charge of the strong rooms and he carried the keys of the treasury on his person. Family members wanting to wear jewellery for an occasion or use silverware for a ceremony had to approach the faithful Gaurayya, who kept meticulous records of which jewel was taken, by whom and in what condition. He also scrutinised each piece when it was returned to him and recorded the condition in which it was returned. In fact, that was the custom followed in most deodis in Hyderabad; even the Nizam entrusted the family valuables to the care of a faithful clerk whose job it was to maintain a meticulous record of the same.

If the Arab soldiers guarded the front entrance of the deodi, Rajputs guarded the rear where the family shrines were located. Resident jewellers, gold and silver smiths, clerks, librarians, accountants, cooks, entertainers, drivers, farrashes, polishers, men and women servants who served members of the family, and numerous other kinds of attendants worked day and night to keep the rambling deodi going. In the evening, no room was ever locked and all the keys were in the custody of the sipahis of proven loyalty.

Religious festivals like Dussera and Diwali were occasions of great festivity and ceremony. The nine days of Dussera were marked by long rituals and religious ceremonies. Evening and nights were spent singing bhajans and in similar religious engagements. On the last day of festival, the Raja would proceed in a procession of elephants,

drummers, shenaiwalas, armed security gruards and other followers
to the family temple at Lakshmaneshwar Bagh to offer worship. In the
evening, the Nizam would pay a visit to the raja at his deodi to convey
his good wishes to him. On such occasions the Nizam was presented
with a nazar of golden ashrafis by the Raja and his family members
and articles of silver were gifted to the other members in the Nizam's
encourage. The guests were entertained with platters of dry fruits and
delicacies like mewa and mithai. In his turn, at the time of Muharram,
Shamraj Bahadur would send an aalam to the nearby dargah.

Whenever important people came to the city, a visit to the Rai
Rayan Deodi was a must. As such, the deodi received a stream of
dignitaries and prominent men of the time. Some notable persons
who visited the deodi during the time of Shamraj II included the
renowned poet Rabindranath Tagore and the revolutionary writer
Vinayak Damodar Savarkar. Rabindranath Tagore visited the deodi to
enlist the support of the Raja in getting a grant for Shantiniketan.
Savarkar, a freedom fighter, arrived at the deodi on an interesting
mission. He was told that the only available copy of one of his books
happened to be there in the Raja's library. He came to borrow the
book, to have it reprinted and dutifully returned the original to the
Raja. Sarojini Naidu was a friend of the family and a frequent visitor to
the deodi. Another important person who visited the deodi was K.M.
Munshi, the founder of Bharatiya Vidya Bhavan. He came specially to
look at the much-talked-about library of Shamraj. The Raja being a
scholar himself, revelled in the intellectual company that these men
provided.

Raja Shamraj and his wife Rani Ambika were different compared
to the rest of the aristocracy of the city. No doubt, the raja saheb
dressed in finery; he dressed in brocades and expensive jewellery
whenever he attended the court or the state banquets. However, at
home he led a simple and austere life and he stuck to wearing the
Maharashtrian dhoti and the traditional pagdi. Being high in the
pecking order, he would sit close to the ruler and the chief guest at
state banquets, but as an orthodox Brahmin, he did not eat with the

rest of the guests. He carried gangajal with him and refrained from shaking hands with anyone; he did a respectful pranam from a distance. The Nizam, who was familiar with the noble's orthodox ways, did not take offence and instead he respected the raja's religious sentiments.

In spite of their brahminical orthodoxy, the Rai Rayans were modern in their outlook. For example differences of faith and caste did not stand in the way of their offering help to others in times of need. During the flood in the year 1908, the family members of some Muslim nobles, whose deodis were damaged, took shelter in the Rai Rayan Deodi. Rani Ambika was the daughter of a Winsurkar chief; Winsurkars were the famous sardars of the celebrated Maratha ruler, Shivaji. She was a woman of character and dignity and was also progressive in her outlook. Women of her family mixed freely with men. Girls of the family were educated along with the boys and were encouraged to be modern. Rani Ambika tempered tradition with modernity; she would wear georgette saris, which were in fashion at that time, but in the traditional Marathi style. She joined her husband in performing puja as per the dictates of the Hindu religion but she would also play bridge and mahjong when she had the time. She was the president of the local Lady's Club and a rallying point for women of her neighbourhood. She would take her daughters and daughters-in-law for a drive in the car to the tank bund or on a visit to the families of the other nobility often. The rani led an active social life and maintained cordial relations with the ladies of both the Hindu and the Muslim families. This was all in marked contrast to the lives of the women in other deodis.

Raja Shamraj and Rani Ambika were devoted to each other; they brought up their children with discipline and high moral values. In spite of the fact that the Rai Rayans served the Nizams and lived in feudal Hyderabad, they were nationalistic, fiercely patriotic and were inspired by freedom fighters like Bal Gangadhar Tilak, Gopalkrishna Gokhale and Mahatma Gandhi and they avidly followed the political developments in the country. Rani Ambika was a student of Sri Aurobindo and followed his teachings. Though extremely wealthy, the couple was not carried away by the trappings of power and position.

They led a life of simplicity and were rooted to the ground. They kept their children away from the idle and dissolute world of the Hyderabadi nobility.

The abolition of the jagirs devastated the Rai Rayans like all the other nobles in the city. However, being educated, the descendents of the family did not go under when their jagirs were taken away.

ᔕ

Today the deodi of the family is divided into independent two-room tenements. Parts of the once sprawling structure were demolished when the heirs divided the ancestral property. The artifacts of the museum so lovingly put together by the raja including marble statues, Chinese artifacts, clocks and ivory pieces were sold for a mere Rs 50,000. The land on which the deodi stood and generations of Rai Rayans lived was divided into small plots and sold. Today a warren of shabby tenements replaces the once formal gardens.

When we went in search of the deodi, we had to request at least ten different householders to permit us to see what was left of the original structure. Fortunately, at least some of the attractive features of the deodi, like the intricate stucco work, the decorated false ceilings, the pavilion where the Rai Rayan takhat was placed at one time and even the massive strong room that the daftardars once used for keeping the state revenues have survived, perhaps more by default than by any deliberate intention to preserve them. However, ripped out of the context in which they once existed, today they fail to make any sense, other than being of academic interest. Of particular interest is the section of the deodi, where we located the strong room of the Rai Rayans.

ᔕ

It was eight in the morning. We had been on the road for more than a couple of hours by then. The three of us must have made a strange combination. A tall and lanky Praful with his camera, blonde and blue jeans-clad Robert and I, dusty, hot and terribly dishevelled. We had seen most of the tenements by then and we had come to the end of our search. It was a commentary on the amiable disposition of the people who lived there that they should cheerfully let us, utter strangers, walk into their homes at such an awkward hour and allow us to inspect their interiors. In fact, they were most friendly and informative. They pointed out bits and pieces of the original structure that still remained.

We knocked at the door of what appeared to be a large unit of a house as compared to the others. The young owner, his eyes heavy with sleep, opened the door to our guilty knocking. He scratched his head in bewilderment when we asked to see the inside of his home. Having asked us a few gruff but legitimate questions about who we were and what business we had in his house, and after being satisfied that we were perfectly harmless, he shook off his sleep and agreed to take us around his part of the deodi. We stepped in tentatively, not sure what to look for. To be said to their credit, the new occupants of these rooms had carefully retained whatever decorations that they could save.

It was somewhat dark inside, since all the windows were shut. The walls were painted in a florid blue and multi coloured pictures of gods and goddesses adorned the walls. Clothes festooned every possible nail on the wall and a mosquito net covered the rest of the room. In all that confusion, it took me a while to size up the room. I had seen pictures of that part of the deodi and was hopeful of finding some original features, a decorated niche or perhaps a stucco decoration somewhere. Right in the middle of the room, staring me full in the face was something that looked suspiciously like a pavilion. I could not believe my eyes. A closer examination revealed that it indeed was the pavilion, where generations of Rai Rayans sat in state and received guests! It was just that it was altered beyond recognition. The once alabaster-like fluted pillars were painted in gaudy colours of red, green and yellow to suit the taste of the present owner. In a classic case of recycling or reusing an old structure for a new purpose, a TV and its stand occupied the place where the Rai Rayan musnad once stood. The original stucco work of the pavilion was in a perfect condition!

The ceiling of the deodi too was in a good shape and the teakwood beams gleamed. The owner was very enthusiastic about the wood. It is very valuable, he told us, it was all Rangoon teak and he was getting interesting enquiries and offers for it. He knew the value of good wood, he told us importantly and 'he' was not going to sell anything in a hurry. Once he got the right price, he planned to build his mother and himself a proper house.

We walked down the steps, past a couple of rooms. Located one floor below and a little to the right was the strong room. We were surprised to find that the vault was in a perfect condition; it appeared to be made of solid iron, with a very robust and a complicated locking system. It was surprisingly large, the size of a regular bedroom in a modern flat. We could not walk in to examine it further, for the present occupants were using it as a puja room. It was painted a bright yellow and in a corner stood the pedestal, where the idols of family gods and goddesses stood.

We trudged two floors up, led by our young guide, who was by now quite animated by the novelty of impressing utter strangers with the attractions of his home. We entered a large room, which was half demolished. The roof had already disappeared but the walls still stood. I immediately recognised the stucco work on the walls. It was the Chandrabhuvan, the modern drawing room of Raja Shamraj. Praful managed to take a few shots of what was left of the once grand drawing room. The demolition was to be completed that very day, we were informed. The workers had to move on to another structure. They were busy men and some more demolitions were in the offing. We asked him whether it was another old deodi or was it another part of the same deodi? The young man scratched his head again and said he was not sure. 'Did it matter?' he asked.

We climbed another flight of steps to the terrace. We could clearly see the main gateway of the deodi and it looked beautiful against the blue sky. Praful clicked his camera furiously; he was trying to get a shot of the gateway with the pigeons rising from it. From the vantage point of the Rai Rayan terrace the skyline looked quite spectacular. The Charminar shimmered in the morning sun.

The best-kept part of the original deodi, however, was the old kitchen and the deogarh of Renuka Mata. It was what Moro Pant and Naro Pant must have built some century and a half ago. The interiors were cool and shaded by the time we reached that part of the deodi. The pujari had just finished puja and the deity was covered with flowers, haldi and kumkum; incense burned in a silver holder. The pujari had at some point of that morning, done sandhya vandan and had left the peedha and the silver plate in a corner. A lone picture of Raja Shamraj, taken in happier times, hung on the wall. Within the deep folds of the puja mandir one could neither hear the din of traffic nor the noise of the busy market outside.

Raja Saheb rarely stirred out of the house after the jagirs were taken away and the Nizam stopped being the Nizam. Rani Ambika's death, after fifty-three years of companionship, was the last straw. Raja Shamraj gave up his title and signed his name as Renuka Das. Thereafter, he seldom referred to the old times again.

The Malwala Palace

One of the most painful blows to heritage conservation in the city in recent times was the demolition of the Malwala Palace. It was painful because it happened well after conservation as a concept had become popular in the city. An extensive survey of heritage structures had taken place; grading buildings into categories in terms of antiquity, historical value and architectural merit had been completed and laws had been passed at the instance of the heritage-sensitive officials of Hyderabad Urban Development Authority. Heritage activists had been closely monitoring the perils the old structures were being subjected to in the city. Given that so much awareness had been generated, one would have expected that the demolition of one of the most beautiful and prized structures in the city could have been prevented. Instead, the city woke up to the disturbing news one day, in the year 2000, that the palace had been demolished, quietly and surreptitiously.

The threat of demolition had been hovering over the palace for a year by then. Rumours had been circulating that a some of the owners were contemplating pulling the deodi down. While the land on which the deodi stood was valuable, even more valuable was the Rangoon teak, which was used in the construction of the building. One heard that the owners were planning, along with real estate agents to demolish the beautiful structures to dispose of the wood. There were others, also heirs to the property, who wanted to save the building. There was an ongoing tussle between the two sections, one wanting to demolish the structure and the other wanting to save it for posterity. One of them, in fact, had gone to the court and the court had directed the government 'not to alter the structure until further orders.' The governmental agencies swung into action at that point but a little too late. In spite of all these attempts, on one rainy day, while the city stayed indoors, and its guard was lowered, tragedy struck the beautiful palace, acclaimed as the most beautiful in the city. 'The Prince among Palaces is no more,' screamed a newspaper the next day, on 22 August, in the year 2000.

Once the Malwala Palace was razed to the ground, the blame game started. Heritage conservation bodies as well as activists pointed accusing fingers at one another. The prospective builders were barred from entering the site. The palace, broken walls, sagging ceilings and the rubble and all, stands today, mocking conservationists and civic authorities as a sad reminder of their utter failure in saving the heritage of the city.

When Robert, Praful and I visited the palace or, more correctly, what remained of it, the sky was grey and brooding with heavy clouds. It was the monsoon season and the city was awash in a gentle spray. We marched on bravely, hoping that the rain would not hamper our walk. It didn't. The high point of our excursion was to be the Malwala Palace. We walked past the Sardar Mahal, the one-time palace of the Nizam. It looked dirty and unkempt in its new avatar as the Office of the Hyderabad Municipal Corporation. The Malwala Palace lies at the end of Maidan Road, one of the radial roads of Charminar and it overlooks Alijah Kotla, a one-time residence of a royal scion. The very location of the palace declares the status and the importance the Malwalas commanded in the state of Hyderabad. The palace gate looks impressive, it stands high and robust, perhaps more than usual because the Malwalas, as the very name suggests, were revenue collectors of the Nizam, a job they shared with their senior counterparts, the daftardars of the Rai Rayan family. Since the state revenues and their records were kept under safe custody in the deodi, the gate had to be very strong. It had an elaborate locking/safety system. Uptil about fifty years ago, two men used to struggle to open and close the gates, we are told. The members of the Malwala family continued to live in the palace long after Hyderabad ceased to be a princely state, and for years after they lost their jagirs, power and wealth.

When we entered the massive gates of the palace, a lone dog barked and the chowkidar barred our entry. This area is out of bounds he said, spitting the neem twig he was chewing. 'Sarkar ka hukum hai', he said. After a bit of pleading and a promise not to disturb anything, he grudgingly allowed us inside. As if we were going to walk away with either the rubble or the crumbling lime plaster! We walked in, followed by a bunch of children, obviously the chowkidar's brood. An old man, sleeping under the eves of the peshi, which was still intact shook himself from sleep and lit a beedi. A rickshaw was parked askew in a corner and a couple of cycles stood next to the gate. The appearance of the forecourt was one of neglect and decay. It bore no semblance to the power and authority it once commanded. The chowkidar obviously lived on the premises; a make-shift screen of gunny bags hid his living quarters. We gingerly picked our way around, past the masonry and broken bricks.

Some years ago, when the Nizam's writ ran and the Malwalas were still powerful, naubat played from the upper floors of the impressive entrance of the deodi. Officials thronged to that very spot to transact business. Visitors to the city vied for invitations to attend the famous banquets thrown by the Malwalas and those that did not merit an invitation requested permission to visit the deodi's beautiful premises. The palace, as it is called today was built by Raja Ram Pershad Lala Bahadur in 1845. The style of architecture employed was locally termed 'regional Mughal variation', which is essentially Rajasthani with a distinct local flavour. The palace grounds were vertically divided into public and private parts by a high wall. The offices were located in the first official enclosure; the reception rooms built in the European style were obviously added at a later point. The public space was further divided into courtyards, the inner and the outer. In the inner courtyard in the upper floor were located the three drawing rooms, furnished with expensive European furniture, marble statues, artifacts and standing chandeliers called farrashes. Below the drawing rooms, was the library. The long and spacious side galleries displayed miniature paintings said to be a few hundred in number, and a variety of weapons. The star attraction of the weaponry section was a complete chain mail suit, said to have belonged to Tipu Sultan. A well-stocked bar was located in one of the rooms.

In this enclosure stood the diwan khana, the showpiece of the palace, in fact, of the entire city, famous for its beauty and elegance. The wooden dalan of the diwan khana had the typical multi-foliated arches, supported by delicate ornamental wooden pillars. The arches tapered down and culminated into graceful birds, a motif so common to the wooden dalans of Hyderabad. The roof as well as the walls of the wooden structure were lacquered and decorated with floral designs. From the roof hung three gigantic chandeliers made of red and white glass. In front of the main dalan was the pesh-dalan, smaller in proportion but equally beautiful and equipped with chandeliers. The walls were covered with Italian paintings and Venetian mirrors, mounted in gilt frames. Ornamental brackets of rare charm and elegance supported the side galleries.

This was where the large social gatherings of the Malwalas were held. This part of the deodi was the first to give way in the year 1960. A large chunk of the roof caved in, even while the family was in residence. A chandelier of large proportions had crashed to the floor and shattered to smithereens.

In the middle of the charming courtyard was a large fountain with its lotus-shaped basin. A well in the courtyard and a hydraulic system of water pipes supplied water to the fountains. The long hall above the diwan khana was the dining room. It had a dining table that could seat one hundred people, it is said. On its walls hung huge Venetian mirrors and on its sides stood massive sideboards. Between the dining room and the miniature painting gallery was the billiards room, appointed in typical British colonial style. The décor was Rajasthani but the furnishings were European.

Some seventy years ago, the Malwala Palace was a major attraction in the city. The family's hospitality was legendary. Gatherings routinely included rajas and maharajas from different parts of the country along with the heads of states and other such distinguished people. Of the long list of dignitaries who visited the palace were the maharajas of Mysore, Kashmir, Baroda, Jaipur and at a later time, film stars and sports personalities. Members of the family were keen sportsmen and they were invited to serve as ADCs to the royal family. Europeans, particularly the British, would visit the palace during the Dussera festival, accompanied by their womenfolk, for whom a visit to the palace was a long-awaited treat. They would turn up in their long evening gowns, looking wide-eyed. They would ask to be shown around the palace. They were entertained in the drawing rooms while a military band regaled them with western music. Goan cooks turned out European food, while the Hyderabadi cooks dished out authentic local fare. Drinking and feasting went on until the wee hours of the morning.

The liquor served in the palace was the Malwalas' special brew. The family received a farman, permitting them to distil their own brand. The bhatti khanas were located at a short distance from the family quarters. The Malwalas made a variety of drinks made from flowers like kewda, rose and jasmine and fruits like tarbuj; a special drink was made of wheat. However, the one unique, mildly alcoholic drink that they made was 'theetar ki sherbat,' a drink made of patridge meat. There was a special process through which the drink was made. The stomach of the patridge was cleaned and filled either with sugar or gud. It was stirred and allowed to ferment for eight days after a wine culture was introduced. At the end of that period, once it was filtered, the drink was ready for consumption.

Other Kayastha families too were licensed to brew liquor in their residences but in smaller quantities. In the Kayastha families of

Hyderabad of those days, it was considered a matter of prestige to be permitted to brew liquor. Old timers tell us that a family's social standing was measured in terms of the number of vats of liquor that they could produce. None, however, equalled the Malwalas in either the variety or the quality and most importantly the quantity of liquor that they could brew.

Behind the diwan khana was the long puja room. It was used on festivals like Gokulashtami and Vijayadasami, occasions of great rejoicing and community gatherings. The entire Mathur caste of the Kayastha community met at the palace on such occasions. In true Hyderabadi spirit, the Malwalas took equal interest in Muslim as well as Hindu festivals. The palace would be illuminated on the birthday of the Prophet Mohammad and alms would be given away on that occasion. The month of Muharram was also a busy time at the palace. The langar procession, which started at the diwan's residence, passed in front of the Malwala Palace as well, after saluting the Nizam on its way. Prince Azam Jah, the heir apparent, was the special invitee of the day, the prince and his friends would watch the display from the balcony of the palace. During that time, tazias were displayed and shelters were set up to give water to the processionists. The elephant carrying the aalams would stop in front of the palace; the residents made offerings of dhatti.

In the deodis of Hyderabad, much attention was paid to the comfort and beautification of the dalans, diwan khanas and the drawing rooms but the living quarters of the inmates were small and cramped. At the Malwala Palace, a very narrow passage led to the living quarters of the family. The segregation of the sexes was not too pronounced in the palace and separate apartments were provided for the married sons and their families. The master and the mistress of the deodi, referred to as the raja and the rani, occupied the largest apartment. Unlike in the deodis of the Muslim nobles, there were no separate quarters for men and women. Some two generations earlier, the women did not mix with the men on social occasions and they did not attend dinners or any such social gatherings at the palace. When any entertainment, like singing and dancing, took place in the diwan khana, the women sat in the balconies behind chilmans and viewed the proceedings. A modicum of segregation was observed even at a slightly later date. For example, during religious ceremonies, women were seated in the puja khana of the goddess Bhavani, whereas men were seated in the shaadi khana, which was a big hall.

The family shaadi khana and the puja khana were the focal points of the private sections of the deodi. The shaadi khana, decorated with carved wooden arches and pillars, was where the brides worshipped the family deity on arrival at their husband's home. As the heads of the Kayastha clan, the Malwalas ran a separate school for the Kayastha community which was located on the property, just beyond the offices. No wedding in the Kayastha community would take place in the city, without the bridal party receiving either a member of the Malwala family come to attend the ceremony or at the least, a tray of gifts and blessings duly conveyed to the bride and the groom, from the palace.

The wealth and power of the Malwalas declined considerably during the time of Salar Jung I, because of his financial reforms. In spite of such a set back, the family managed to maintain its dignity. The resilience of the family was such that even the tumult of the Razakar movement, the Police Action and the subsequent abolition of the princely state of Hyderabad did not cloud their enthusiasm or hospitality. The Malwalas continued to entertain and receive distinguished visitors to the palace. In fact, because they were Hindu nobles no suspicion could be attached to them during those troubled days of communal tension. On the contrary, they alone were able to entertain the officers of the Indian army along with their other friends. However, the trouble for the family lay elsewhere. It was the abolition of the jagirs that dealt a severe blow to them and in that regard they were no different from the other nobles in the city.

After the abolition of the jagirs, the drama that was enacted in the other deodis unfolded in the Malwala family too. With the main source of their income cut off, the heirs to the family fortunes fought over the property and the matter went to court. Powerful lawyers from the family of Sir Tej Bahadur Sapru fought the cases. The legal wrangles led to demolitions and the living quarters of the family, adjoining the official courtyard were the first to go. The old structures were demolished and the land was sold to the 'developers.' A multi-storied building came up in its place. Valuable furniture, expensive art pieces like miniature paintings, chandeliers, cut-glass items, books and similar valuables with which the palace was studded were either sold or apportioned. The hesitation was over the diwan khana, which had already been declared a heritage structure. It had decayed a lot by that time and a section of the family felt that it could not maintain the structure. Finally pragmatism and dire need dictated action. The dalan and the rest of the palace were demolished quietly, while the city and the heritage watchers were kept in the dark.

∿

The site that greeted our eyes was heartbreaking. Little trace of the once beautiful diwan khana remained. Bare walls, devoid of plaster or paint, galleries with sagging floors, wooden colonnades that seemed to serve no purpose and a severely damaged fountain greeted us. Bricks and rubble were strewn everywhere. This was no slow decay caused by age and neglect. This was wanton destruction done in secret, under the cover of darkness.

If the government had wanted to step in and salvage the palace it could have done so before matters went too far. The beautiful diwan khana could have been conserved as a representative of such dalans in Hyderabad. Obviously the government had other preoccupations. The state talks of heritage tourism long after much of the heritage of the city has been erased. The demolition of heritage structures continues in the city even today. Buildings, which are adjudged as the 'best conserved' heritage structures, have made way for shopping malls. There seems to be no deterrent to demolitions or a motivation provided for conservation. Such is the frenzy of urbanisation in the modern cities and the apathy of successive governments to heritage.

The Decline

🜲

It took me almost a year to get to meet Nawab Askar Ali Khan
(identity changed on request). He was a scion of one of the prominent
families of the city. His was one of the very wealthy families before the
abolition of the jagirs; it was also one of the hardest hit by the abolition.
To my repeated requests for a meeting his stock answer was, 'I have
nothing to say, I do not want to dwell in the past.'

Finally when he relented, his grudging invitation came with the
rider, 'It is not too often that we have visitors these days; I have forgotten
how to entertain.' 'Also,' he warned, 'my house is not too comfortable;
please come in the evening when it is a little cooler.'

Nawab Saheb, as he is called is quite advanced in years. He lives in
an old-style bungalow in one of the many alleys of the busy
Himayatnagar. The bungalow was in a derelict state; its paint was
peeling off and wet patches disfigured the walls. Barring a fountain
gone dry and a few broken-down garden seats, the small front yard
was bare. I was shown into a handsome living room. It was a fair-sized
room with an attractive ceiling with stucco work and large airy windows,
bare of furniture; a single chaise de lounge with a matching footrest
stood in a corner, its upholstery frayed. The grimy walls carried

markings of large portraits and paintings that had since been removed and the walls were pock-marked with nail holes. The only decoration in the room was the collection of mounted porcelain, bearing some faint insignia; the gold-rimmed Sevres porcelain was heavily chipped and discoloured.

A woman of advanced years, perhaps a family retainer, entered the room with a tray in hand. She looked me up and down as she handed me a glass of water. 'Sarkar abhi ayenge,' she said, staring at me quizzically; 'Kya piyenge, chai ke nimbu pani?'

I turned as I heard a shuffling sound outside the room and moments later, two servants helped Askar Ali Khan into the room. The nawab cursed and muttered under his breath as the two men lowered him into the sofa. One of the men adjusted his shawl and the other settled his feet on the low stool. The woman stalked out of the room barely acknowledging her master. 'Send in some tea' he shouted at her retreating back, 'and some biscuits!' He waved me into the plastic chair that was quickly placed for me.

'Maaf karna, Madam,' he said, gasping. 'I am an old man and not agile any more, I need help even to get ready. I am sorry I was not ready to receive you.'

Nawab Askar Ali Khan must have been a magnificent specimen of a man in his prime. Even at that advanced age, he retained his good looks, and had a high forehead, piercing eyes and a thick mop of gray hair. He wore a crumpled white kurta and a pajama. An expensive but frayed shawl covered his legs. When he was a little composed he turned his attention to me.

'So you live at Bella Vista,' he said sharply, fixing me with a steady gaze, 'I do hope you will be happy there. The owner of the palace brought ruin upon himself as well as Hyderabad. It is not a happy place.' I was taken aback by his caustic remark and not knowing how to respond to his attack, I spluttered and muttered something under my breath. After that initial hiccup, I steered the conversation to the old city.

'What can I tell you about Hyderabad, everything is gone now, our culture, our people and homes, gone, destroyed, bulldozed. Sab barbad ho gaya hai. The Hyderabad of my days is dead; I do not recognise the present Hyderabad. Now the very sight of the old city hurts. Where there used to be beautiful palaces and deodis, there are motor mechanic shops now and where the gardens and orchards once stood you have ugly tenements and vulgar shaadi khanas. There is no respect or courtesy any more. There is brashness and ugliness all around. We did not foresee such a future for the city.' Sweat glistened on his forehead.

'What do you want to know about our lives?' he asked wearily. 'You cannot even begin to understand our times. There was grace and beauty in our lives, there was courtesy and concern for all. People were broad-minded and tolerant. Every one is fighting over religion now. In our times we were very religious but we did not wear our faiths on our sleeves. People received respect and positions because of their background and what they stood for; not because of their religion. In my grandfather's deodi we played Holi, we celebrated Diwali and also Christmas. The Muslim nobles of our days did not eat beef in deference to their Hindu brethren. People like Maharaja Kishen Pershad were respected for their virtues and he was an example for all of us for his model behaviour and refinement. Raja Shamraj Bahadur would carry gangajal to the dinner table at state banquets at Falaknuma Palace. Being an orthodox Brahmin, he would not touch anything served at the table but the Nizam respected his sentiments and did not take offence. Can you even imagine anything like that happening now?

'Before the abolition, our jagir used to fetch us a large income.' He continued after a moment. 'Ours was a joint family and as usual celebrations of any kind were grand affairs. I remember my cousin's bismillah ceremony, it was held when I was six years old. It was celebrated with a great deal of pomp. A lot of people were invited; members of the Paigah families and high officials were among the important invitees. Even Sarkar (the Nizam) was expected to attend the ceremony at one stage. Every one was excited over his visit. A large amount of money was spent on the festivities. The celebrations included grand dinners, nautch, music and fireworks.'

Nawab Askar Ali Khan talked so softly that I had to move my chair closer to him to hear him properly. He did not seem to notice.

'When we were children, most of us went to the Aliya School to begin with. All the male members of the family were sent to the school together. In the beginning, we used to go to the school in horse-drawn coaches. Later, we went in motorcars. Some children were under the supervision of their personal teachers, even at the school. Every attempt was made by their families to make sure of their exclusivity. Sometimes separate rooms were provided at the school for the children of some premier nobles like the Asman Jahi Paigah children, who had their lunch in private in a different room at the School. The children of the Vicar-ul-Umra family were westernised because they studied in England. I heard it said that when Nawab Wali-ud-Daula Bahadur returned from London after completing his education, he addressed his father, Nawab Vicar-ul-Umrah as "Hello Dad!" This highly displeased the nawab. This incident was the subject of discussion in most families for days and days. Being so familiar with one's parents, particularly the father, was frowned at. This incident was repeated again and again in our families to highlight the importance of maintaining traditions and teaching the right etiquette to the children. The children of the Shamraj family went to the local school but sat apart, on sofas, while the rest of the children sat on benches. In the early days, they used to go to the school on elephants, I believe, but that was much before my time.'

The arrival of tea distracted Askar Ali Khan. There was a flurry of activity; four people entered in a procession; one carried tea, the other a plate of biscuits and the third person carried a plastic stool. Askar Ali scolded the woman for not using a tray cloth, the manservant for sloshing the tea onto the saucer and fussed over where to place the stool for my convenience. He turned to me and apologised that the tea service was not elegant enough. The excitement seemed to have tired him and he leaned against the cushions and closed his eyes. I leaned forward anxiously; but he waved my enquiries away.

'Our families were more down to earth. We were taught Persian, Arabic and Urdu at home,' he continued sipping his tea. 'Some families appointed highly qualified English governesses, who, in addition to giving general training, instructed the children in pronouncing English words correctly. They were taught table manners and all that. For most of us of course, it was important that we communicate with the Englishmen of the Residency properly. After all, that was the power centre in our day and our elders were anxious that the British should accept us as equals. Our teachers taught us by a play-way method. Education was given a lot of importance in my family. In that respect we were different from the others. I know of a Paigah family where some adults felt that there was no need for a Paigah child to get educated! That sort of attitude was common in certain old-fashioned families, but not mine.

'In my family, when the children were old enough to go to the school, they were sent to a separate house. There they were provided all the comforts. It was like a hostel, where the young boys could focus on their studies without being distracted. Some families did not approve of their children mixing with other children, that was the reason why they educated them at home. There were others who sent their children to the school but they did not want their children to talk to any one and they had to go home once they finished with the school. Later the Jagirdar College was established which admitted only the children of the jagirdars. It was a great leveller and we had good teachers who drilled some sense into our heads; the English teachers of the college insisted that all the students should mix freely. I am thankful for the modern education that I got in the college. We learnt to play games like tennis, polo, cricket and billiards. All those who were tutored privately in their palaces and deodis, I must say, continued to be very narrow-minded.'

'Some of the nobles were highly educated and very cultured. Inayat Jung had one of the best libraries in the city. He had very rare books. In addition to printed material, he had a very big collection of manuscripts, farmans, dating back to the Mughal period, particularly related to Aurangzeb and Hyderabad. One big room was full of books and they were sent to the archives at Delhi. They are preserved there in what is called the Inayat Jung corner. Idara too got some of them. The Surai Yar Jung Deodi in Yakatpura also had a big collection of books. He had the richest collection of English literature, particularly fiction. Nothing is left now. Nawab Mahboob Ali Khan, son of Shah Yar Jung, had a palace in Yakatpura, Bada Bazar, which is intact. Tairo was his pen name. He translated a lot of poetry and was a very good painter. His paintings were sought after and were sold the moment they were ready. He too had an excellent collection of books. I am told that all of them have disappeared from the deodi now. Another deodi, which took pride in its library was Raja Shamraj's deodi. Raja Saheb was a scholar. Now there is neither the deodi nor the library.'

I looked at my watch. It was dark outside. I did not want to interrupt the Nawab. He seemed in a mood to talk. But leave I must. I took my leave reluctantly, with the date for our next meeting firmly fixed.

The next time I reached the bungalow, I found that Nawab Saheb was waiting for me; washed and brushed and legs stretched, in his customary seat.

'Forgive me if I do not stand up,' he apologised and waved me to the chair placed next to him. He seemed to be in better spirits today, there was an extra twinkle in his eye.

'We Hyderabadis are very particular about etiquette. The old Hyderabad was all about courtesy. The mores and norms of etiquette were drilled into us right from our childhood. How to receive a guest, how to pay respect, and how to behave on different occasions, were all taught to us from the very beginning. Maharaja Kishen Pershad set high standards in courtly manners. He was our role model. Although he was the prime minister of the state, he would be as courteous to young people as he was to older people. He would always be appropriately dressed while receiving a nobleman.

'We Hyderabadis are acutely conscious of our tahzeeb and resent any dilution of it by newcomers. Respect for the spoken language, the manner of sitting in the presence of elders, proper dress, and salutation are all part of the tahzeeb. The culture of an individual is reflected in the language he speaks and it is different for different people. There are strict rules about wishing others. We were told that one responded to the salaam of a servant without nodding one's head. But a salaam to the elders or men of equal status is more elaborate, and the bowing is lower. A salaam to a prince or the ruler of the state was always the most difficult, one had to bend very low, and do the salaam, slowly and gracefully, just so.' Nawab Saheb swept his arm in a wide arc, demonstrating the salaam. I looked on fascinated, I thought I had never seen anything so graceful yet so dignified. He seemed transported in time. His eyes twinkled.

'We had to sit still, our palms held together and listen respectfully when any one important or an elder spoke to us.' He continued. 'Even in present-day Hyderabad, one can spot an old Hyderabadi of a good family, particularly a member of the old nobility, by the way he conducts himself. Hyderabadi nobles believe that behaviour and breeding are what set a person of high birth apart. In my childhood it was customary for the sons of the nobles to appear before their parents and pay respects every morning. It was also traditional to address one's father as 'sarkar'; none of the modern frivolity of being familiar with one's parents. Above all, we did not dare to address our children or our wives in the presence of our parents. H.E.H. (His Exalted Highness, the Nizam) never spoke to any of his family members directly. There was always an intermediary through whom he communicated. All those traditions were common in our families.

'Reception formalities were elaborate and we lived in fear that we may do something wrong when a guest of honour visited the deodi.

When great people like Maharaja Kishen Pershad or Salar Jung Bahadur came visiting, the reception formalities were endless. Greeting on arrival and leave taking would be very long drawn out affairs. There is one incident that did the rounds in Hyderabad concerning Kamal Yar Jung whom every one held in awe, for he was considered to be very urbane.

'Once,' we were told, 'a distinguished gathering of nobles was at a reception given in the honour of Mr Crofton, the then secretary of the Revenue Department. When dinner was almost over, Nawab Kamal Yar Jung rose to leave even before the chief guest left. Now, that was against all norms of courtesy. Kamal Yar Jung was an extremely polished man and all those who noticed his mistake were shocked. Soon the Nawab himself realised what he did. He cleverly made up for it by turning around as if to examine the paintings, and adroitly drawing the guest into a conversation over the merits of European paintings until it was time for every one to leave. He saw the guest into the car and the rest of the visitors heaved a sigh of relief. Only a man of Kamal Yar Jung's stature could manage a tricky situation like that. Every one in Hyderabad, including the British, was very conscious of the nuances of the Hyderabadi etiquette and strictly followed the rules. An omission or a commission, intended or unintended, however trivial, could cause a serious diplomatic row. We were told that when the Paigah nobles were deputed by H.E.H. to represent him at the Residency, the Resident took care to receive them with appropriate courtesy.

'Similarly a person of noble birth had to accost a person below his station in a particular way and infringement of the manner did not go down well either. Once, Nawab Yousuf Ali Khan Salar Jung III was going to the Secunderabad Club in his car. When his car entered the Tank Bund Road, he saw a Rolls Royce at a distance, driving towards him. He recognised it as that of Prince Azam Jah, the heir to the musnad. When the car came close, Nawab Saheb stood up and did the customary salaam. That evening he got a phone call from one of the local tradesmen, who apologised profusely for misleading him. What transpired was that the Rolls Royce belonged not to the prince but to the tradesman, and the wealthy trader realised that he had been mistaken for the prince! I am told that the Nawab Saheb was both embarrassed and furious!'

Somewhere in the depths of the house a clock struck. It was getting dark already. As if on cue, tea arrived, though with a little less ceremony today. Instead of the woman, the manservant brought the tray. As I stirred in the sugar, Nawab Saheb leaned forward and confided. 'Half the servants have not reported for duty today, there is a wedding somewhere, and it is an excuse for them to abscond from work.' One thing I noticed whenever I visited the nobility in Hyderabad was the number of retainers that each household seemed to employ even in this modern age!

'Servants are not what they used to be.' Nawab Saheb said, sipping tea. 'It may sound strange to you, but in the olden days they were our confidants and we were very close to them. Though we were kept from mixing with the lower classes, our household servants were given a special place in our lives. You see, we did not have too many friends and did not mix with people. Only on special occasions would we go to the houses of other nobles. Even when we did visit friends, there was a certain barrier of formality with everyone. It was only with one's own servants that one was very free. At times the children of the servants were all that we had to play with. However, you had to be careful with whom you talked freely; old and faithful family servants were safe but you could not chat with the coachman, a driver, a watchman, a footman or any one who mixed with other people's servants.'

I had to interrupt him for a moment. 'I heard that the old Hyderabadi families kept slaves...', I said hesitantly, but that was one question I needed to ask. It had been on my mind. '...Is it true?'

The nawab paused for a moment. He stroked his chin thoughtfully. 'I do not know what to say to that. What we had was not slavery in the real sense. True, families lived with us for generations; but they lived happily. We were generous to them. They enjoyed all the privileges except eating with us. They were our only contact with the rest of the world. There are a number of instances that can be quoted to show how favours were showered on the servants. One of the nobles of Hyderabad gave away a part of his jagir to his anna. That locality is called Annajiguda even today. After we lost our jagirs, it was our faithful servants who stayed with us. All the other sycophants and hangers on left us; it was a case of the proverbial deserting of the sinking ship. They fleeced us as long as we had money and power, and disappeared the moment we lost both whereas our servants' loyalty for us remained unshakable till the end. They were with us in our hour of need and were our only solace.

'It was different with the smaller jagirdars. They were cruel and exploitative of their servants and people in their jagirs. They would take free labour, demand gifts and nazars and exploit the people mercilessly. They exacted money from their subjects under various pretexts such as marriages, bismillah ceremonies, birth of children, etc. Most of those nobles were uneducated and illiterate. I should not be saying these things to a lady like you but these men were so dissolute that no woman was safe with them. They had concubines by the dozen and were very vulgar in their behaviour and speech. That was the reason we had to be careful not to mix with them. They were no better than the ordinary people.' I looked down to hide my smile.

'Today nobody seems to believe that class is important, but to my mind class does matter. Look at the nobles of the upper class in Hyderabad, they may be naïve and foolish in money matters but you cannot fault them on their behaviour, dignity, refinement and generosity. In fact they vied with one another in being called 'generous or magnanimous.' Take the case of the maharaja (Kishen Pershad). The old noble was so generous that all his wealth went into paying poor poets, scholars and students. Yes, our people were unworldly, but they were never petty or mean.

'When we were children we rarely visited our jagirs. We were sent there only when there was an epidemic of plague, which was not uncommon. All of us would move to the jagirs and stay in the country for fresh air. The mango season was the other time we would go to the villages. There used to be a terrific variety of fruit. Hunting was the other reason for going to the rural areas. When the adults took guests, particularly the British, on hunting expeditions, preparations would be made for days on end and a whole township would come up overnight. The villagers took every care to make our stay enjoyable. The food on such occasions was generally local. Looking back, they gave us more care and affection than we cared to acknowledge. By the way, I was a very good shot. I shot my first tiger when I was barely fifteen years old.' The nawab's eyes shone with pride and I looked away. It was difficult not to like this man, but every now and then he would make a statement that would outrage one's sensitivities. He, however, seemed to be in high spirits.

'Talking of food,' he reminisced, on a cheerful note, 'we were brought up on a very healthy diet. There was no limit to the variety of dishes that our cooks turned out. No effort was spared and expense was never a consideration. I heard that, even cattle were fed on badam so that the milk meant for the Nizam's table had a badam flavour. I am not an expert on cooking but I know enough to give you a taste.

'Along with the rich Mughlai food, the local food was popular among the nobility. Perhaps some of our dishes were Mughal variations, I am not sure of that. For example we have what is called chakna and it is a concoction of all the vegetables, cooked with or without goat meat. It is eaten with jowar ki roti to the accompaniment of liquor. The khichdi of Hyderabad too is very famous. Kulti kut, made of horse gram, marag, a winter soup made of lamb meat which was originally Arabian in origin and of course, nehari, meat cooked on a slow fire through the night and eaten for breakfast, paya, a soup of lamb eaten with Hyderabadi bread called sheermal – all these were great favourites. Then, there is haleem from Iran and harees from Arabia, both were popular in Hyderabad, these dishes are forgotten in their place of origin, but they are available and also popular in Hyderabad. My mother sometimes would send us special dishes from the zenana.'

The old noble went into a kind of reverie; he closed his eyes and stroked his chin absent mindedly. I sat quietly, not wanting to disturb his thoughts. It was quite late but I had no intention of leaving. After a couple of minutes, he shook himself and started talking softly, as if to himself.

'The abolition of jagirs was a rude shock to us. When it happened, we were stunned and did not know how to react. Things happened too fast. When the jagirs were abolished, we hoped that we would get the twenty-five years of compensation in a lump sum, and that would have helped us to tide over the difficult times. That did not happen either. Even today, I still cannot believe that our jagirs, our palaces, our cars, servants and wealth have really gone, I keep wondering if it is a bad dream from which I will wake up one day.

'Now, fifty-odd years after all that happened, I can be philosophical about it. I realise that we had none but themselves to blame. We lived in a world of our own, in a make-believe world. Instead of taking care of our jagirs we clamoured for titles to satisfy our egos. Titles in fact meant nothing; they sounded grand, and were awarded not because a noble had distinguished himself in anything but as a matter of course and led to jealousy and much rivalry. Frantic efforts were made by uncles and aunts, entreaties and requests were submitted to the palace and channels of influence were activated. And finally when the reward came, there were great celebrations and back-slapping. Occasions for rewarding nobles were when the ruler celebrated his birthday or held special durbar at the time of Id or some such festivity. The revelry thereafter too was with borrowed money.

'Money was a dirty word for the nobles. Thinking of money was considered poor taste. Whatever purchases any of us made were usually from the two famous shops, of Messrs Mir Hasan and Mohammad Younus at Abids Road. We would go to Secunderabad to John Burton for our suits. The bills were sent to the deodi for settlement. There was no question of handling money directly. Believe me, madam, the first time I thought of money was when my father died and I had become the head of the family.

It was then that for the first time in my life, I came to know about the salary of a cook. After his death, I realised that we were heavily in debt and that we were living lavishly on borrowed money. I wonder if my father knew the state of our finances either. Most of the servants had to go and the deodi had to be given up, and we moved into this house.

By the time I realised how hollow our so-called wealth was and how meagre our resources were, it was too late. Creditors haunted us. My family's wealth dried up before my very eyes. There was nothing left intact in our lives, neither dignity nor peace of mind.'

Nawab Askar Ali Khan leaned back in his chair, his eyes closed and his brow creased. He seemed oblivious to my presence in the room. We sat silently for a long time in the dimly lit room. Somewhere, a clock ticked. After a while, a servant appeared at the door. He hesitated for a moment and then with tender care, he helped the aging noble to his feet. A lump rose to my throat. Clutching my papers, I tiptoed out of the house.

Najeeb Sultana

Najeeb Sultana* stood at the entrance of her home, the pallu of her red silk saree, draped gracefully round her shoulders. A string of pearls clung to her neck and a large antique ruby flashed on her ring finger. The courtyard of Najeeb's home was bathed in sunshine; it had rained the previous night and the air carried the promise of more rain. Drops of water glistened on the bright yellow alamanda flowers and sunlight filtered through the overgrown fronds of the bottlebrush shrubs. A fountain, gone dry, stood in the centre. Ornamental plants and creepers shaded the deep verandahs from sun and glare. I stood still, taking in the beauty of the scene in front of me. At that moment it did not matter that the tiled roof of the house was giving away or that the plaster of the walls had peeled to reveal the inner brickwork; all one noticed was the charm of the courtyard and the residence beyond. It was like an island of beauty and grace contrasted with the dusty crowded ugliness of Malakpet.

The Khans occupied what was left of their once sprawling ancestral home, the Saram Jung Deodi. Najeeb Sultana and her husband, Syed Ahmad Ali Khan, tenaciously clinging to their part of the inheritance

---

* Najeeb Sultana passed away suddenly, subsequent to my visit to her deodi.

when we visited them in the year 2003, long after major portions of the deodi had been sliced off and sold out to make way for modern dwellings.

'This was the zenani portion of the deodi,' said Najeeb, leading us upstairs to her portion of the residence. The crumbling zenana was partitioned between two brothers. 'We are trying hard to preserve what we are left with. As you can see it is falling apart; we fix one portion of the house and another portion collapses and the roof leaks. You see that balcony, it is sinking; we cannot keep any furniture there since it cannot take the weight. It takes all our resources just to keep the building from collapsing. I don't know how long we can keep it going like this.'

I looked around the house, fascinated. It was just a suite of rooms, consisting of a verandah, the central hall, the dining section and a bedroom. It was the rear end of the original deodi, which had long since vanished. The building indeed was pretty ramshackle and was badly in need of restoration. But what caught my eye at that moment was not so much the state of the structure, but the way the rooms were done up. They were charming and graceful without any modern affectation. Family photographs tinted in sepia covered the walls interspersed by miniature paintings, tapestries and chinaware. Antique tables were covered with a confusion of indoor plants and knick knacks; worn-out rugs covered the floors and a variety of statuary was strewn all over with a studied carelessness. I noticed clever attempts at improvisation wherever there was something to hide. A crack in the flooring was covered by a strategically placed rug and what appeared to be red sandstone jaalis of the balcony were in fact, cement jaalis, painted in terracotta red to make them look like sandstone. The overall effect of the arrangement was one of great charm and harmony. Najeeb and Ahmad Ali Khan took us round the flat, pointing to a painting here and a porcelain vase there. 'These are all that came down to us,' Najeeb said, 'pieces of value were sold long ago. When the regime changed and the jagirs were abolished, the floor was knocked down from under our feet, and household articles like vases, statues and paintings were sold in Hyderabad by the hundreds, all in secret. Most of them in fact, have left the country.'

I could see the effort it took to maintain their home the way they were used to. Najeeb and Ahmad Ali's situation more or less summed up the lot of the nobility in the city. Some went under and some put up a fight, but sooner or later they all had to give up. I could not imagine Najeeb and Ahmad Ali Khan in a modern flat. The very thought seemed incongruous.

After a tour of the house, we settled down to tea in the attractive dining room.

Over cups of hot tea Najeeb told me, 'The family originally lived in the ancestral deodi in the old city. It was cramped and uncomfortable. It suited the old people but it was not suitable for the modern way of living. My father-in-law's grandfather built a modern deodi in the then fashionable Malakpet area. This place had become important and fashionable ever since Mahboob Ali Khan built the Mahboob Mansion and a race course in the neighbourhood. The new deodi, true to form, retained all the features of a traditional deodi, like a massive main gate, the public and private courtyards, the ornamented dalans for receiving distinguished visitors and for social occasions. Pandals would be erected and the open spaces covered for ceremonies like nikkahs or when a visit by the royal family was expected. There was strict segregation of the sexes with separate quarters for men and women. Finally, there were the bawarchi khanas, the baggi and motor khanas built at some distance. The deodi had three courtyards for the women and two for the men. The men of the family used the main gate while women used the side gate. They seldom went out of the deodi. Weddings and visits to the parents were special occasions when they ventured out. The gate was guarded by the pehra of Sikhs from Punjab and also the Arabs. The bawarchi khana produced two types of cuisines. One was traditional food, which was a mix of Mughlai and typical traditional dishes of Hyderabad, and the other was European. The Goanese cook produced continental food while the local cooks turned out traditional dishes.

'The deodi was sumptuously provided for. My father-in-law and his father were connoisseurs of art and the deodi used to overflow with art objects. We had French furniture. I believe large banquets were given in the deodi. There used to be many photographs in the family, showing all these events; I do not know where they are now. But all that was before our times. Once the property was divided among the brothers, parts of the deodi were demolished and the land was sold off. I belong to a different generation.

'Then there was my own grandfather's deodi, where I grew up; it was near Maula Ali. My grandfather, Nawab Sultan Ali Khan, was an honorary elephant hunter,' said Najeeb, pushing a plate of Osmania biscuits (named after the last Nizam, who is said to have favoured them) towards me. 'He used to be called upon to tackle rogue elephants. Every now and then wild elephants used to turn rogues and spoil crops and attack villages, particularly in Maharashtra. My grandfather was well known for hunting down such animals. At the age of eighty-two, he created the Asian record in shooting. Men in my family were very good sportsmen. They played tennis, went hunting and were keen horsemen. My father was a well-known rider; he was invited by the turf clubs all over the country to advise them. Men also kept pigeons, parakeets, peacocks, dogs, and even cheetahs. Going on a hunt was like an expedition. They would go riding an elephant, take hunting dogs, and a huge retinue used to follow them. The carcasses of hunted animals would be carried by bois.

'Our deodi had two hundred rooms, built on twenty five acres of land; there used to be a huge gate and then a courtyard, the offices were situated in the courtyard; the munshis who looked after the payments to forces and other affairs of the estate sat in these offices. And then there was the paddock and finally the deodi. There were separate quarters for men and women. They were like two different worlds. Each had its own rhythm; if by any chance any male member, generally the members of the family, entered the zenana, prior intimation had to be given to the zenana, so that the women were prepared. Mostly eunuchs were employed as the go-betweens for the two sections.

'My grandfather's offices and reception rooms were located in the mardana. There were several kothis, one inside the other. Each kothi had its own courtyard. There used to be tennis courts in the men's courtyards. There were huge halls, surrounded by verandas, where rows and rows of sofas were placed. My grandfather used to conduct his daily work and receive delegations there. There was also the baradari in the men's quarter where my grandfather used to entertain important guests on special occasions. It was decorated with large chandeliers, French furniture and European decorations. Grand parties were thrown there. Englishmen and women and military officers and their wives used to attend these parties. If the master of the house was a minister or held any other important position in the court, the household would be geared to support his position.

'I grew up mostly in the zenana, under the care of my grandmother. There were many children to play with. We had a lot of fun, at least as children. My grandmother was the mistress of the zenana and she presided over the goings-on there. Life in the zenana was traditional. Men might have been influenced by a western style of living but the women stuck to tradition. In fact, it was they who continued the traditions in the family. There used to be huge halls, where she received people. The floors of these rooms were covered by farrashes; takhats were placed to seat the lady guests who came to meet her. There used to be a lot of activity in the zenana of the deodi, perhaps because there were so many people. There used to be scores of servants to serve the family members. When relatives came to visit, their visits did not last hours but days. The courtyards in the zenana had rose bushes, hauzes, fountains, and a huge swing in which eight people could swing. Even adult women would swing in it. Boys stayed with the mothers in the zenana until they grew up. Once they started going to school, they moved out and lived separately in the mardana.

'A lot of activity went on in the zenana. The most important occupation of course, was cooking. It used to go on the whole day and took much of the ladies' time. Meals were generally very elaborate.

Even though it was the servants who cooked, the ladies of the deodi personally supervised and took pride in turning out delicacies. There used to be such a variety of food that could be prepared, that a lot of discussion and effort went into planning a meal.

'We used to have khichdi, ande, qeema and murgi, etc. for nashta, then, there were a variety of rotis to choose from, like sheermal, kulcha, and parathe, and a variety of meetha like gajar ka mitha, puran poli, ande ka lauz, kheer, kaddu ki kheer and so on. The women of the family were experts at making jams, jellies and murabbas. These were eaten with fresh cream. There was one very elaborately prepared dish called mutabak, which was a favourite with everybody. Thin roti, ground lamb, a layer of eggs, saffron, chutney and hari mirchi, kothmir and pudina were all arranged in layers and baked in a lagan. There was another dish that Hyderabad was famous for. A Salim bakra stuffed with yakhni. Then a chicken was stuffed with boiled eggs and yakhni and in turn the lamb was stuffed with the chicken. The lamb was then sewn and barbecued. Tutak was a favourite dish as well. A paste was made with rava, ghee and minced meat was stuffed into the flattened paste, in the shape of eggs and baked in the oven.

'A delicacy which has not survived in Hyderabad is called rasaval, which is basically rice cooked in sugar-cane juice. For some reason this tradition has not been passed on. In winters we would be invited to nimish parties in the Kayastha homes. Milk was boiled with sugar, cardamom and saffron and exposed to the dew of the winter nights. The cream, which came to the top, would be churned and set in earthen-ware bowls and served on banana leaves.

'Families had favourite recipes, which they kept as closely guarded secrets and passed on from generation to generation.

'Women ate separately and the chief begum presided over the meals. Eating was a ritual following an elaborate procedure assisted by well-trained servants. A printed cloth with not only interesting designs but also with Persian couplets called dastarkhan would be spread on the floor, around which the members of the family would sit. Water was poured from an aftaba and hands were washed in a sailafchi, a silver bowl with a tray with holes, into which water drained, decorated with leaves so that water did not splash. All these silver articles were used everyday and were kept shining. There used to be a hookah too for the women's use in the zenana. Nowadays silver does not stay bright any more in Hyderabad, it tarnishes quickly because of the pollution in the Musi river.

'In the deodis, sewing and stitching also went on round the year. A lot of zari work and kamdani would be done. Families from Benares would stay with us and my grandmother would get the work done for the entire deodi. She personally supervised the colours, the designs and the texture of the material used. Saris had to be embroidered, the musnads of my grandfather, pillows, gau takias, tray cloths, khada dupattas, all these had to be done up in fine karchob work. Embossed work done in pure gold and silver thread was used for musnads and flat work for the rest. The families from Benares would stay as long as there was work and then move somewhere else in the city. Sometimes the women in the deodi would join the zari workers to learn the designs or some stitches.

'The women were very religious and prayed five times a day. Religious training was also given to them. Life in the zenana was quite hectic and we were always busy; there was a lot of entertainment; the servant girls received training in singing and they would entertain us. Nobody ever got bored; life was like a picnic.

'There used to be a lot of entertainment for the men. Women were permitted to witness some of it. Qawwals used to be invited to entertain in the deodi; Aziz Ahmad Warsi, a very famous qawwal, used to visit the deodi often and rendered the compositions of Amjad, Wali Deccani and Amir Khusro. Ghazal compositions of the last Nizam, Mir Osman Ali Khan and the junior prince, Moazzam Jah would be rendered by M.A. Rauf and his son Arif. These were the famous singers of Hyderabad. Women would sit behind the chilmans and enjoy the music. Bade Ghulam Ali Khan used to visit our deodi and sing to a distinguished audience. Akhtari Bai Faizabadi, the famous ghazal singer, later known as Begum Akhtar, used to visit Hyderabad often and she sang regularly in the court of the junior prince, whose pen name was 'Shajih.' Her famous ghazal, "khoob parda hai ke chilman se lage baithe hai, saaf chupte bhi nahi, saamne aate bhi nahi" fits the Hyderabadi women.

'Poetry writing was another great interest and hobby in Hyderabad. But this was forbidden for women. Men took pride in writing shairi. Even if women wrote poetry, they kept it very quiet. The only case of a woman writing poetry and being openly appreciated by men was Mahalaqa Bai Chanda, the famous courtesan who lived during the time of Maharaja Chandu Lal. In my time, if any member of the zenana wrote poetry, it could be appreciated only in the zenana. Writing poetry was not easy even for men, it was a long drawn out process and it was difficult to get recognition. Great people like Maharaja Kishen Pershad did not need to make an effort to be appreciated but otherwise it was difficult to get an appreciative audience. To begin with, if one wrote a poem, he had to have it approved by his ustad, then the poet had to find someone to compose the music, then find a singer to render it and finally find an audience to listen to it and appreciate it. However, in some families poetry was not favoured even for men. It was associated with looseness of character, which I think was unfortunate. It was considered respectable to be sportsmen, but not to be poets.

'Then there were the religious gatherings for Shiites called majlis. Women were sometimes permitted to witness famous majlis sessions when singers from Lucknow and Rampur came to render marsiya. There used to be such excitement on these occasions, we would sit behind the chilmans and listen to the recitation. Very often the women in the zenana had their own majlis. The majlis sessions in the Inayat Jung Deodi are famous even today.

'On the rare occasions when women went out of the deodis, the travel preparations took a lot of effort because visits were not casual affairs; if they went anywhere it was at the least for a few days and they took a retinue of servants with them. Women travelled in pretty shakrams, drawn by either horses or bullocks, there would be a toshak spread in it. In the early years they went in mainas, carried by bois. Motorcars came to Hyderabad sometime around 1910 and were not too common.'

The call of the muezzin for the evening prayers broke our conversation. Najeeb Sultana quickly covered her head and withdrew into the bedroom; and I walked out to the terrace to admire the view from her rooftop. The old city turned quite magical, almost medieval when the call of the muezzin from several mosques reverberated in the evening air. Pigeons suddenly rose into the blue sky and fluttered down slowly, like clouds.

Najeeb resumed her narration after her prayer. 'Women used to be invited to sing and to entertain the male guests in the deodis. Nautch and mujra were held on special occasions, in some families, not in all the deodis. The mujra would be held in the middle of a large hall and the men used to sit all around. Those who attended these sessions would carry gifts of money for the singers and the dancers. Drinking, mujras and women destroyed half the nawabs of Hyderabad. Some times the tawaif became the wife and the whole family lost its social standing. Hyderabad had its share of tawaifs; they used to reside in a locality called Mahboob ki Mehendi. Half the barbadi in the city was because of the tawaifs. They would fleece the men who gave away large sums of money, expensive pieces of jewellery, property and even their jagirs to these women. Men had easy incomes, no occupations, a lot of leisure, and no other diversion. Not all the men in the deodis were educated and most of them ceased to occupy any positions in the court. So they were idle for the most part. These men got into bad habits early in life and continued them into their old age.'

The insistent ring of the telephone interrupted our conversation. Najeeb went to answer the phone while I walked across to the table where she had spread her wedding finery to show me. The gold embroidery felt rough to my touch and the brilliant red silk was soft with age. Dressed in such brilliant clothes and wearing her antique jewellery, Najeeb must have made an attractive bride. Najeeb had not yet talked about her jewellery. I made a mental note that I must remind her.

Hyderabad has always been famous for its gems and jewellery right from the Qutub Shahi period. It was from the village Kolluru, which was a part of the Golconda kingdom that the world-famous Kohinoor diamond, which originally weighed 756 carats, and the other famous diamonds like Hope, Pitt and the Nizam were found. During the Qutub Shahi rule and in the subsequent times too, the streets of Charminar were lined with shops where diamonds were cut and polished. Apart from diamonds; garnets, amethysts, topaz and agate too were sold in Hyderabad. Next in popularity to the gems were the pearls, mostly from Basra; they were graded, pierced and strung together. Many jewellers and artisans migrated to Hyderabad from the Mughal court during the Asaf Jahi rule; hence the strong Mughal influence on the Hyderabadi jewellery.

My thoughts strayed to the very important event that held the city in its thrall. The Nizam's jewellery had been on display in the Salar Jung Museum just recently and it was the talk of the town. There were fierce whispers about the inappropriateness of displaying Sarkar's family jewels in his diwan's museum. Never mind that the present museum is a modern structure and not the Diwan's Residence, as it was referred to. 'They should be placed in Nazri Bagh', whispered the lady who sat next to me at the inaugural ceremony. She was a scion of a noble family and bristled with indignation at the perceived insult to the Nizam. 'That was where Sarkar himself kept them. Do you know he never let the floors of the vaults be swept, ever, so that he could make out if any one walked on it?' In a city where nobility of birth took primacy over everything else in life, the location of the display of the jewels was indeed a matter of grave concern. 'This is just a fraction of what the Nizam really possessed.' I was further informed. 'Most of it has been taken out of the country.'

A month or so later, while I walked around admiring the jewellery in the Salar Jung Museum, one of the staffers of the Museum I was acquainted with accosted me. 'The princess came here yesterday,' he said, brimming with pride. 'I watched her as she was wheeled around.' By now Princess Durru Shehvar was well into her nineties and rarely came out of her home Chamlija in Banjara Hills. 'She is so dignified and beautiful even at this age,' the museum staffer informed me. 'Not a muscle moved in her face and she sat so erect.'

∿

'Tell me about your jewellery,' I said to Najeeb. I would have liked to see some of her jewellery but I thought asking her to show her valuables would be an imposition. Najeeb excused herself and disappeared into the bedroom. She returned a moment later with a photograph. 'I wanted to show you this photo, this is the wedding photograph of my friend. You can see all the jewellery that women used to wear.' It was the photo of a bride, decked from head to foot in a jumble of gold, pearls and emeralds. Najeeb sat next to me and named the various ornaments.

'Men competed with women in wearing jewellery in the olden days,' she dimpled. 'They would wear gem-encrusted sarpeches on their dastars, bajuband on the sleeves, and bugloos round the waist. Even swords were decorated with gems and sherwanis had buttons made of diamonds, enamel, mother of pearl or bidri work.

'As for women, jewellery making was a major preoccupation in the zenanas. We had our own jewellers, attached to the deodis. As for most girls, my jewellery-making started the moment I was born, my mother tells me. You had to wear the kind of jewellery that was in keeping with the dignity of the family. We used mostly emeralds, pearls and uncut diamonds in Hyderabad. South Indians preferred rubies to emeralds. Ladies of the Nizam's family wore jewellery from head to foot. The entire assemblage of such jewellery was called sarapa or saaj. Sarapa started with a tikka worn on the parting of one's hair, a jhoomar worn on the right side of the head, karanphool in the ear balanced by strings of pearls, then a lachcha, a jugni and a satlada round the neck and ended it all with anklets called sone ke kabutar, worn on one's foot. This is a modest collection. Those who could afford to, wore many more things and the list is endless.'

ᔐ

When I spoke to Najeeb a few months after our visit to her home, she told me that a deal was being finalised to demolish her home and turn it over to 'developers.' It is inevitable, she told me sadly; it was going to happen sooner or later. The rest of the family wanted it that way and the land would fetch a handsome price.

Afterword

کہاں ہے میرا حیدرآباد ۔۔۔

اے میرے شہر کہاں ہے تو ؟ میرا وہ خوبصورت شہر جو بارونق تھا، جہاں باغات تھے، تالاب تھے جو صدیوں پرانی چنالوں سے گھرا تھا، جس میں ایک خاص ہنگیں تھا، جہاں لوگوں میں تہذیب اور مروت رچی بسی تھی۔ وہ وقت کہاں چلا گیا جہاں ہم ایک دوسرے کے پیارو وادی کے زیر سایہ پل کر بڑے ہوے ۔ لوگ صرف لوگ تھے، مذہبی معاملہ تھا جو بھی ان اُنٹ رشتوں میں حائل نہیں ہوا۔ ہماری گنگا جمنی تہذیب سارے ملک میں مشہور ہے ۔ ہماری شناخت یہ ہے کہ ہم صرف اور صرف حیدر آبادی ہیں۔ عید تہوار ہم نے ساتھ ساتھ منائے ۔ کیا دسہرہ کیا دیوالی، عیدالفطر بقر عید، سب ہماری اپنی عیدیں تھیں۔ محرم میں سب ہی ماتم کرتے، ہر بزرگ کا احترام کرنا، ہر ایک سے بغل گیر ہو کر ملنا، یہ ہماری تہذیب تھی۔

اب حالات کیوں بدل رہے ہیں! بھائی کو بھائی سے نفرت کرنا کون سکھا رہا ہے؟ جو بھی ہو، ان لوگوں کی رگوں میں حیدر آبادی خون نہیں دوڑ رہا ہے۔ ایسا کیوں ہو رہا ہے؟ حیدر آبادیوں میں حیدر آبادیت کیوں ختم ہو رہی ہے؟ کیوں؟ شہر کا حلیہ الگ بدل رہا ہے۔ سکون کیسے غائب ہو گیا ہے۔

بازار اپنی جگہ تھے جہاں لوگ خریداری کرتے ۔ عابد روڈ جہاں میوسات، کتابیں، جوتے اور دیگر سامان ضروریات فراہم کیے جاتے ۔ شادی بیاہ خواہ ہندو ہو یا مسلمان خریداری ہمیں لاڈ بازار لے جاتی جہاں عطر، چوڑیوں کے علاوہ کار چوب اور کامدانی کی ساڑیاں اور دوپٹے بنوائے جاتے ۔ پتھر گٹی سے شیردانیوں کے لیے کم خواب، جامہ دار، اور ہر دوار و ساڑیوں میں بناری، بچو کی، منجر، ناش وغیرہ خریدے جاتے ۔ مظلم جاہی مارکیٹ سے گوشت، مرغی، مچھلی، انڈے، بڑ کاری، دودھ، دہی، بالائی غرض ہر قسم کے کھانے کی اشیاء خریدی جاتیں۔

رہائشی علاقے پرسکون ہوا کرتے، گھر گھر تھے اور بازار، بازار۔۔۔۔ میرے حیدر آباد اب نہیں تجھے کہاں تلاش کروں؟ ان اونچے اونچے شاپنگ مالس کے پیچھے؟ پرانے گھروں، ڈیوڑھیوں سب کو زمین دوز کر دیا جا رہا ہے، سڑکوں کو کشادہ کرنے تاریخ کو ایک جھٹکے میں مٹایا جا رہا ہے ۔ لاڈ بازار جیسے صدیوں پرانے بازار کی دکانوں کو نیا بنایا جا رہا ہے۔ جن دکانوں کی پرانی وضع دار کاریاں ان دکانوں کی زینت ہوا کرتی تھیں انہیں ہٹا کر shutters لگائے جا رہے ہیں ۔ چار مینار ذرا فلک کی زیادتی سے کانپ رہا ہے، بالکل اسی طرح جیسے کہ میرا دل میرے شہر کی حالتِ زار دیکھ کر کانپ رہا ہے، رو رہا ہے۔

ہمارے زمانے میں تفریح کی مشاغل گھر میں قوالی یا غزلیں سننا ہوتا اور پھر مشاعرے، کلاسیکی موسیقی کے پروگرام اپنے بڑوں کے ساتھ زنانے میں بیٹھ کر لطف اندوز ہوتے ۔ اسی طرح اپنے عزیزوں سے ملتے، مزے مزے کی باتیں ہوتیں۔ بڑی خوبصورت شامیں ہوتیں کسی شام باغ عام کی سیر یا بھی بھار حسین ساگر کے کنارے پرنو کرانی اور اپنی سہیلیوں کے ساتھ گھومنے جاتے ۔ ہم تین تین دیویوں کے نام سے جانے جاتے ؛ سونا مرزا، اندرا دھن راج گیر اور میں (لکشمی دیوی راج)! کبھی یوں بھی ہوتا کہ ہم سکندر آباد اگریزی سینما دیکھنے یا پھر کرکٹ میچن یا پارسی دوستوں سے ملنے چلے جاتے ۔ سکندر آباد میں چوں کہ اگریزی زیادہ رہا کرتے تھے ۔ اسی وجہ سے وہاں رہنے والے بہت زیادہ اگریزیت پسند تھے اور ہم بالکل خالص حیدر آبادی! ہم ملتے جلتے بھی سے تھے لیکن گھر آتے ہی اپنی اصلیت پر آ جاتے یعنی سرد ہا تیک لیا اور بڑوں کے آگے جھک کر نظریں نیچی کیے بیٹھ جاتے جو ہماری حیدر آبادی تہذیب تھی۔

کہاں ڈھونڈوں تجھے اے میرے شہر۔۔۔ ملٹی پلکس، Fast Food Joints، جابجا بن رہے ہیں ۔ جن کی وجہ سے اب گھر کم نظر آتے ہیں ۔ مانصاہب کا تالاب، صرف نام رہ گیا ہے ایک کالونی بن گئی ہے ۔ پرانی عمارتیں، پرانے لوگ بھی جا چکے ہیں ۔ ہم نے بڑی کاوشوں سے نا پپلی کی سرائے کو بچا لیا ورنہ وہاں بھی ایک شاپنگ مال بننے والا تھا۔

مانا کہ زندگی کو چلتے رہنا ہے مگر اس کا یہ مطلب تو نہیں کہ تاریخ کو مٹا دیا جائے! ہمارے درتے کو ختم کیا جائے! کیا پرانے شہر کے بنیادی کردار کو برقرار رکھ کر نیا شہر بسایا نہیں جا سکتا؟

آج صرف پرانی یادیں باقی رہ گئی ہیں ۔ اے میرے شہر حیدر آباد، تیری یادیں جو بھی کاب رو رو کرستاتی ہیں ۔۔۔۔

یاد ماضی عذاب ہے یارب ۔۔۔۔

لکشمی دیوی راج

❖

The original Urdu version of the Afterword by Smt Lakshmi Devi Raj.

Whither My Hyderabad?

Where is my beloved Hyderabad? Where is that beautiful city, which was so full of gardens, lakes and open spaces? That picturesque city enclosed by the fascinating primeval rock formations, which seemed as though a child had stopped playing midway and left his toys lying around? The city where there was grace and grandeur, where there was courtesy and concern? Where have those times that we all lived and loved gone?

We called ours a ganga-jamuni culture. We were bound together by bonds stronger than faith. Affection, warmth and tenderness were the qualities that nurtured us. Festivals were celebrated round the year, never mind one's creed or culture. Dussera, Diwali or Sankranti, were all meant to be enjoyed whether one was Hindu or not. Id brought celebrations not for one community but for the entire city. We were all Hyderabadis and faiths were personal. Were we less devout then or were we more human? Why is the 'Hyderabadiat' which is the blend of cultures and people being diluted? What went wrong? And when?

The old Hyderabad had its fabled markets. Weddings, whether Hindu or Muslim, rich or poor, meant trips to Laad Bazar, where along with itar and bangles, karchob sarees and dupattas were sold. Pattargatti was for fabrics for sherwanis—himroo, kamkhwab and jamavar; and the sarees of Benarasi tanchoi, mushajjar and taash (gold tissue). Trips to Vithaldas were for uncut diamonds and jadat jewellery with Basra pearls, rubies, and emeralds.

I bemoan the change that is sweeping the old city, a change that is robbing the old Hyderabad of its charm. Old houses and deodis are razed regularly, roads are widened erasing centuries of history in one stroke. Attempts are made to modernise even Laad Bazar. 'It is too narrow,' they say, 'the old dukans are too cramped'. The graceful arches are being replaced by rolling shutters. Unregulated traffic crowds and pollutes the city's streets. The majestic Charminar shudders and trembles with the rush of traffic, much like my own heart, which weeps for the sorry state in which the old city is today.

In my days entertainment meant qawwalis, ghazals, mushaira and classical music. Sitting in the zenanas, with friends and relatives, we savoured the magical moments, laden with melody. Bagh-e-Aam (public garden) was for leisurely strolls and the Tank Bund, for evening drives. The farthest we went was to Secunderabad to meet our Christian and Parsi friends. The influence of the Europeans was stronger there. Those who lived in Secunderabad thought themselves superior; we lived in Mughlai Hyderabad, old and charming. We were a threesome, Sunna Mirza, Indra Dhanrajgir and I. We would zip around the twin cities without a care but enter our homes demurely, heads covered and eyes cast down; for we had to live up to the cliché, the girls of good families could neither be seen nor heard.

Where do I look for you now, my childhood friend? Multiplexes have edged out old homes and fast food joints have taken over even the celebrated lakes. Maa Saheb ka talaab is a sprawling residential colony and Bagh-e-Aam is crowded with buildings. All the old landmarks have gone and so have the old people. It took all our strength to save the Nampally Sarai from turning into a shopping centre.

I do not expect magical moments to last forever. Life moves on and the old gives way to the new. In that process, should all the traces of the past be erased forcibly and irrevocably? Can't the old co-exist with the new, in some measure?

Only memories remain of my beloved old Hyderabad; only memories which trouble me at night.

Where do I go now, to love, to cry and to a share a joy?

Translated by Rani Sarma

Vithaldas: A famous jewellery shop of Hyderabad.
jadat jewellery: Jewellery encrusted with gems, particularly uncut diamonds
dukan: a shop
Tank Bund: The bund of Hussain Sagar Lake, which connects the two cities of Hyderabad and Secunderabad.

Glossary

aalam	:	A standard, the sacred symbols representing the Prophet, his sons, and others important to Shia Muslims
Ab kuch bhi nahi bacha hai	:	Now there is nothing left
Abbasi	:	A particular kind of weapon
abdaar khana	:	A water point where people could get a drink of fresh water
adaab	:	Respectful greetings
aftaba	:	A water jug
aina khana	:	A room adorned with mirrors
Ala Hazrat	:	The great or respected Sir, the Nizam
ambari	:	The decorative chair (sometimes covered) placed on an elephant to carry a person, or people
andar ana mana hai	:	Entry is forbidden
ande ke lauz	:	A sweet dish made of eggs
annas	:	One fourth of a rupee which is now out of use.
arzbegee	:	An applicant; *arz* is an application
ashrafia or ashrafees	:	A gold sovereign
atta	:	Flour
ayah	:	A nanny who takes care of children
azaan	:	The muslim call for prayer
badam	:	Almond

baggi khana	:	A shed that houses carriages
baolis	:	Step-wells
baradari	:	A pavilion with twelve doors
Bathakamam	:	A festival celebrated by the Hindu women of Telengana, a region in the erstwhile state of Hyderabad and a part present Andhra Pradesh
bawarchi khana	:	Kitchen
beedi	:	A leaf which is rolled and smoked like a cigarette
begum	:	A Muslim noblewoman
bela	:	Area
Bengalis	:	The people of Bengal
besan	:	Powdered Bengal gram
bhajan	:	The rendering of Hindu devotional compositions
bhatti khana	:	A large oven, a distillery
bhi darte the, sarkar se	:	Was also afraid of Sir
Bidri	:	Bidri is an art from Hyderabad which takes its meaning from the town of Bidar, located near Hyderabad. Bidri is a form of surface ornamentation in black colours, which never fades and is coated with silver and gold coverings.
Bismillah	:	The Muslim ceremony to mark the beginning of a child's initiation into studies of Islam
Boi	:	Palanquin bearers
Bonalu	:	A festival of the rural women of the state of Hyderabad
borse ke jawan	:	Soldiers attired in traditional uniforms
Brahmin	:	A Hindu belonging to the priestly caste
bugloos	:	A local adaption of the English word, buckle. A ceremonial belt of velvet or brocade required to be worn in the presence of royalty
chabutra	:	A raised platform where people sit, either in a garden or in an open place
chaiwala	:	A tea vendor
chaman	:	A garden
chamar	:	The yak's tail. A royal insignia bestowed as a royal favour
chameli	:	A variety of jasmine
chandan	:	Sandalwood
Char dhams	:	The four holy shrines of the Hindus
charpai	:	A light bedstead

chattri	:	An umbrella
chaubdar	:	A mace bearer, an attendant
chaval	:	Rice
chilman	:	A thin curtain made of bamboo
chouth	:	One fourth of the revenue paid as a tax to the government
chowkidar	:	A watchman
chutney	:	A sauce
crore	:	A hundred lakhs
daftardar	:	A person in charge of the office
dalan	:	An ornamental verandah-like pillared pavilion.
dargah	:	The tomb of a saint, venerated by the people of all faiths
darwaza	:	A door or a gate
dastar	:	A form of headdress worn in the presence of the Nizam and other members of the royal family.
dastarkhan	:	A cloth spread over the carpet for a traditional meal.
deodidar	:	The caretaker of a deodi
der raat tak chalta tha	:	Went on till late at night
deval	:	A temple
dhatti	:	A cloth that is tied to the sacred standard as thanksgiving or to invoke the blessings of the gods
dhobi	:	A washerman
dhoti	:	The traditional Indian lower garment worn by men.
Dipavali	:	An important Hindu festival
diwan khana	:	An official reception room
Diwan	:	The prime minister
diya	:	An oil lamp
Do rangi chhod ke, ek rang hoja/pighalkar moam hoja ya sang hoja	:	Do not be of two colours, choose any one/Either become stone or melt into wax
doodh shareek bhai behen	:	'Milk participant brother and sister'. At the time of suckling a child of a deodi, if the wet nurse suckles a child of her own at the same time, the two children are given the quaint epithet.
durbar	:	A room where court is held by the ruler, a noble or a feudal lord
durri	:	A rug, inferior to a carpet
farman	:	A royal order
farrash khana	:	A storeroom for carpets, floor rugs etc

farrash	:	A thin rug for the floor
farrashes	:	Sweepers
gaddi	:	A throne
gajar ka meetha/halwa	:	a sweet dish made of grated carrots
gangajal	:	Water from the river Ganges, considered to be sacred by the Hindus.
Ganga-jamuni	:	The river Ganges and Yamuna, the latter being the tributary of the former. They are considered to be inseparable. The composite culture of Hyderabad, where the Hindus and Muslims lived in harmony and evolved a common culture is described as Ganga Jamuni culture.
gau takia	:	A bolster, round cushions to lean on
General Choudhury	:	General Choudhury led the Indian armies in the Police Action of September 1948 against the forces of Hyderabad. Major General El Edroos, the Commander of the Hyderabad forces surrendered unconditionally to General Choudhury. Choudhury took over as the Military Governor to begin with and handed over control of the state to a civilian governor following the Nizam's accession to the Union.
ghagras	:	A traditional Indian skirt
ghazal	:	A form of Persian verse, poetry, generally romantic in nature
ghee	:	Clarified butter
gilli danda	:	An amateur sport, similar to cricket that is popular among the Indian youth
Gokulashtami	:	A Hindu festival
gud	:	Jaggery
gulab posh	:	A rose water sprinkler, generally made of silver
hajjam	:	A barber
haldi	:	Turmeric powder, considered to be auspicious for the Hindus, used in Hindu ceremonies
naleem	:	Lamb meat cooked in the traditional Hyderabadi style.
harathi	:	A Hindu religious ritual
narees	:	A dish made of chicken stock, almonds, cashewnuts, pista, yogurt, wheat and lentil
hari mirch	:	Green chillies
hauda	:	A seat carried by an elephant, used for carrying royalty

hauz	:	A water tank
haveli	:	A palace
Hazrat	:	A honorific expression like 'reverend'
Holi	:	A Hindu harvest festival
hookah	:	A tobacco pipe with a long flexible tube connected to a container where the smoke is cooled by passing it through water
Idara-e-Adabiat-e-Urdu	:	A centre for the study of Urdu literature
Imli	:	Tamarind
insaniyat aur pyar mohabbat	:	Humanity and love
Irani kanjhar	:	A traditional hunting weapon
itar or *itr*	:	A perfume
itardan	:	A portable box where perfumes are stored
jaali	:	A screen, made of wood or stone
jagir	:	A grant of revenue land; often to a high official or for the purpose of maintaining troops
jagirdar	:	The grantee of a jagir
jalsa	:	A meeting or a gathering
jamia	:	Traditional hunting weaponry
jharokha	:	A window
jhoomar	:	Jewellery
jillu khana	:	A room at the entrance of a deodi or a palace, where visitors would alight a horse, an elephant or a carriage
jowar ki roti	:	A kind of bread made from grain grown in the drought-stricken part of India, considered to poor man's food
jugni	:	A necklace
juhi	:	Jasmine
juloos	:	A procession
kabutar bazi	:	A game with pigeons; when a pigeon is released, and if the pigeon brings a bird of some other flock back, it is a point in favour of the owner. But if the pigeon goes to some other flock, it is a point against the owner.
kacheri	:	An office
kaddu ki kheer	:	A milk pudding in which a vegetables are added to make it thick and add some flavour to it
kamarband	:	An ornamental waist band
kamdani	:	A kind of embroidery

karanphool	: Earrings
karchob	: Raised embroidery generally done with gold thread.
karsevaks	: Refers to those who offer services for free (volunteers) to a religious cause, particularly to Hindutva.
katori	: Small bowls that surround a dinner plate and are used for different curries
Kayastha	: A community of traditional account keepers
kewda	: A flower
khada dupatta	: An upper garment worn by women
khasdan	: A box-like container where the prepared paan is kept and is made of silver or gold.
khazana	: A strong room
kheer	: A milk pudding
khichdi	: A dish made of rice, yellow gram, spices and clarified butter
Khilafat movement (1919-1924)	: In the aftermath of World War I when the treaty of Versailles led to the dismemberment of the Ottoman Turkish Empire and posed a threat to the office of the Caliph, the Muslims in India launched the Khilafat Movement in protest; subsequently it became a part of the Indian freedom movement.
Khoob maatham hota tha	: Great sorrow was expressed
Khoob parda hai ke chilman se lage baithe hai/saaf chupte bhi nahi, saamne aate bhi nahi	: You are sitting tantalisingly behind a beautiful screen/ You neither can be seen openly nor you hide totally
khoya, khova	: Condensed milk used in sweetmeats
khus	: Aromatic roots which have a cooling effect, used to flavour a drink or woven into curtains used during the hot summer months to shield the interiors.
khutbah	: A prayer
kothi or koti	: A palace, a mansion
kothmir	: A herb used in Indian cooking
kotwal	: A police chief
kulcha	: A type of bread
kuldevta	: A family deity
kumkum	: Vermilion powder

kurta	:	A traditional knee-length shirt
Kya piyenge, chai ke nimbu pani?	:	What would you like to drink? Tea or lemonade?
lachcha	:	A necklace
lagan	:	An improvised oven; a flat bottomed plate is kept on red-hot coals and the dish to be baked is placed on it; another plate is inverted on the dish and burning coals are placed on it as well, providing dry heat.
lakhs	:	A hundred thousand
Lakkad kot	:	A mansion built of wood
maaf karna	:	Forgive me
maali	:	A gardener
maatham	:	Expressing sorrow
machans	:	An elevated shelter made for hunting expeditions, generally on a tree to get a clear view of the animals
Madrasis	:	People from the city of Madras, now renamed Chennai
maghrab	:	A traditional hunting weapon
mahal	:	A palace
mahant	:	An officiating priest of a temple
mahathma	:	A great soul
maina	:	A palanquin
majlis	:	Prayer meetings held by Shia Muslims during Muharram, focused on the martyrdom of the Prophet's grandsons; often held in private homes and open to all.
mama	:	An elderly trusted female servant
mandi	:	A bazaar, market
mandir	:	A temple
mansabdaar or *munsabdaar*	:	The recipient of a royal grant, entrusted with the maintenance of troops.
Marathas	:	Soldiers and people belonging to the region of Maharashtra.
Marathi	:	An adjective that refers to anything of Maharashtrian origin
mardana	:	The men's section of a house or a deodi
marsiya	:	The narration of the story of the martyrdom of Hassan and Hussain
masala	:	Spices, condiments
masnad or *musnad*	:	A richly adorned cloth of silk or velvet with matching pillows and a carpet, a kind of a throne

math	:	A Hindu religious establishment
meetha	:	Dessert
mewa	:	An Indian sweet dish
mez khana	:	A room where tables and other furniture are stored
mithai	:	Indian sweets
mohur	:	A gold coin
morchel	:	An arrangement of peacock feathers, a royal insignia
motor khana	:	A garage
muezzin	:	The man who gives the call for prayers
mujra	:	A form of entertainment which includes dance and song and also poetry recitation
mullahs	:	A Muslim cleric
munshi	:	A private secretary, a teacher
murabba	:	A preserve
murgi	:	A hen, fowl
murthi	:	An idol
mushaira	:	A gathering of poets, where the poets read out their compositions
Mussavir	:	An artist
mutavalli	:	A caretaker
myna	:	A bird that can be taught to talk
Myseram	:	The regiment of Monsieur Raymond, a French mercenary who was in the employment of the fourth Nizam. His name was adapted to sound like an Indian name.
Naka	:	A police station
naqqar	:	A large-sized drum
nashta	:	Breakfast
naubat khana	:	A room where drums and the accompanying wind instruments were kept and from which naubat was played.
naubat	:	Traditional music played during ceremonial occasions and sometimes to indicate the time for prayers or the time of the day.
nautch	:	A dance performed by the community of entertainers and frowned at by the orthodox society
Nawab	:	A noble, an honorific title
naya makan	:	New house
nazar	:	An offering of coins as a token of respect, a gift

neemajama	:	A traditional dress
nikkah	:	Marriage
nimish	:	A sweet dish made with milk, sugar and saffron
paandan	:	A box made of silver and highly ornamented, used for storing the ingredients used in a paan
pachcheesi	:	A traditional dice game
pagdi	:	A turban, an Indian headdress
Paigahs	:	Premier nobles
pairavikars	:	One who pursues an official matter, a lobbyist
paithani	:	It is a variety of sari, named after the Paithan region in state in Maharashtra where they are woven by hand.
palki	:	A palanquin
pallu	:	The edge oh the sari that hangs from the left shoulder
Panch mahalla	:	Five palaces
pandals	:	A large tent or a canopy
pardah	:	A curtain used by the women in a zenana who want to conceal themselves.
Parsis	:	Descendants of the Zoroastrians who were driven out of Persia in the fourteenth century, and given refuge in India
patang bazi	:	Kite flying
Pathans	:	People from Punjab
patta	:	A grant of land
pattedars	:	A small landowner who is bestowed with land by the ruler
peedhas	:	Very low wooden seats
pehra	:	To keep vigil, to provide security
peshi	:	To be on attendance
peshkar	:	An administrative officer in charge of the royal treasury and the army. This position was hereditary in Hyderabad.
Police Action of 1948	:	After Independence in 1947, the State of Hyderabad under Osman Ali Khan chose not to join the Indian union, but to remain independent. The Indian government which did not approve of the stand of the Nizam sent in armies on 13 September 1948 to force the annexation of Hyderabad to the Indian union. Within five days, the state of Hyderabad was defeated and

		subsequently annexed to the Indian union. This operation was called 'operation polo' or the police action
porambok	:	Public land, government land
pranam	:	The traditional salutation of the Hindus
prasad	:	Offerings made to Hindu gods
pudina	:	Mint
puja	:	The Hindu form of worship
pujari	:	A temple priest
Punjabis	:	The people of Punjab
Puran Poli	:	A sweet meat
purana makan	:	Old house
Purani Haveli	:	The old palace
purdah	:	A system of secluding women from the men
qasida	:	An ode, poetry written in praise of someone
qawwalis	:	Religious sufi songs
qawwals	:	Artistes who render religious sufi songs
qeema	:	Spicy seasoned minced meat
Rai Rayan	:	A premier noble
rajanagaru	:	The ruler's abode
rava	:	A roughly pound mixture of wheat and maize
Razakar movement	:	Razakars were a militant Muslim organisation led by Qasim Razvi. They vehemently opposed Hyderabad's union with the Indian Republic and resorted to violence against the Hindu population of the state in an attempt to intimidate them, till the Indian government intervened and annexed Hyderabad in 1948.
Rohillas	:	Soldiers of Rohilkhand which is located in UP
roshan khana	:	The room from where a person from the community of barbers, lit up the torches for the various parts of the deodi
roti	:	flat bread
Round Table Conference (September-December 1931)	:	During the freedom struggle of India, three Round Table Conferences were held in England to resolve the political deadlock in India and to frame the constitution acceptable to the people. The representatives of Hyderabad, who attended the weddings of the two Hyderabadi princes at Nice, were in Europe to attend the second Round Table Conference.
rubaaiyaat	:	A poem of four lines

saab	:	An adaptation of 'saheb' which means sir
Sab barbad ho gaya	:	Everything is destroyed
sadhu	:	A monk
sailafchi	:	A basin in which hands are washed; the basin has a lid with holes, through which the water drains. It is also decorated with leaves to make it more attractive.
sailapas	:	Traditional hunting weapons
salaam	:	To salute
salim bakra	:	A whole young lamb
samasthans	:	An ancient principality ruled by a Hindu prince which existed prior to the Nizam's
sanad	:	A certificate, proof
sandhya vandana	:	Salutation of the dawn, a ritual observed by Brahmins and performed thrice a day
sangrahalay	:	A museum
santh	:	A saint
sarai	:	An inn
sardar	:	A chief
Sarkar abhi ayenge	:	Sir will come now
sarkar	:	The ruler
sarpech	:	A gem-encrusted gold ornament worn on the traditional headgear by the nobles
sati	:	An archaic Hindu custom in which the wife burnt herself on the funeral pyre of her husband
satlada	:	A necklace which has seven strings
sawar	:	A cavalry trooper
sehra	:	The veil of flowers, or pearls that a bridegroom wears during the wedding ceremony
shaadi khana	:	A marriage hall
Shad	:	To be happy, it was the *nom-de-plume* of Maharaja Kishen Pershad,
Shahgird-e-khas Asaf Jah	:	A special student of Asaf Jah
shahukar	:	A wealthy man, a trader
shairi	:	Poetry
shakram	:	Colourful and comfortable closed bullock carts, drawn by bullocks or horses
Shams-ul-Umarah	:	'A sun among nobles', a title given to a Paigah noble
sheermal	:	A kind of bread

shehnai or shahnai	:	A wind instrument, played on auspicious occasions
sherwani	:	A traditional long coat worn by men on formal occasions
Siddis	:	The people of Sudan who migrated and settled in Hyderabad and were employed by the Nizam
Sikhs	:	People who follow the Sikh religion
sipahi	:	A soldier
subedar	:	A viceroy
Subsidiary Alliance	:	The Subsidiary Alliance was introduced by Lord Wellesley, the Governor-General of India, in the early years of the nineteenth century. As per the Alliance, an Indian ruler's security needs would be taken care of by the British, who would place a British contingent at the disposal of the ruler. In return the ruler would have to disband his own army and also pay for the British troops. The Nizam of Hyderabad was the first Indian ruler to accept such an alliance.
tazia	:	A flag or a standard
tahzeeb	:	Culture
takhat or takht	:	A throne
tarbuj	:	Watermelon
tawaif	:	A prostitute
thekhana	:	Cool underground rooms
tikka	:	An ornament worn on the parting of hair by women
toran	:	Strings of flowers and mango leaves used as decorations during auspicious and festive occasions
tosha khana	:	A pantry
toshak	:	A soft cloth, a coverlet
tukdian ladna	:	A pigeon fight
ugaldan	:	A spittoon
Umra-e-uzzam	:	Premier nobles
Unani	:	An Ionian system of medicine brought to India by the Arabs it continues to be practiced in India, particularly in Hyderabad
ustad	:	A teacher
vakils	:	A representative, advocates, lawyers
Vedic *pundits*	:	Learned men who recite the ancient Hindu scripture, the vedas
Vijayadasami	:	An important Hindu festival

wada	:	A neighbourhood, a settlement or a village
waraq	:	Silver foil
watandar	:	A local landlord, who is vested with the responsibility of organising land-tax collection in a cluster of villages.
Woh jamana guzar gaya hai	:	That age has gone
yakhni	:	Aromatic rice cooked with nuts, spices and saffron
Zafar Pultan	:	The victorious platoon
zari	:	Gold thread embroidery
zat	:	A foot soldier
zenana	:	The women's quarters in a deodi

Bibliography

A lecture given by Nawab Mir Moazam Husain at Salar Jung Museum in the year 2003, on the occasion of Salar Jung Day.

A.K. Imadi 'The Nobles of Hyderabad - A study in social change',a doctoral thesis, Osmania University, Department of Sociology, 1977.

Ashraf, Dawood Syed Dr, *The Seventh Nizam of Hyderabad – An Archival Appraisal*, Moazzam Hussain Foundation, Hyderabad, 2002.

Bawa V.K., *Hyderabad and Salar Jung the First*, S. Chand & Company Ltd, 1996.

Bawa, V.K., *The Last Nizam: The Life and Times of Mir Osman Ali Khan*, Viking, Penguin Books India Pvt Ltd, 1992.

Campbell, Claude A., *Glimpses of the Nizam's Dominions*, 1898, Historical Publishing Company, Philadelphia Press, USA.

City Improvement Board (CIB) records (set up in 1912).

Hussain, Meherunissa, *Nashad Asifi - The Unhappy Prince*, Vikas Publishing House, 1991.

'Hyderabad Affairs', *Times of India*, 21 December 1875.

Jung, Yar Mujeeb 'After The Black Buck With Cheetah (a peek into the past)', *Siasat Fortnightly*, 16-30 June 2003, Vol.8, No 12.

Khalidi Omar, 'The Ottoman Royal Family in Hyderabad, Deccan India.', Agha Khan Program for Islamic Architecture, Massachusetts Institute of Technology, Cambridge, USA.

Leonard, Isaksen Karen, *Social History of an Indian Caste– The Kayasths of Hyderabad*, Orient Longman, 1993.

Luther, Narendra, *The Nizam Who Wasn't*, Creative Point, Hyderabad, 1996.

Lynton, Ronken Harriet and Rajan, Mohini, *The Days of the Beloved*, Orient Longman Ltd, 1987.

Mudiraja, Krishnaswamy, *Pictorial Hyderabad*, Vol I & II, Chandrakanth Press, Hyderabad, 1934.

Municipal Survey Maps of 1913, 1914 and 1915.

Naidu, Ratna, *Old Cities and New Predicaments*, Sage Publications, 1990.

Prinsep Val. C. A.R.A, *Imperial India*, London Chapman and Hall, 1879.

The Power of Glory, Deccan Books, a division of Deccan Chronicle, 1998.

The *Hindu*, Hyderabad Edition, 22 August 2000.

Trench, Chenevix Charles, *Viceroy's Agent*, Jonathan Cape, 32 Bedford Square, London 1987.

Yazdan, Zubaida, *Hyderabad during the Residency of Henry Russell*, University Press, Oxford, 1976.

INTERVIEWS IN HYDERABAD

Ahteram Ali Khan, the heir of the Salar Jung family and a trustee of the Salar Jung Museum.

Asghar Ali Husain, a member of the Inayat Jung family.

Dr Audhesh Bawa, a scholar in Urdu and a one time resident of the old city.

Dr Sadiq Naqvi, Professor, Department of History, Osmania University, Hyderabad.

Dr Sheila Karan and Mr Iqbal Karan, descendents of the Malwala family.

Dr Zeenat Sazida, Reader, Department of Urdu, Osmania University, Hyderabad.

Najeeb Sultana and Syed Ahmad Ali Khan, members of the Hyderbadi nobility and owners of the crumbling Saram Jung Deodi in Malakpet.

Nawab Farkhunda Ali Khan, a nephew of Salar Jung III.

Nawab Mir Moazam Husain and Begum Meherunissa, of the Khan Khanan and Fakhr-ul-Mulk families.

Rasheed-ud-din Khan, an old retainer who worked at the Diwan Deodi and later employed by the Salar Jung Museum.

Shyam Saincher, the great grandson of the hereditary Peshkar, Maharja Kishen Pershad.

Smt Lakshmi Devi Raj, Member, Urdu Academy; an old Hyderabadi and a connoisseur of arts.

Smt Mangala Devi Bhale Rao, daughter-in-law of the Rai Rayan, Raja Shamraj II.

Index